PLAYING WITH FIRE

ALSO BY NANCY PRICE

NOVELS

A NATURAL DEATH
AN ACCOMPLISHED WOMAN
SLEEPING WITH THE ENEMY
NIGHT WOMAN
NO ONE KNOWS
L'INCENDIAIRE
(Published in French)
UN ÉCART DE JEUNESSE
(Published in French)
L'ENFANT DU MENSONGE
(Published in French)
200 MEN, ONE WOMAN
STOLEN AWAY

POETRY

TWO VOICES AND A MOON

PLAYING WITH FIRE

A novel by
NANCY PRICE

A Malmarie Press Book
Malmarie, Inc.
Kissimmee, Florida

Copyright © 2012 by Nancy Price

All rights reserved. No part of this book may be reproduced in any form or by any electronic or mechanical means including information storage and retrieval systems without permission in writing from the publisher, except by a reviewer who may quote brief passages in a review.

The names, incidents, places and characters in this book are the product of the author's imagination. Any resemblance to actual events, locales, or persons alive or dead, is completely coincidental.

First Printing

Malmarie Press and colophon are registered trademarks of Malmarie, Inc.

ISBN-10: 0-9744818-3-1
ISBN-13: 978-0-9744818-3-8
Library of Congress Control Number: 2012939495
First Malmarie Press hardcover printing 2012
Illustrated by the author

For universities, colleges, schools and organizations: Quantity discounts are available on bulk purchases of this book for educational use, gift purchases, or as premiums for increasing magazine subscriptions and renewals. Please contact Malmarie, Inc., 1301 Hidden Harbor Lane, Kissimmee, Florida 34746.

E-mail: nancypricebooks@aol.com   Website: nancypricebooks.com

ACKNOWLEDGEMENTS

My children, Catherine and David Thompson, and also my good friends, Amy Lockard, Barbara Lounsberry and Michael James Carroll have read this novel in manuscript and offered many perceptive suggestions. My son John's widow, Charlotte Thompson, and her family: Derrick, Sugaree, Lauren and Andrew Gillikin, have helped me, and so have Julie and Richard Westin. I thank them all.

This book is dedicated to my son, David Malcolm Thompson. I could never have completed it without his loving care and constant encouragement.

PLAYING WITH FIRE

1

A week before his wedding, Tom Hancock walked home from work in the hot sun and deep city shade of June. He slung his coat over his shoulder. A breeze blowing from miles of Iowa cornfields felt good on his damp chest.

Tom stopped at a jewelry store window to look at silver-backed brushes gleaming on satin. A woman in the store watched the handsome man gazing in. His face seemed sad above the sterling surfaces, as if he could never buy what he saw, but when he glanced up, his eyes, gray as the silver, glowed.

Shouts came to Tom on the June breeze as he walked on and turned a corner. Protesters had been in Waterloo all day. They wore white skull masks and carried heavy pails, and they yelled about the Nuremberg trials: "Find the rest of the killers! They burned thousands of Jews!"

Tom stopped suddenly in a crowd of late shoppers and workers going home. A few women watched him, but he stared at a young woman with brown hair like a shawl on her shoulders. He said something under his breath and started toward her. Pale and still, she watched him come.

"Raina," he said.

Raina said nothing.

Tom looked around him, then took Raina's arm. "Come to my place," he said, and the two hurried away, running into the shadows of an alley.

Skull-faced men in the square shouted about dead children, and swung the pails they carried: red water unfurled from the pails like flags. The crowd backed away from scarlet bleeding into the street.

Raina followed Tom up flights of stairs. Tom's room was hot, and smelled of the tuna sandwich he'd had for lunch. He put his arms around Raina and murmured, "Don't cry." Shouts from the square ricocheted down the street under his window.

Raina pulled away from him to take off her hat and strip off her gloves. "Two years," she said, and wiped her cheeks with both hands. "I'd just checked in at the hotel and was taking a walk until I could phone you."

Raina looked at the room's two chairs, a table, and a narrow bed. "You live *here*? Oh yes—Emily said you were a store clerk!"

"Only job I could find."

Raina laughed. "With a college degree? But now you're working for a rich girl's father! Going to be his son and inherit the business?"

How beautiful she was. She lifted her long, heavy hair from her shoulders with both hands, a movement so familiar that Tom had to look away. "You're marrying Vince," he said. "Aunt Emily told me."

"I'm still living in our little room, our one little room," Raina said, taking his hand in hers, kissing the palm.

"What's going on?" Tom pulled his hand away.

"I'll hide with you here. One last week. Before I stay with Emily, and you marry." Tears welled from Raina's eyes again. "What's your Anne Bonner like?"

"Sweet. Smart. I love her," Tom said.

"So she's not pretty."

"I didn't say that."

"Didn't have to. Anne's fat?"

"No."

"Thin," Raina said in a businesslike tone. "Plain. Rich."

She stared at a stuffed toy soldier on the bedside table, then snatched it up. "Our Queen's guard!" she said in a choked voice. "You kept him." The soldier's eyes were black beads, and the strap of his tall busby was a gag across his mouth.

"And I kept your goodbye note that came with him," Tom said.

Raina put the toy back on the table, and the Queen's guard stood at attention as she unbuttoned her dress and let it fall. "You remember. You bought him for me. You said we'd have a London honeymoon and see the Changing of the Guard at Buckingham Palace, and find out if the guards really do look straight ahead and never speak, no matter what." Her voice was soft. "Like this little toy, guarding our secret, you said."

"Raina—"

"You're so lucky," Raina said. "You're marrying money."

Tom said nothing. He had taken his coat off; that was all.

"Emily wrote about your big new house Anne's father has built for you—all finished and furnished by the time you're home from your honeymoon." Raina unhooked her bra and threw it with her shoes into a corner.

"You didn't want anybody poor, like me," Tom said.

Raina gave him a look under the fall of her shining hair. He saw tears in her eyes. "I don't want anybody like Vince, either," she said. "I didn't want Billy, or even Bob Delbridge. I couldn't marry them. They weren't you."

"So?" Tom said in a hard voice.

"It's been perfectly obvious to me for a long time." She gave a sob like a hiccup.

"I'm sorry," Tom said. The shouting in the square was louder; the skull-faced protesters were turning into the street below. He stepped closer to her, but Raina lifted her head, swiped at her wet eyes, pushed her panties, garters and hose down and off, and was beautiful and naked in light from the street. "I have such bad luck." She glared at Tom. "And I'm in for more, obviously—you haven't even taken off your shirt."

Tom met her angry eyes with his cold gray ones. Raina said, "You'll have to put on a little act when you marry this Anne Bonner. I'll just be *the daughter of your Aunt Emily's best friend, coming for a visit*." She grabbed the toy palace guard and hugged him to her bare breasts. "And we'll be *acquaintances*. That's all."

"You can't stay here."

The room was fragrant with the perfume Tom remembered. "I want to be waiting for you every night," Raina said. Her brown eyes looked almost black, veiled by her long lashes. "You can go to your toast-the-happy-bride-and-groom parties—I don't care. You'll know I'm here in your room, waiting. And our guardsman will never say a word."

"So we pretend to be just friends?" Tom said. "Why not tell Anne we were lovers? She'd expect I might have had some experience— we're twenty-eight—"

"No!" Raina cried. "You're supposed to be a gentleman. You can't kiss and tell." Her voice trembled. "You left me—"

"You wanted money, lots of it, right away. We could have married."

"I know!" Raina cried. "I know!"

"Put on your clothes." Tom picked up Raina's dress. "I'll take you to the hotel."

"Tom..." Raina ran to him, and he put his arms around her under her warm, silky, slippery fall of hair.

"I hurt so much," Raina whispered, and kissed him over and over. "I don't love anyone but you. There's still time—let's run away. I was so stupid."

Tom let her go. "Get dressed."

Raina covered her face with her hands. He saw tears drip from her chin.

In a little while her face and her voice were under control. She dropped her hands and turned away. "I left my suitcase at the hotel, but I can't stay there, pay all that money."

"I've got money."

"No! I'll call Emily."

"I'm having dinner with her tonight at seven," Tom said.

The telephone was by the bed. Raina found her purse, propped it on her bare knees, rummaged in it until she had the right number, and dialed it, never looking at Tom. "Emily?" she said. Her voice was still a little rough from crying. "It's Raina."

Tom could hear Emily's tiny voice chirping in surprise.

"Here," Raina said. "In town. A week early, I'm afraid." Listening to Emily, she picked up her black bra without a look at Tom standing before her. "I know you're just back from Paris, not even unpacked, but could you possibly take me in? Oh, how wonderful."

Raina's hose dangled from a dresser knob; they had kept the shape of her calves and thighs. "At seven?" Raina asked Emily. Tom put her hose, panties and garters on the bed beside Raina.

"I'll come," Raina said. "I'll be glad to see Tom again." She lifted her breasts one by one into her bra, then jammed the phone receiver between cheek and shoulder while she fastened the bra hooks.

Tom put her dress on the bed beside her. She watched him bring her round sailor hat and gloves; he paired her shoes neatly on the rug by her feet, as if small things were something he could do.

She doubled up on the edge of his bed. "And we'll be *acquaintances*. That's all."

Chanting and shouts filled the street outside as Raina said goodbye to Emily, then called a taxi.

Tom's room seemed very small after Raina put down the phone; they avoided each other's eyes and heard the skull-faced men pass by, turn a corner. The street below rang with echoes for a moment, until the echoes died beneath the ordinary sounds of traffic.

Tom looked out his window while Raina finished dressing, then sat in one chair while she sat in the other. "If you marry Anne Bonner, you'll never have to work again?" Raina said.

"I'll work. I'll be Daniel Bonner's property manager and foundation director."

"Working for your father-in-law," Raina said.

Tom watched her fiddle with the catch of her purse. "It's so hot in here. Do you want a glass of cold water? I don't have any ice."

"No," Raina said. "Thanks."

Silence lengthened between them. Finally Tom said: "So you got your B.A.? And a job?"

"In Reeno's gallery. That little place on Henter Street. I thought I'd get gallery experience, and I did—dodging Reeno. I got pretty good at that, until I'd had enough. I started my M.A. but didn't have enough money, so I worked as a window-dresser at Harriman's Men's Wear." Raina's tone was bitter. "Harriman's put me in the window in shorts and a tight T-shirt, and men pushed their noses against the glass to watch me put underwear on plastic mannequins. A degree in art history, and all I could get was a job dressing men in public."

The Queen's guard, tossed on the bed, watched them; the strap across his mouth kept his face expressionless. Tom couldn't see Raina's face: her sailor hat hid it. She spread her long fingers on her knees. He remembered that gesture; he had never liked those long fingernails of hers. When she was nervous, she picked the nail polish from those talons and left red shreds behind her on sinks, on the rug…

"Emily told me you lost your mother and father," Raina said. "I'm sorry."

"July of 'forty-six. After you sent your goodbye note. A truck crossed the center line and that was it."

"So you came to Iowa, and Emily found you a rich wife. She's prouder of you and Anne Bonner than she ever was of you and me," Raina said. "There's so much *money* involved."

Tom said, "Here's your taxi."

Raina jumped up. Halfway out the door, she turned back. "It's all money," she said to him. "That's all it ever is."

"I love Anne," Tom said.

"And she's got the money!" Raina cried. She ran past a battered baby carriage and tricycle near Tom's door and down the stairs that smelled of old dinners. Muddy sand on the steps grated under her shoes.

Tom watched from his window as Raina's taxi pulled away from the curb. Her scent hung in the room, the expensive scent she bought even when she couldn't buy food. In his Berkeley days, he'd been like a hungry kid hiding in a college boy's clothes, following that perfume of hers, stunned by sex. He shut his eyes and breathed in her scent until it faded away. The toy soldier, face-down on the bed, still stood on guard in his gold, red and black.

Raina.

Tom locked his door behind him. *I don't love anyone but you.* He drove to streets where suburban houses, set in wide lawns, were half hidden behind hedges and iron railings.

Tom parked in his aunt's drive and ran up her front steps two at a time, a florist box in his arms. Clara Pedersen, his aunt's housekeeper, opened the door. "Welcome home," Tom said to her. "How do you like keeping house in America again after Paris? Are you spoiled?"

"Am I unpacked—that's the question," Clara said. "Boxes all over the kitchen."

"Come in, come in," Emily Snyder called.

Tom looked in a hall mirror to smooth his hair, straighten his tie. There was no lipstick on his face.

Tom found his aunt Emily before the plate glass wall of her "garden room." She came to kiss him: a small, fashionable widow, inquisitive and quick. The filagree earrings she always wore glittered.

Tom kissed her. "Sorry I couldn't meet your train." He looked around him. "You've been gone months. Now it seems as if you never left."

"And you're almost a married man." She opened the florist's box. "Roses. How thoughtful." Clara brought wine and glasses, and took away the roses.

"Put your feet up." Emily poured their wine. "We'll toast the happy day."

Tom settled before the garden window with Emily, sighed, and put his shining boots on a hassock.

"Tired?" Emily asked.

"M-m-m," Tom said. Summer light shimmered in his half-shut eyes.

"The Nordstrom party was a success, I hear. Now for the bachelor party... rehearsal dinner...Big Day..." Emily raised her glass. "To happiness for you and Anne."

They sipped for a while in companionable silence, looking at the garden.

"Your parents would have been pleased," Emily said. For a moment there was silence again. "Worried?"

Tom glanced at her, shrugged, and ran a hand through his black hair. "You're the only family I have. I count on you."

Emily raised her eyebrows.

"To keep me from making a fool of myself. This isn't California," Tom said.

"Iowa's not a foreign country."

"But I'm a foreigner."

"You're joking."

"Anne and Daniel Bonner..." Tom stopped, hunting for what he meant. "They don't...act the way you'd expect. The way I'd expect, I mean. Or the way I used to expect the rich to be."

"Well," Emily said, with a pause to think. "It's our good old farm values: work hard, keep an honest tongue, marry a woman who's got straight legs and a strong back, don't show off."

"It's their life-style."

"They don't show off."

"Why?" Tom said.

"You mean they ought to be enjoying themselves? Skiing, gambling, driving fast cars, getting drunk, lying on beaches." Emily was laughing; her earrings glittered. "None of that for you. Do the Bonners ever go to a movie?"

"Not often."

"Do they listen to classical music, hour after hour?"

"I'm used to it now. I like it."

"Reading books? Gardening? Ever since you two were engaged, you've gone to every play and opera and concert and museum show within five hundred miles, haven't you?"

Tom looked sheepish. "At first it was…"

"Boring?"

"Well," Tom said, "not exactly."

"Not exactly your thing at all."

"But after a few months…" Tom's voice trailed off, then his gray eyes met Emily's brown ones. "I count on you," he said in a low voice. "Give me a nudge if you see me on thin ice."

"You won't be. You're smart," Emily said. "Lord, you're handsome enough. What don't you have, except money? And they've got that."

"Daniel Bonner's got that," Tom said, watching reflected sunlight cast circles on the ceiling and sparkle in Emily's diamond rings. She had folded her narrow hands on her narrow knees, and looked like an ordinary woman of forty-five who saw nothing more than the flowerbeds in her garden.

"Daniel approves of you," Emily said, and glanced at his thoughtful face, admiring it. He had his mother's eyes. If his ears stuck out a bit, who in the world would notice?

"Daniel seems to approve of my navy service, at least," Tom said. "I heard him tell his friends: 'Tom's cruiser was in battles at Tarawa and Wake and the Marshalls, and helped rescue the *Franklin* at sea.'"

Clara brought Tom's rosebuds in a cut glass vase; when she was gone, Tom watched the petals begin to unfurl. "Daniel's so… cool toward Anne. It hurts her; I can see it. But he's spending so much on our wedding."

"That's to impress the town."

"And our new house is almost finished."

"That's to impress people, too: 'the Bonner Homes,'" Emily said. "I imagine Anne agrees with every idea Daniel has for your house? She does anything she can to please him?"

"Yes."

"She's trying to make him love her."

"My boss at Morse Brothers said, *So you're dating Bonfire's daughter? He burned down his competition once. Keep your eye on him.*" Tom scowled. "I told you: I'm a foreigner."

11

"Anne's a foreigner here, too," Emily said. "Shut away miles from town...sent off to college."

"She's not what you think," Tom said.

"Who is?" Emily poured more wine in their glasses. "I'm constantly amazed at the people I think I know—catch a glimpse of their real selves, and you'll see they're just like children inside, yearning for something." She sat back in her chair and glanced at him. "I had a phone call today, and I'm mystified."

"You? Mystified? Impossible."

"You won't believe this." Emily put her wine glass down as if she needed both hands to deal with such a riddle. "An old friend from your California days—and mine—came here by train this afternoon. She'll be at dinner tonight, and she'll stay with me for a while." She was watching Tom. "Raina Weigel."

His face showed her nothing.

"She worked at a gallery after she graduated. Then she was a window-dresser. She started working on her M.A.. Every now and then she called to say she was going to marry, but she didn't. A month ago she wrote to tell me she was engaged to Vince Courson, that rich fellow with the beach house. The next week she called to say she was coming here for your wedding, and would I be able to put her up? Now she's here in town, a week early." Emily's voice had a prodding edge. "I don't know what to think."

Tom didn't answer. He turned his face away. Emily's sharp eyes moved over him as she said, "I've never told anyone you and Raina were... anything but acquaintances."

"You knew her mother for years, didn't you? You were best friends." Tom's eyes were on his wine glass.

"You know what I mean. Why has she come now, when you're being married?" Something about the way Tom sat with his face turned away softened Emily's voice. "When you'll have a honeymoon abroad, and your new house..."

"Maybe her heart's broken," Tom said. "She hasn't got anyone else to go to, has she? Her mother wasn't married, and didn't leave Raina anything. She's never had enough money."

Emily's darting glance had scorn in it; her earrings glittered as she turned her head. "She was a fool. She could have had you."

The doorbell rang. They heard Clara go to answer it, and then a young woman's voice.

"Raina," Emily said. She watched Tom as they stood up; he showed nothing more than polite interest. The same look was in

Raina's beautiful eyes as she came in.

"Such a marvelous hat!" Emily said as they hugged each other. "You're pretty as ever—so much like your dear mother. Here's Tom."

"I haven't seen you for so long," Raina said to Tom, pulling off her white gloves and putting her hat on a table. "Emily wrote about your wedding next Saturday. Congratulations." Her eyes were bright and a little red. "And you're taking me in, dear Emily. How much that means to me."

Tom watched Raina settle herself on the couch beside Emily, perching on the edge of it as if she were a guest not sure of a welcome. She said to Emily, "So you've just left Paris? Some old friends of yours in San Francisco told me to give you their love: the Atkinsons, and Rene Herbert, and Patrick." Again her polite, bland expression exactly matched Tom's.

They settled themselves at the dinner table, and Emily's look sharpened, listening to the two of them playing a game of "Do-You-Remember?" Raina smiled at Emily and said, "When I met your nephew, he thought he was too poor to ask me for a date."

For a moment—while Emily's eyes were on the serving cart at her elbow—Raina turned a lover's face to Tom: her eyes narrowed and glowed; she lifted her heavy hair from her shoulders with both hands.

Emily turned back to the table. Raina's expression was the cool, teasing look of a former friend. "Tom didn't know that I was living on a meal a day," she told Emily. "Didn't see that I wore the same sweater and skirt to every class at Berkeley, can you imagine? He didn't even notice."

"I can imagine," Emily said.

There was a moment of silence, then Emily said to Raina: "And you aren't marrying Vince?"

Vince's name, dropped into the conversation, caused small adjustments in the expressions of everyone at the table. But Raina, in the next second, said his name twice over. "Vince. Vince. No, I'm not. I can't. I've known that for a long time."

Clara came to carry away their dinner plates. When the pantry door shut behind her, Raina said to Tom: "So you came to Emily's town. She wrote that you found a job."

"As a salesman in a men's wear store," Tom said. "Until I started working for Anne's father. And what have you been doing since you graduated? When was it? 'Forty seven?"

Emily watched as Raina told about her work at the Reeno's gallery. "You remember that place, don't you?" she asked Emily. "The job wasn't so bad, but Reeno was. Finally I'd had enough. So I started my M.A., but I didn't have enough money, so I got a job at Harriman's. A window dresser, can you imagine—when I had a B.A. in art history?"

Emily smiled. She had caught their dutiful tone. They were asking each other questions and giving answers by rote, like old married people who keep their secrets and perform for guests, never expecting each other to be interested or surprised.

3

The church sanctuary, full of wedding guests and organ music, was bright, but the church parlor seemed brighter still when Raina followed Emily through the parlor door. The big room was lit by Anne Bonner's glow of white satin, white lace, white ruffles, white tulle. She looked fragile and young, almost hidden under bridal finery: pale face and big blue eyes. The brightness surrounding her cast a faint shimmer on anyone who approached; Emily caught that reflection as she went nearer, and Raina's long hair was silvered with it.

"Who's *that*?" one bridesmaid said to another, staring at Raina in her vivid flowered dress. "That *long hair*. And that *gorgeous* hat."

"I should call you 'Mother,'" Anne said to Emily. "You're the closest thing to a mother that Tom and I have." She held out her huge bouquet with a laugh. "I'd hug you, but 'see what careless love has done.' I'm swaddled and smothered in matrimony already."

"How lovely you look," Emily said. "I want you to meet the daughter of a good friend of mine: Raina Weigel from San Francisco. She's staying with me just now."

Anne smiled at Raina. "I'm so glad you're here for our wedding."

"I hope you'll be very happy," Raina said.

"You haven't met Tom yet, have you?" Anne said. "I *will* be happy—you can't imagine how wonderful he is."

"Raina and Tom met at my house..." Emily began, but a tall, middle-aged man walked up, coming just close enough to Anne so that Raina could see he was more than a friend. Then he turned his cold, strange eyes on her, and they were as blue as Anne's.

"Raina, this is Daniel Bonner, Anne's father," Emily said. "Daniel, Raina Weigel's a friend of mine from California."

"The procession's forming," one of the bridesmaids called.

Anne took her father's arm; the wedding party fell silent and waited in their places.

Emily, sitting with Raina in a church pew, heard the crowd hush; the organ began to play. She watched Tom and his best man enter, splendid in their tuxedos, to wait for the bride. Now and then Emily glanced at Raina, and Raina's eyes were always on Tom; she hardly seemed to notice Anne and Daniel Bonner pacing down the aisle after the bridesmaids.

A young man sang. Daniel gave the bride away. Vows were given and rings exchanged. Raina watched Tom, her hands twisted in her lap. The groom kissed the bride. The bridal party walked down the aisle and out.

Raina watched. Emily never saw her expression change. When the bridal party was gone, Raina's eyes were very bright, that was all. She followed Emily into the warm summer dusk.

Emily found her car. They waited in line to leave the church lot. "Daniel's using the whole Rolinger Gallery for the wedding reception and dinner," Emily said when they reached the street. "I wrote you about the Rolinger when Daniel built it and gave it to the city. He named it for his mother—her maiden name. He can use it for entertaining any time he pleases."

"Only the best for Anne's wedding," Raina said.

"Not quite. I think it's for Tom: his son and heir. Daniel's never cared much for Anne."

"Why not?"

"Who knows?" Emily shrugged. "Anne wasn't like her mother. Patricia was beautiful. *Such a plain child*, I've heard Patricia say about Anne, as if some bird had put the wrong egg in her nest." The line of cars let Emily enter it; she pulled into the street. "Bringing home Tom was the first thing Anne's done that's made Daniel care for her, I think." She glanced at Raina. "Do you ever see your father?"

"I don't even know where he is." Suddenly Raina's eyes filled with tears.

"My dear," Emily said in a gentle voice.

Raina gave one low sob, shook her head, blotted her eyes and swallowed several times. "He didn't want me. Same old story, I guess," she said in a muffled voice.

Emily swung her car into the Gallery parking lot that was filling rapidly. Wedding guests came from darkness to the bright, roofed courtyard; they chattered and drank champagne in the galleries.

The bridal party welcomed guests in the lobby. "Raina," Anne said when she saw her, "will you be here when we come back from our honeymoon?"

For a moment Raina's eyes met Tom's.

"You'll have to come visit us," Anne said.

Other guests were waiting to speak to the bride and groom. "I... don't know," Raina said; she wished them happiness, took a glass of champagne from a waiter and moved away, not meeting Emily's eyes.

"I've been hiding you at home," Emily said to Raina, "but tonight you'll meet anybody who's anybody in town. They're all here." She began to walk from group to group, Raina beside her. "This is Raina Weigel, my dear friend's daughter from San Francisco," she told each cluster of people, and gave their names to Raina without a stumble or stammer.

Faces that often looked bored by such introductions were not bored now, Emily noticed. People opened their ranks as she approached, and stopped talking to hear her say, "Raina Weigel." When Raina walked off to examine a painting, she wasn't alone for long: a man left a group to talk with her. Another man brought her more champagne.

Emily glanced over the crowd. Tom had made friends in town: young people surrounded the bride and groom. Emily's eyes narrowed as she caught sight of Daniel Bonner. The reception line had scattered; he stood by himself, the usual expressionless look on his face. It was his eyes, Emily thought: Daniel Bonner's ice-blue eyes. His feelings showed there for a second, sometimes, if you could catch their glint. It was not comfortable to have those eyes fixed on you.

Raina came to Emily. "They've announced supper, and they'd like you and me to go in with the bridal party," Raina said.

The main gallery shone with tables covered in white linen, crystal and silver. Tom and Anne were seated on the dais beneath a fiery painting of nude dancers.

Emily and Raina sat at the nearby table. Emily introduced

Raina to several men seated there and said, "Raina is doing graduate work at Berkeley." There was joking at the dais table; she heard Tom's laugh ring out.

"Art history," Raina said, answering a question. "I'll get my master's degree." The orchestra played something by Mozart. Raina cut beef on her plate into very small pieces. She ate one or two of them. She drank some water. After a while a waiter took her plate away. Miniature wedding cakes bearing miniscule brides and grooms were put before each guest. The scent of coffee filled the gallery.

The tiny wedding couple on Raina's miniature cake were ankle-deep in pink frosting. "We may have a surprise tonight," a man across the table said. He watched Raina topple her cake's bride and groom face-first into icing. "You've heard Daniel Bonner's giving his Van Roche to the museum?"

Raina said yes, she had. She left her cake on the plate, drank a little coffee and watched Anne sitting beside Tom. Anne had a nice figure and lovely deep blue eyes. Her nose was all right, and her teeth were even, but not much makeup, and that hair...

The tapping of a spoon on a glass hushed conversations and the orchestra. Anne sat through toasts to the bride, toasts to the groom, speeches, laughter and clapping. Tom sat through it with her, wearing his well-tailored tuxedo as if he didn't hate it, but she knew he did, playing his part so well for her father's friends in her father's town. Only Anne saw the beads of perspiration at the edge of his dark hair, and the nervous jerks of his hand where his new gold and diamond ring glittered. When their eyes met, she smiled and said in a whisper, "I'm numb. Are you? I'm squeezed and pinned and sprayed and stuck here like that big bouquet."

"Numb," Tom said. "Yes." He watched Anne's delicate profile against the bridal veil. The corners of her full lips were drawn in, as if her nerves, too, were tight.

"And not truthful," Anne said.

"Why?"

"We're pretending, aren't we?" Anne asked. "How many of these people do we know? But here we sit, smiling as if we're glad this crowd is here, pretending we're having a good time, pretending it's fun being 'the groom' and 'the bride.'"

"I love you," Tom said, and raised his dark eyebrows as if to show even more of his eyes' steady, deepening gray.

Anne's eyes lifted and shone as she whispered that she loved him, too. When Tom turned back to the room full of people, his ringed hand found and held hers.

The director of the Gallery rose to stand before a draped easel. He praised the gifts of Daniel Bonner to the Gallery and to the city. "It's a great honor," he said, "to announce yet another fine addition to a collection which is quickly becoming the pride of the state."

Daniel joined him. "This painting, 'Lightning On A Landscape' by Van Roche, is a gift to the Gallery on this happy occasion, in Tom and Anne's name," he said.

Anne and Tom made their way to Daniel's side. Most of the women were watching Tom. Emily saw Anne cover her mouth and chin with her fingers for a moment; it was a habit of hers...did she feel she wasn't pretty?

The director pulled the covering from the easel beside him, and two men held the painting at shoulder height.

The eighteenth-century landscape was thick with the electric dark Van Roche was master of—huddled trees were green-black, cliffs were gray-black, fields of grain were smoky yellow and brown, and all of it lay under an immense black storm cloud. A ragged stroke of lightning split that darkness, making ruins on a cliff stand out, white as bones.

The wedding guests murmured, then clapped. Daniel, Tom and Anne were lit by the sudden, harsh light of flashbulbs from photographers crouched before them.

When the newlyweds had danced alone on a shining new gallery floor, other couples joined them. Anne waltzed with her father. Tom came to Emily, who sat with Raina along the wall. "Won't you be my partner?" Tom asked Emily. "It's a waltz, and you like waltzes."

"I like to eat, that's the problem," Emily said with a sigh. "I've had too much good food. Ask Raina."

The three looked at each other for a second. Tom raised his eyebrows. Raina took his outstretched hand. She said nothing until they were in step, moving together without words; then she whispered, "I can't stand it."

"For old time's sake," Tom said, his eyes on Anne dancing with her father. She had wound her veil around one arm, so that she seemed to be dancing with two partners: Daniel Bonner and a bundle of white tulle.

Raina's face nearly touched the bridegroom's white carnation. "I should have stayed on the coast two thousand miles away," she said, her voice trembling.

"Yes," Tom said.

They danced to the end of the waltz, revolving in perfect time among the other dancers, as silent as two dead leaves spinning together. Raina didn't hear the music stop, until Tom moved out of her arms and another man stepped in. The new man's lips were moving; she looked up at him as if she had just waked from sleep, and saw Daniel Bonner.

Daniel had said something about Emily. "Emily was my mother's high school friend, and she's taken me in to stay with her," Raina said.

Daniel's eyes at close range had an easy, cool, flirtatious light, as though he danced with her at the center of a world he owned. "You met Tom at Emily's house in San Francisco," he said.

"Now and then," Raina said.

Daniel Bonner said nothing more, so that her last words seemed to echo in her ears until the music stopped.

Tom Hancock danced with wives of businessmen—businessmen he had waited on at Morse Brothers. Daniel danced with the bridesmaids, until he took Anne in his arms again. He said, "I miss your mother tonight. We married, and Patricia brought me everything: herself, a new life, a fine job, a beautiful house." His eyes were a bleak blue.

"Yes," Anne said. "I miss her. All my life I've missed her."

They stopped dancing as Tom tapped Daniel on the shoulder.

"I'll take Anne away from you, sir, if you don't mind," Tom said. "It's almost ten. Anne and I should probably change our clothes and slip away."

Music spilled into the June evening with light from the long, low Gallery. Anne and Tom, dressed in street clothes, ran through a rain of rice to their taxi and waved goodbye.

For a few moments after they drove away, the newlyweds were silent; then, as if on cue, they both sighed deep sighs, and then laughed. "We're through it," Anne said.

"It's over," Tom said. "Now for our hotel, a drink, and then a nice cool shower."

"Yes," Anne said in a grateful tone. She straightened her hat, and rice spilled from the brim. "Creature comforts."

"All of them," Tom murmured as he kissed her. "We'll have every one."

Tom had already registered at their hotel; they could take an elevator like any married couple. Their suitcases stood in the bridal suite, where a huge bed waited in rosy lamplight. Anne took off her hat and gloves, unpacked her clothes and laid her white nightgown on the bed. The mirror showed her a young woman covering her mouth with her fingers.

But Tom was calling her; he'd mixed drinks for them. Anne finished hers faster than she'd meant to; Tom mixed more. Anne watched the lamps of their suite grow softer and the colors grow brighter.

"I've run our bath," Tom said. Anne joined him at the bathroom door and laughed at the huge, pink, round pool, bubbling and fragrant, with rose petals on the water and fancy bottles along the rim, piles of towels, and twin showers above.

"C'mon," Tom said. "I'll be in before you are!" He began to strip, and Anne did, too; they tossed their clothes on brass racks. In a minute or two they were naked and splashing among rose petals in the warm, scented water.

Anne had dreaded taking her clothes off, but it turned into a game where lights were low; she shut her eyes and felt Tom's hands slide over her. It was so easy in the water, so comfortable when your body was half-hidden and you could touch someone else back, gingerly, a little at a time, while you kissed and murmured love words.

Tom's arms and chest were hard and muscled. It was hard for Anne to think that women went to bed and make love to human beings so big and bony...nobody ever talked about that. Didn't you get bruised every time you rolled against a man?

They splashed in the fragrant water, turning over each other like otters at play, murmuring and kissing. "You're so beautiful, so beautiful," Tom said, and kissed her all over, diving under rose petals, until she had to do the same for him. Petals slid down her cheeks and breasts, and caught in his thick black hair. The drinks and the warm, sweet-smelling water wrapped Anne in a dream as comforting as the big towel Tom put around her when they splashed out of the tub. They dried each other, climbed into bed, and her satin nightgown slid to the floor.

Anne crept close to Tom against the astonishing parts of his body...to think that he carried them around under his clothes...

she had seen pictures, of course, but the shape of them in her hands made her feel a kind of pity: they were so heavy and awkward and odd to wear all your life.

But she wasn't afraid. Under his kisses she felt what he was doing and threw her arms around his neck, and didn't cry out, and when he asked if it was hurting her, she shook her head and whispered, "I love you" over and over against his shoulder.

"I love you, too," Tom said when they lay side by side again, Anne's sleepy head on his arm. "You'll enjoy making love when you're used to it and it doesn't hurt. Wait and see." So he had known how she was feeling.

They were still for a while, kissing now and then, almost too tired and too relaxed to fall asleep. Finally Anne said, "I feel so...different. I was dreading being here with you. I was. Being embarrassed, being naked...it's an awful shock when you've lived with women all your life. Everybody thinks making love ought to seem natural, but I never thought it would be..." She stared straight ahead of her, then turned and kissed him. "Until now."

Tom held her tight. Anne rubbed her cheek against his shoulder, gave a small blissful sound and went to sleep in a few breaths.

Tom smoothed her fine, soft, damp hair. If a woman with dark eyes swam in his memory, whispering *I don't love anyone but you*, she floated in one dimension like oil slick on water, her thin colors eddying away.

In a minute or two they were splashing among rose petals.

4

A week later Emily Snyder joined her housekeeper at a card table. Clara Pedersen looked up and said, "You're happy."

"Raina's going back to California on Tuesday," Emily said.

"Well, I should hope so." Clara was a large, middle-aged woman whose thick-rimmed glasses were large, too. They slid down her nose and she pushed them back with an absent-minded poke.

Emily dumped dominoes out of their wooden box with more noise than usual. "I was worried. So were you."

Their eyes met across the card table. Clara looked thoughtful. "She'll be gone when the newlyweds get back from the honeymoon."

Emily looked grim. "At least I won't have to lie."

"If you hadn't moved to San Francisco—"

"I didn't want to. My dear Wendell did." Emily gave Clara her darting, bird-like glance. "And, of course, I thought they'd marry."

"No money, I suppose," Clara said.

"Raina wrote about where she lived in Berkeley. I couldn't believe it," Emily said. "She'd found a broom closet in a run-down house near the campus. A broom closet! She said that she slept with her head against one wall and her feet against the other. Cooked on an electric plate on the floor. They let her rent it for fifteen dollars a month, if she promised not to tell anybody she was there. And I think Tom…stayed there, too, you know…some of the time."

Clara won the game. Emily mixed the dominoes and they set

up new lines before them on the table. After a while Clara pushed her glasses up with a poke and said, "Tom wouldn't risk losing everything he's got now."

They looked at each other, then at the dominoes before them. Clara sighed. "Well. Raina's going."

They settled down to an interesting hand in the game they had invented, a game where every domino that was half blank could, at any time, become three pieces in one: a blank, or its single number, or its double number. For a while, struggling with all the combinations of fives, they forgot Raina and Tom.

Clara won again. They mixed the heavy brass-studded dominoes with scrapes and clicks and set them up for the next game. Emily said, "No secrets to worry about, except…"

"Except for the reason Raina's going back to California," Clara said. She could finish most of Emily's sentences, and often did. After long practice, Emily might pause halfway to let her do it. Once in a while Emily stopped halfway when company was present, but then Clara, always alert to her several roles, played her third role and was a blank.

"I've got the double six," Emily said, looking at the dominoes she'd drawn.

"You've given her the money to finish her master's degree." Clara laughed at the guilty look on Emily's face. "That's the secret. You've given her the money to get her into school way out in California. And, of course, we won't have to put up with her."

"Untidy," Emily said. She shook her head and her filigree earrings twinkled. "Absolutely no idea of keeping things in order."

Clara maintained a diplomatic silence.

"Maybe she'll meet a man out there," Emily said. "He'd have to be…"

"Rich," Clara said.

After a while Emily said, "I gave her the money for Tom's sake. Raina's so…"

For a moment the two women gazed at each other over the dominoes, an identical speculative look in their eyes.

"You're worried," Emily said in a while. "You think Bonner's going to put Tom on his payroll and then proceed to make his life miserable?"

Clara said, "There's that. Yes." She looked at Emily over her thick-rimmed glasses. "But the important thing is: does Tom love Anne? Or is it the Bonner money he's interested in?"

"Well!" Emily said. "He certainly hasn't said a word..." she looked at Clara sidewise with a little smile. "Aren't you asking a lot of a young man who was just a clerk in a store?"

"Asking a lot? All I want him to do is to love Anne. She's a prize, all by herself."

Emily paused, then said tentatively, "Anne's a nice girl and you're fond of her, I know. She's helped you out, hasn't she? Helped your relatives, too?"

"I've known her since she was seven." Clara hadn't looked at her dominoes, or touched them. "I could tell you..." her voice trailed off.

"She's certainly nothing like her father—"

"No!" Clara said in a loud, unfamiliar voice. She pushed her glasses higher on her nose with a determined poke. "You don't really know what Anne's like. You're Tom's only relative. You might be able to help Anne somehow."

"Well, I will." Emily looked surprised. "Of course I will, but why would she need help from me? She certainly doesn't need money."

For a moment Clara moved her dominoes about as if arranging words in her mind. "The first day I saw Anne, I was so sorry for her," she said. "I almost cried, sometimes, watching her."

"Sorry? Oh—of course. The year her mother died. A horrible accident."

"The summer of 'thirty-two," Clara said. "I'd just come to work for Daniel and Patricia at their new house. I was housekeeper and cook. Bill Hanson was gardener—the Bonners were wild about gardening."

"Bonner took forever getting that house built," Emily said.

"Bill Hanson and I..." Clara took a breath and went on, 'we talked about Anne. It was so sad. A seven-year-old, and no one to love her."

"Not her father and mother?"

"No. I could see it right away, and so could Bill. Anne tiptoed around them...tried to whisper when she talked to them. And they had almost nothing to do with her. You'd have thought Patricia and Daniel were newlyweds, the way they cuddled and kissed. They were gone most of the time, or wandering around their new 'estate,' planning how they were going to garden, garden, garden and buy, buy, buy."

"Waterloo folks called Daniel 'Bonfire Bonner' by then," Emily said.

"That little girl could read books, whole books, at seven—how she loved books! She read *The Secret Garden* to Bill and me while the three of us had dinner in the kitchen. The Bonners ate in style in the dining room, if they were home. Anne loved *The Secret Garden*. She said she wanted her own garden."

Clara sighed. "One morning I saw the Bonners from the kitchen window. I could hear them; they were planning the terraces down to the river and laughing. Anne brought her box camera and took their picture—Daniel looking like a pirate in a picture book: that dark hair, bushy eyebrows, and Patricia in his arms, smiling up at him, a marcelled blond. I heard Anne ask them if she could have a garden. She asked in the soft voice she always used when she talked to them. She said it twice: 'Could I please have a garden, too?' And they didn't listen. They never even looked at her. They walked away, still talking about terraces and espaliered fruit trees." Clara shook her head. "She wanted that garden."

"She never got one?" Emily said.

"Oh!" Clara cried. "If only she hadn't! But she came and asked Bill and me if we could keep a secret. 'I've found a place for my garden!' she said. So off the three of us went to the big meadow on one end of Bonner's property near the highway, and Hanson dug her a twelve-foot-square garden there—took out a lot of big stones and piled them under an oak tree. He gave Anne seeds and hid a barrel of water for her, and she watered that garden and weeded that garden, and by July she had zinnias and marigolds in bud. She talked and talked about how she'd surprise her parents with her secret garden when it was all in bloom."

Clara sighed. "And then one morning that child climbed the big oak tree there. She told me she'd wanted to see how her garden looked to the birds. But she climbed too high, and when she looked down she just froze, and started to scream. She screamed and screamed until she couldn't make a sound, but we didn't hear her: I was in the kitchen, and Patricia was reading in the front garden. Daniel was in Waterloo.

"Finally it was lunch time, and her mother went looking for Anne and found her. Patricia was five months pregnant, and I've never known why she climbed that tree to get Anne down—why didn't she go for Bill Hanson? But she climbed, and a big branch on that oak was rotten, and Patricia went down head-first on the pile of stones Bill had piled there."

"Oh, my!" Emily said. "We never heard about that! Not a word! They just told everybody that Patricia had fallen and hit her head. Such a tragedy, we all said. She wasn't even thirty. And Bonner took it very hard, we thought. He didn't go to his office for months afterward."

Clara stirred her dominoes on the table. "I'll never forget finding Patricia. When I saw her smashed up and dead, I went running and yelling for Hanson, and he came with a ladder and climbed to Anne. She couldn't loosen her hands from the oak trunk, or shove her sandals out of the tree crotch, but he was patient; he talked to her until she let go and put her arms around his neck, and he brought her down with her face pressed against his shoulder so she couldn't see her mother."

"Oh my," Emily said. "Oh my."

"I gave Anne some warm milk and we put her to bed. I didn't know what to do. Bill said, 'After you call the doctor, call Bonner at his office. Tell him there's been a death in his family, and then hang up, as if you're beside yourself.'

"'But he doesn't have any other family,' I told him. 'Not that I ever heard of.'

"'Never mind,' Bill said. 'And if he calls back, don't answer the phone. Can't tell him on the phone that his wife's dead, and the baby, too.'"

Emily stared across the table at Clara. "How terrible!"

"Bill and I were out in the hall, but Anne must have heard us, because she called to me: 'Where was the baby? Where was the baby?' She wanted to know how there could have been a dead baby. She cried and cried, and said she'd climbed too high in the oak and was scared, and her mother had tried to get her down, and the branch cracked and her mother fell, and where was the baby?

"So I called their doctor—Bateman—he lived close by, just along the river. He came right away, and they carried Patricia home. And Bonner drove from his office," Clara said. "Wondering all the way, I suppose, whether it was Anne who was dead, or Patricia."

"Awful," Emily said. "Simply awful."

"We heard Bonner's car coming, so I went out on the drive with Bill. Anne must have heard the car, too—she came just as Bonner climbed from it, and she ran to him with her arms out, crying. And the look he gave her! It stopped the child as if she'd run into a wall."

There were tears behind Clara's dark-rimmed glasses. "Bonner yelled at Anne: *Why couldn't it have been you?*"

Emily left the table to stand at the window, staring at garden flowers swaying in a hot wind. Clara sat at the table, her head propped on her hand, and said again: *Why couldn't it have been you?*

"What did Bonner do then," Emily asked without turning.

"He yelled, 'Mrs. Bonner? It's Mrs. Bonner?'" Clara said. "I couldn't bear to tell him it was—I just told him that Anne had a secret garden in the meadow, and she had climbed a tree beside it and couldn't get down…that she was stuck up there for a long time, and Mrs. Bonner must have heard her crying and climbed the tree, and a branch broke. I said we'd brought Mrs. Bonner in and put her on her bed. He ran into the house, and we heard moans and sobbing, and then he slammed his bedroom door.

"We looked for Anne, but we couldn't find her—not in the house, not in the woods. Finally I opened the closet door in her bedroom. There she was, hugging her stuffed animals and crying in the dark. I coaxed her out; she was trembling all over. She couldn't eat any lunch, but I held her on my lap for a long time. At first Bonner kept to his bedroom after the doctor left and the police came. The funeral home took the body away. Afterwards, Bonner roamed the house all afternoon, drinking from a bottle. We could see Anne sitting on a bench in one of the gardens. 'That's a good place for her,' Bill said. 'It's peaceful there.'"

Clara sighed. "We never should have let Anne go out of the house. It looked like a storm was coming before dark, so Bill went out to call for her. Finally he found Anne, and he didn't know what to do: Anne was crouched at the edge of the meadow watching Bonner in the middle of her secret garden. He was pulling up every flower—zinnias— marigolds—yelling, throwing them in the air, stamping on them!"

"Ruined it?" Emily came back to the table. "Anne's garden?"

"Bonner ran off then," Clara said. "Anne was crying and crying. She found her trowel, and Bill brought his shovel and they buried the smashed garden. But she saved some of the flowers that weren't muddy and laid them on the grass. 'It wasn't your fault,' she kept saying to the flowers. 'You wouldn't ever have hurt her. Why would you hurt her? It wasn't your fault.'"

The two women sat without speaking for a while.

Finally Emily said, "So you decided to live at Bonner's all the time?"

She would surprise her parents with her secret garden when it was all in bloom.

"I couldn't leave Anne," Clara said. "Bill never lived there; he had a house in Cedar Falls. Bonner paid plenty for a housekeeper, and I didn't have anybody else to live with, and I wanted to send my niece and nephew to college. Bonner acted as if Anne didn't exist, but that was nothing new. She really lived with Bill and me, not him. When Bonner was home, he talked on the telephone or read the papers, and after a few months he rented an apartment in town, 'to be near his business,' he said. Finally he sent Anne off to a girl's school in the east. Anne wrote me every week, and I wrote her, and she came home summers, so we had good times."

"You've been like a mother to her," Emily said.

"And then Bonner sent her to Cornell College, and the poor girl was so happy. You know why? She told me: 'Dad doesn't want me too far away—Cornell's only ninety miles from him.' Imagine that." Clara scowled at Emily.

"She wrote me letters about how Cornell was almost a girls' school by then—the boys were going to war by every train. The coeds had to be in the dorm by seven forty-five every night, so she sat in tiny dorm rooms and heard girls talk about engagement rings and wedding dresses and silverware patterns. If they couldn't get married, they'd have to be a secretary or a teacher or a nurse. They talked about sex, she told me; they called it 'making love,' and 'losing your reputation,' and said it really meant 'losing your virginity.'

"They asked Anne how many boys she'd kissed, and couldn't believe she hadn't kissed one. She had a few dates with service men stationed at the college. She held hands with one of them in the Mt. Vernon movie balcony, and she kissed another at the dormitory door so she could say she had. She majored in English, and spent summers with college friends she made—that's when I came to work for you.

"Bonner spent more time on his gardens than he ever spent with his daughter—he was out in all weathers, spring, summer and fall, digging in the dirt with Bill Hanson. We thought the war would go on forever. When Anne graduated, she asked her father what she should do next, and all he said was, 'Suit yourself,' and went back to his espaliered trees and grafting and mulching…"

"And then she met Tom," Emily said.

"She knows how I love her," Clara said. "We still spend time together…you know we do. She can talk about anything with me. A few weeks ago she said, 'Was my mother pregnant when she died? I remember asking and asking, Where's the baby? And the baby was a boy? Once I heard my father say, *I've lost a son*."

Clara sighed. "I had to answer her. I said, 'It was a boy. Your father made the doctor tell him.'"

The two women were quiet for a while, watching afternoon shade deepen the garden's green.

Emily said at last, "How very sad. How awful. And we never heard about it. Not one word."

"I've told her," Clara said. "Over and over I've said to her: 'It wasn't your fault. Ever. It was the tree. The branch broke. That's all.'"

5

The wake of the great ocean liner cut a gash in the sea, until—almost at the horizon—the ocean healed itself, fading in haze. Tom and Anne watched, leaning on the rail, planning their month in London and Rome.

Wind from the Atlantic snapped Anne's headscarf like a flag, and when Tom kissed her, he tasted salt on her lips.

In a few days rough weather half-emptied the ship's dining rooms, lounges and ballroom. Tom had ridden a navy cruiser through storms; he wasn't seasick. Neither was Anne. They wandered from deck to deck, laughing to find themselves rising like birds aloft on one step, only to come down with more than their weight on the next.

Sunshine met them when they stepped from their train in London. They stared at a city still scarred by war. Piles of rubble lined streets. Beautiful row houses showed sky through their shattered windows: blue eyes in a skull. Crosses and flags and dying bouquets of flowers marked where bodies still lay under ruins. "Americans!" a woman in a restaurant snarled when she heard them talking. "You made a mint of money, you did! Sent us junk on Lend-Lease!"

London's galleries and plays and sights surrounded Tom and Anne. They saw very little of it. They ordered breakfast and lunch and supper in their Chelsea hotel room, and spent the days in bed.

"We're crazy," they told each other, and didn't care. They were out of their country and out of their everyday bodies, making one out of two, hidden from every eye.

"You're so..." Tom said one day, and stopped, faced with a hundred clichés. "I love you," he said. "That's all. Do you know you hum after you make love?"

"Do I?" Anne said, and giggled. "Well, I'm happy. I'm home. You're my home. I've never really had one."

Days went by, but at last they sat up in bed, looked at each other, and laughed. "We *are* in *London*," Anne said.

"Some of the most fascinating objects in the whole world are out there," Tom said.

So they sighed, put on their clothes, and went out to see.

The National Gallery, the Victoria and Albert, the Museum of Natural History... Tom and Anne roamed London, and kissed in doorways, and behind famous statues, and under Nelson's monument in Trafalgar Square. After one long morning, they went back to their hotel and their bed, while double-decked red buses rumbled along King's Road below their window.

"You read my mind... you do," Tom murmured in Anne's ear.

"You'd had one museum too many," Anne said, holding him tight and rocking them back and forth under the sheet. "You kept looking at the nudes. I saw you." She giggled. "You weren't interested in anything but naked women."

"You're amazing," Tom said.

"I'm hungry," Anne said. "Nobody ever told me making love was such hard work. I'm eating enough for two—" she stopped, her eyes wide. "Do you suppose I am?"

"What?"

"Eating for two?"

"You said you wanted—"

"I do. I do. If there's anything in the world I'd like to be and have never been, it's pregnant," Anne said. "I want to trundle around like somebody with a wheelbarrow— with the baby going first through doors and me following after. I want to do absolutely nothing for nine months and produce a human being who looks exactly like you. Can you think..." her eyes were very blue, "...of any other miracle like that?"

"Yes, I can," Tom said, running his hand along Anne's soft cheek. "And she's hungry. Time for lunch."

Anne watched Tom walk across their bedroom. She'd seen men in swim trunks and wondered: wasn't it hot, having hair on your chest and arms and legs all the time? It must prickle under your pants and your shirtsleeves. Wouldn't you button that hair into buttonholes and zip it in zippers? How could your hands ever feel clean when they were so fuzzy? And men's hair grew while they slept; they woke in the morning to find it on their chins again. There Tom was, rubbing his face as he looked in the mirror. Perhaps she got hungry when she made love, and he grew whiskers?

He was so handsome. Anne smiled. Above his hipbones he had angular ridges like the shape of a shield or the shell of a turtle.

"Hurry up, you exquisite creature, you can't eat in a sheet." Tom got into his shorts and pants and stood over her. Anne remembered he hadn't even blinked the first time he saw her wearing nothing but her rings, so he'd already seen his first naked woman. Maybe more than one.

Anne got out of bed, thinking how much she didn't like to think about Tom's women. She dressed in a hurry and barely glanced in mirrors as she passed, but when she put on lipstick and a hat, she had to face the mirror and see ordinary-looking Anne Hancock, rumpled and much-kissed, with eyes that Tom said were "so blue, so beautiful." Maybe they were, but she saw the looks women gave Tom as he passed. "And how did she get *him*?" their eyes said as they ran over Anne Hancock.

As if to underscore her thoughts, there was Tom before her, dressed to leave, his billfold in his hand. "I'm not used to finding all this cash in my pocket," he said, counting a sheaf of big pound notes.

He didn't see the look in Anne's eyes. Anne turned her back on him and his billfold. "It won't seem like so much money when you're at the Foundation, choosing ten worthy causes from a thousand," she said.

"I hope I can earn this kind of keep."

"You'll make Dad happy. I think he can't bear listening to the woes of poor people. He was too poor too long, fought his way up, went through so much," Anne said. Tom held her dress jacket for her, and followed her out to King's Road.

They walked in sunny Chelsea along blocks of little shops, then turned down Danvers Street toward Cheyne Walk and the Thames. Suddenly Anne stopped, turned back and looked down. Far below the railings and the street, a garden bloomed against a cellar wall below ground. A woman was watering her plants at the bottom of that stone well.

Anne leaned over the railing. "I've heard of a sunken garden, but never one as deep as yours," Anne called. The woman looked up, surrounded by her flowers. Anne smiled, and she smiled back. "It's beautiful, and so unlikely," Anne said.

"Likely," the woman said. "If you consider the sun. Straight overhead this time of day, and plenty of light otherwise."

"I'll remember you," Anne said to her, and walked on with Tom.

"People smile at you. They like you. Haven't you noticed?" Tom said to Anne. "They come to talk to you when we're at plays and concerts and dinners. We ought to have some housewarmings when we're settled at home. Daniel doesn't entertain much, does he?"

"Sometimes I think people in town resent Dad's success," Anne said. "He doesn't have any close friends—not ones who come to visit, anyway." As they came to Cheyne Walk, red double-decked buses going opposite ways along the Thames missed each other by a foot or two. "I suppose he's made enemies."

Tom said nothing.

"Here's Crosby Hall," Anne said, looking at her guidebook and then at the great stone building. "Built in 1466—they moved it here from Bishopgate, if you can imagine, to Sir Thomas More's garden. Now it's a 'hostel for female graduates.'" They went down a walk to look at Crosby Hall's oriel window, and she said, "Dad's a fighter. He grew up on the streets. He thinks those who aren't for you are against you."

The Albert Bridge spread its cobweb of piers and cables above boats on the Thames. Anne and Tom strolled along Cheyne Walk watching the river, and were watched by old men on sidewalk benches as they went into the *King's Head and Eight Bells*.

The pub was dim, but rich with rows of bottles and the sparkle of glasses hung upside down above the bar. In the back room a woman waited behind a display case that held a whole turkey, roasted and golden, and a sliced ham. There was beef beside it, red at heart, and plump croissants beside chunks of baked-brown potato. All was set off with the greens of lettuce and peas and the whites of sliced bread.

Tom told the woman what they wanted, and she heaped their plates. Anne sat at one of the small, battered tables and watched him. He was so handsome and he was smart, aware from the beginning of what he didn't know and had to learn. He'd be director of a foundation...

Her love for him shone in her eyes. "Delightful," she said, picking up her napkin as Tom set her plate before her. "Delicious."

Tom joined her in a first swallow from their tall glasses. "The cider?"

"The cider. The love-making," Anne said, smiling into his lash-shadowed gray eyes. "Being here in London with you."

Tom took her hands, turned them over, and kissed the palm of each one. "I always wanted a honeymoon in London..." he hesitated. "And going to see the Changing of the Guard."

"Let's go," Anne said. "Tomorrow. Then you'll know whether watching the queen's palace guards stamp up and down in tall black hats and red coats makes a honeymoon complete."

"Yes," Tom said, holding her hands tight for a moment.

So the next day, a rainy day, they stood with a crowd to see the Changing of the Guard. When the ceremony was over the sun came out, and a man on the street uncovered his cart of cheap trinkets: British flags, cardboard models of the queen's coach, Westminster Abbey postcards, and rows of guardsman dolls in red and black. The button eyes of the dolls watched Tom as he passed. Their toy mouths were shut tight under the straps of their tall black hats.

"Sunshine!" Anne said. "And while we're enjoying ourselves, Dad's hard at work finishing our house."

"For you," Tom said. She heard the reassurance in his voice.

"No," Anne said. "I don't think so. He wants to set you up in his business. We'll need to entertain. You're the son he never had, and he's delighted with you."

The private Bonner road, winding through forest trees, ran past Daniel's house and ended at another—a long, low stone house on the river bluff, surrounded by lawns, gardens and forest. Woodland joined the houses with its gravel paths from garden to garden. At each back patio, flights of stairs and terraces led down to the river's wrinkled silk.

On an early August morning Daniel drove down his forest road with a car full of florist bouquets for every room in the new house. He roamed the place for a last time. On his way to the station, he drove slowly, looking back at the house in its woodland as long as he could see it.

When the train hissed to a stop at Waterloo, Anne saw him standing alone on the platform.

"Nobody here to meet us but Daniel?" Tom said. "That's a strange homecoming."

Anne smiled as she gathered up her purse and coat. "He's worked on our new house for us for a year. Now it's ready, and he wants to show it to us all by himself."

Tom watched as Anne kissed her father.

Daniel shook hands with Tom. "Welcome home," he said.

"Roses!" Anne said when she found them in Daniel's car. "For me?"

"For you," Daniel said.

Anne blushed with pleasure. "So lovely." She held the pink roses to her pink face for a moment.

Iowa's summer greens were deep on both sides of the highway. "Have you got somewhere for us to stay?" Anne said in a teasing voice as they turned on Daniel's private road.

"A temporary place," Daniel said. "Remember, nothing is permanent. Anything you two don't like can be changed."

Anne gave a muffled cry as they passed Daniel's house on a road that had once been only a rutted path. In a few moments sunlight crossed the river, fell through an opening in the trees, and tinted a driveway pink, and a winding walk. It flooded over the low stone house backed by forest. "Home," Anne said softly to Tom. "Home."

Tom got out of the car to open Anne's door, and looked at Daniel across the car top. "I've never in my life had anything like this," he said. "I hope to pay you back—it will take years. I can't think of the right words to thank you."

"Don't even try," Daniel said. "You'll have to carry Anne over the doorstep. Can't break any traditions."

Anne went over the doorsill in Tom's arms; he kissed her and put her down in sunset light streaming through two-story living-room windows into the round hall. "It's all here," Anne whispered. She looked from the back view of river and trees to the woodlands and road at the front. "Everything, just as we planned it."

"There's your water sprite statue," Daniel said to Anne.

"You've worked so hard on this." Anne's arm was around Tom, but her eyes were on Daniel. "Oh, look!" she cried. "The beautiful dining room...and the kitchen! You put in those imported cupboards just because Tom admired them...and the tile and curtains to match..."

The master bedroom was in the vivid colors Tom and Anne had

chosen. "Wonderful view," Tom said, and went through a French door to the bedroom's walled garden. Summer flowers spread their scent on the air as the day cooled and bees still hummed among them.

"You can lay out the rest of the gardens to plant next spring," Daniel said, coming to stand on the flagstones with Tom. "I had this one filled with the obvious annuals, but we wanted an English cottage garden, you remember." Anne watched the men from the master bedroom. A big bed's embroidered white canopy and curtains stirred in breeze from the open door.

She followed the men from one bedroom to another. "The stained glass angels," Tom said. "The window seats," Anne said. When they came into the patio room, Anne clapped her hands in delight. "My light carts! You've brought the violets! All my African violets." The flowers glowed under lights: blue, pink, white, purple.

The patio was a half-moon of flagstones, with steps descending to the river past newly built terraces. Anne followed Tom and Daniel down to the dock. She followed them up again to the laundry, and the big kitchen where a smiling housekeeper named Mirabelle was making supper. Anne followed them through the garage and the gardener's storage room. "You've given us everything we talked of," Tom said to Daniel.

They drank champagne in the living room, then Mirabelle served dinner in the new dining room on new china and linen. Tom sat at the center of his own home; it surrounded him, softly lighted, rich room after room.

"I'd never imagined I'd own such a place," Tom told his aunt Emily the next day. "Not just the expense of it. Until I visited Daniel's house, I'd never believed homes could be so empty and peaceful."

"No clutter," Emily said.

"I'd lived all my life in that clutter: every surface covered with telephones, family pictures, baskets, boxes, figurines, plastic flowers, decorated plates, souvenirs, piles of magazines, opened mail, candy bars and beer bottles, calendars, trophies, newspapers..."

"You had sense enough not to comment."

"I'd never have chosen what they did. They couldn't have imagined my kind of taste."

"Or perhaps if they could imagine it, they never showed it."

"Never! They planned the new house and the wedding and the wedding trip, and what did they do?" Tom grinned and shrugged his shoulders. "They *included* me, so gently, so thoughtfully: 'Of course you will want...'"

Emily smiled, too. "And of course you wanted it."

"Beyond my wildest dreams! I'd always wanted it, without ever knowing it. I'd never lived that kind of life."

"You might have never lived it."

"And they put me there so gently, like somebody opening a door and saying, 'Where have you been? Why has it taken you so long?'"

Tom watched the trees in Emily's garden move in the wind beyond walls of glass. "But they saw me, you know. As I was when they met me."

"Yes," Emily said. "You can't help that."

Sunlight and shade flickered over their terrace as Anne and Tom finished breakfast the next Sunday. Anne began to open letters piled for their return. "Mr. and Mrs. Thomas Hancock," she said. "From California."

She opened the envelope to read the card and note. "Raina Weigel," she said, handing them to Tom. "She remembered I have violets, and she knows a hybridizer!"

Tom didn't hear her; he had opened Raina's note, and was intent on one paragraph: "I'm enjoying the medieval art seminar, but I have to guard against boredom in the rest of my classes. Berkeley is full of men returning on the G.I. Bill. The old guard on the faculty must feel the place has changed."

Tipping Raina's note to the sunlight, Tom saw the ghost of a dash under each "guard"—nothing more than the impression of a sharp red fingernail. The salutation was "Dear Tom and Anne," and two more grooves had been pressed under "Dear" and "Tom."

"Such an odd name," Anne said. "'Raina.'"

Tom caught a scent he knew; Raina had perfumed the note he held in his hand. "'Raina' means 'Queen,'" he said. "'Raina' is the name of the female lead in Shaw's play, *Arms and the Man*."

Anne took the note to add to her pile. "Or *The Chocolate Soldier*?" she said.

6

"Come and have lunch with me," Anne called one morning when she saw Daniel coming down the path from his house. "We can take a look at my catalogs. You know so much. What should we have in the patio beds, and the terraces—and around the sun dial in the cottage garden?"

"A garden like Sissinghurst, all green and white?" Daniel said, his blue eyes intent under their bushy brows.

They read the catalogs. They went to the local nurseries. In a few days Daniel said, "Do you think you'd like a 'rockery'?" Anne said she would, and for a week Daniel hunted for rocks in farmers' fields and had them hauled to "Anne's gardens." Father and daughter worked in rain or sun with Bill Hanson and his assistant. By late October "Anne's gardens" were ready for planting in the spring, and Tom had run Daniel's business for most of the mornings and many of the afternoons.

"Dad always loved gardening," Anne said to Tom in a contented tone on an October day. "And now we're so close. The trouble is that you've been working too hard. But winter's coming. I think he'll soon go back to the office full time."

But Daniel Bonner had come to like his free mornings…and yet his house seemed too big, and lonely, and Anne was so close. As the months passed, he spent less and less time at work. "Tom's running the business," he told Anne with a grin, and spent the mornings with her. He stayed for lunch to talk of nitrogen…crab grass…slugs…

"I've got my violets," Anne said one day, looking at the hundreds of blooming plants in her "plant room." "But what will you do for a garden all winter long?"

Daniel shrugged. "Dream of spring?"

"You ought to build yourself a greenhouse."

"A greenhouse?"

"Orchids?" Anne said.

"Orchids," Daniel said thoughtfully.

"Your study has a south wall. Make it a glass wall with a door and greenhouse beyond! Look at your orchids from your desk!" Anne clapped her hands in delight.

"You're like my mother." Daniel stared at her.

"Grandma?"

"Caring about everybody. You look like Patricia, and I loved her—she was all I wanted. But you're like my mother inside." There was a stunned look on Daniel's face. "Like my mother."

"And you loved her, too," Anne said, her eyes very blue and her cheeks suddenly flushed with what she felt.

"Yes," Daniel said. "For years she was all I had. She was all I could count on."

Anne couldn't speak. She pushed her chair back and went to look at her plant stands of violets.

"I remember my mother putting ink on the sleeves of my first suit coat to hide the worn edges," Daniel said. "And she wrapped her wedding ring in tape because it had worn thin, too."

"I've never known much about her," Anne said, "except that I'm named for her."

"She didn't live long enough to know that I'd left my friend Bill Drucker and Wasserman Street: no more knives and guns and hanging around corners. She worried about me, the way you do."

"I hate to see you living alone," Anne said.

"She never dreamed that I'd be a machinist's mate in the navy," Daniel said. "And marry Patricia Sadler, and have enough money to buy my mother anything...too late."

Anne came to put her arms around Daniel.

"Mother had a head for business," Daniel said. "She'd have loved to watch me take over Sadler Supply—see all the parts of it that were stupid, unprofitable. Me! Owning a company downtown, sinking the competition!"

"She'd be proud of you," Anne said. She had her head on his shoulder, and couldn't see the look on Daniel's face. He didn't answer her.

"Was Bill Drucker your best friend?" Anne asked.

"The toughest kid on the block," Daniel said.

"What happened to him?"

Daniel gave a laugh with no joy in it. "He was chief of police when I took over Sadler Supply. In a year or two they found him in the river."

"Drowned," Anne said. "Almost all the people you've cared for have died." She tightened her arms around him. It still seemed strange to her to touch Daniel.

"Almost all," Daniel said. "But there's one left." He pulled away from her encircling arms to look into her eyes.

"Two. Tom and me," Anne said. "Think of all you've given us." She kissed him. "You have two."

Daniel designed a greenhouse built beyond his study wall. He hurried the workmen so that it was finished just as autumn turned cold. The sunken floor was pea gravel; a glass roof vent lifted to let heat out. When the vent closed in winter cold, hot water radiators warmed the air. Double-decked tables topped in galvanized bench fabric waited for the orchids.

Anne drove with Daniel to orchid houses in the east, south and west. They were gone for days each time and came back with paphiopedilums with crinkled mustaches, crab-shaped cymbidiums, the small dancing dolls of oncidiums, and phalaenopsis hovering like moths. Father and daughter were close now, speaking in tongues Tom couldn't begin to understand or pronounce as they learned a greenhouse-full of long names: *Polystachya paniculata, Odontoglossum reichenheimii, Cirrhopetalum ornatissimum.*

"Anne's happy," Clara said to Emily. "When I saw her this afternoon, I thought she was nesting, just like a bird. Did she ever feel at home at Daniel's, except that Bill and I were there? But now she's got Tom. A nice boy. Kind. She has Daniel gardening with her, and she just lights up when the two of them are together. You've seen them. Doesn't she? It's the first time he's ever spent ten minutes with her."

The first snow of winter changed every view from the two houses; gardens and woods were framed by every window: fragile etchings. Tom and Anne slogged through drifts, their eyes half shut against the brilliant morning.

"To come back home...to live here, in these woods," Anne said, turning her face to the morning sun. "To let myself begin to remember how it was."

"What a different life I've had," Tom said. "My first eighteen years I lived in a California blue-collar neighborhood where all the houses were the same size, and built about the same time on the same plan. You could play in a friend's house and find the kitchen or bathroom with your eyes shut."

"I can't imagine that," Anne said. "Having a neighborhood."

"Hardly saw my father. He worked a night shift. I didn't understand. I thought for a long time that he didn't like my mother and me. Now I realize he was either working or exhausted."

"You knew your mother best."

"She wanted me to 'make good' in life." Tom's somber face was pink-cheeked with the winter wind. "I wonder what they'd think to see me here, so in love, so settled." He hugged Anne.

She hugged him back and said, "Do you know, Dad's beginning to like me. Really. I think he does."

"Of course he does. How could he ever—"

"See that meadow?" Anne pointed beyond the wood's edge to a wind-blown acre of snow. "I had my own secret garden there. And when I was seven, I climbed that oak..."

It was hard for Anne to go on. The oak spread shadows on snow like blue veins on white skin, running over the meadow and a vanished garden.

Daniel had beaten her flowers into the dirt, she said. Her voice trembled as she told him the words her father had shouted at her when he knew her mother was dead. Tom said, "My God." He held Anne tight, smoothing her hair with his hand. "My God."

One December morning Anne said to Daniel: "After more than a year, I still don't have a baby coming. You and Tom have jobs—isn't it time for me to go to work? Can't I be of some use while I'm waiting?"

Anne found a job as a volunteer in an old Waterloo building that wore a new sign: *Center for Senior Citizens*. Daniel had bought the building to make it into two floors of small apartments. It was nearly full of old people rescued from the streets.

"Dad wants me to help get the Center off to a good start," Anne told Tom. "The Center's one more way for him to pay the community back, I think, for all the good luck he's had with his

The oak spread shadows over a meadow and a vanished garden.

Waterloo business. I've got no training in social work, but I'll try to help the old folks—they've got nobody in the world who wants them."

Anne went to the Center every day.

"She's Daniel Bonner's daughter," a cleaning woman told a new worker on a cold, snowy morning. They peered at Anne around a corner. "He paid for this place."

"So what's she doing here?"

"I like her." The cook had come from the kitchen to join the pair of watchers. "She says if the old codgers won't eat nothing but mashed potatoes and creamed chicken and chocolate pudding, they ought to enjoy their last days."

"What about vitamins?" one cleaning woman said.

"They get them in their food. You'd be surprised where you can put vitamins."

"She's friendly," one cleaning woman said. "Asked did I like my work? I said it fed my kids, so who was I to say if I liked it or not?"

"So what's she doing here, asking do we like our work?"

"She said she hoped I did like it, anyway, and if I wanted different stuff to clean with to let her know because I'm the one doing it."

"She's a 'volunteer.' That's what you call people who don't need money."

"If they don't need money, why don't they stay home? I would," the cook said.

"I told her to get those real nice mops that wring theirselves, and she did."

"Rich people get bored, maybe."

They watched Anne. She stood at a lobby window. Snow was falling again. Beyond the window, a few people hurried along boarded-up storefronts, hiding their faces from the wind.

"Who's that?" the cook asked. A young, well-dressed man came in and went to Anne Bonner.

"Must be her husband," a cleaning woman said.

Anne took Tom's arm. "I'm glad you can substitute for our driver," she said as they left the Center. "I've got the directions."

"Who usually takes you?" Tom asked as they drove away.

"An old black man named George Tredwell," Anne said. "But he's sick today. He was a taxi driver, and he knows every street in Waterloo. Turn left at the next block."

They passed row after row of decaying houses and trash-filled lots. At last they found the house. "I'll go with you," Tom said as he parked.

"She's an old lady," Anne said. "You might frighten her. Will you stay out of sight while we talk?"

The door of the house was battered, and the doorbell didn't seem to be working. Anne knocked. After a moment she pushed the door. It opened on a filthy hall and filthy stairs.

"Mrs. Downey?" Anne called softly. "Louise?"

Tom followed Anne upstairs, but stayed on the landing. Windows there had been broken out; snow blew in. "Mrs. Downey? Are you here?" Anne called as she reached the second floor.

Doors were ajar there; some hung on broken hinges. Anne heard a small sound.

"Mrs. Downey?" Anne stepped into a room's dead, icy air. A platform of wooden boxes in one corner had a heap of blankets and coats on it.

"Louise Downey?" Anne said to the tattered heap. She went closer. A small and very wrinkled face with bright eyes peered from it.

"I hoped you'd be here," Anne said.

"What for? You ain't a relation."

"I'm a friend," Anne said. "Are you warm? I've brought a coat and some blankets, and hot tea."

At the mention of the tea Louise sat up. "Here," Anne said, "Put this coat on and keep warm."

The old woman, thin and bent, put her bony arms in the sleeves and buttoned herself up in the brown coat with a fake fur collar. "Do you mind if I sit down?" Anne asked.

"Help yourself."

There was no furniture in the room. Tom heard their voices clearly: there was a scraping sound as Anne pulled a wooden box across the floor. "Hot tea," she said, sitting on the box and pouring a cup for each of them from her thermos. "It's cold out there. It's snowing again."

"I don't look," Louise said.

Anne gave Louise the tea. Louise's scalp showed through her thin white hair as she bent her head over the hot drink and warmed her hands on the cup.

"Do you have neighbors?" Anne asked.

"Used to have," Louise said. "Used to live here with my man and my neighbors and my kids. Now there's nobody but Bill Boyd on the corner. He brings me food sometimes."

Anne poured more tea. "But you have your children yet, don't you?"

"Two boys, dead before me," Louise said. "And my man, too."

For a moment they were silent. A door somewhere banged back and forth in the wind.

"I work for the Center for Senior Citizens," Anne said. "For older folks who need a home. My name's Anne Hancock. We have free apartments not far from here. You'd have your food cooked and your cleaning done. You could think about whether you'd like to join us."

"You want me to pick up and go." Louise's black eyes were sharp.

"Not unless you want to. We'd be pleased to have you."

"I got my own home here," Louise said.

"I know you have," Anne said. "Maybe you don't want to leave it and live in an apartment."

"I got my own home," Louise said.

"It's awfully cold here."

"It's my place," Louise said. She put her cup on the floor and pointed at the ceiling. "See them cracks up there? They been like my friends. Every time I was having a baby I'd yell at the star up there, see it? And over there's a big spot that looks like an old man with just one eye."

"I see him," Anne said, filling their cups again.

"And I keep my Christmas presents for the boys and Bertie in that closet there," Louise said. "Bertie don't look in the back of the closet. He comes home from the plant and washes up, and I always have his clean shirt and pants for him. He works so late. He's not getting to know his boys. Not well."

Louise didn't seem to see Anne beside her. She finished her tea, burrowed deep in her mound of old blankets and shut her eyes.

"Goodbye, Mrs. Downey," Anne said after a few minutes. "I'll come back tomorrow with more tea." There was no answer from the blankets piled on the wooden boxes. She picked up the cups and the thermos and joined Tom on the landing.

"No old lady?" Tom said.

Anne didn't answer. They went downstairs, and into cold

winter wind. He looked at her. "You're crying?"

"She's starving up there," Anne said with a quaver in her voice. "And she's talking about the past as though her husband and boys are still there, not dead."

Tom took her cold hand in his. "You shouldn't come to places like this."

"No one else will," she said. "Will they?"

"You're…" he pulled her against him and kissed her…"you're so…" he kissed her again. "I love you," he said.

George Tredwell was at the Center when Anne came the next morning. "I told Louise Downey I'd be back to see her today," Anne said. "She liked the tea. And I've got an idea."

Snow had fallen all night. George drove Anne to Louise Downey's house and waited in the car. Anne had a camera over her shoulder, and the thermos and cups in a bag. The wind snatched Louise Downey's door out of Anne's grasp and slammed it against the wall with a shuddering bang.

Anne climbed the stairs and found Louise huddled under blankets. She opened her eyes when Anne bent over her. "It's my house," she said.

"What if I promise that any time you want to come back here, we'll bring you back, no questions asked?" Anne said, holding the thermos where Louise could see it.

Louise sat up to drink her tea. For a while the two sipped from their cups without speaking.

"What if you could roam your house any time you wanted to—take a look at every single corner and ceiling and closet and cupboard?" Anne said at last.

Louise's bright black eyes watched her over the plastic cup.

"What if we go over every single inch of this house?" Anne said. "Each time you tell me there's something you want to keep, I'll take a picture of it. We'll take pictures of what you see from every window, and the back yard, and the street—everything." She held her camera up for Louise to see. "Then I'll make a book of big pictures for you to look at every day. You can keep this house forever, but you won't be hungry or cold or alone any more."

Louise was silent for a while. Anne sat quietly beside her. At last Louise said, "I guess."

Anne packed the cups and thermos in the bag and helped Louise to her feet.

Louise wore the brown coat Anne had given her over a long woolen skirt and a pair of mismatched men's shoes. Anne took pictures of the bedrooms, bathroom and hall. Louise wanted a picture of the dented plaster up and down the drafty stairs. "You couldn't guess what messed up that wall, but it was my husband Bertie with a baseball bat," Louise said. "The night our Joe was burned to death, Bertie just picked up Joe's bat and smashed up and down those stairs, up and down. Up and down. Till he wore out."

Louise yanked her coat cuffs over her withered hands. "He wore out." Her chin quivered, and she took one sharp breath and swallowed hard.

The downstairs rooms were bare. "My boys park their bicycles outside the kitchen door," Louise said, dragging her long skirt through cigarette butts. "Handlebar streaks there on the wall, see?" The flash of Anne's camera lit a floor strewn with beer bottles and a condom, but Louise didn't seem to see anything but the black handlebar marks. "Joe's the smart one. I busted my ankle and he rigged up strings so I could turn things on in this here kitchen. See—there's the hook for the string above the door." The flash of Anne's camera lit the kitchen. Scarred walls showed where a stove and sink had stood. Unheated floors creaked under their feet.

"That's my cupboard," Louise said, scowling at a light blue square on a dingy wall. "My blue china in my blue cupboard." Anne's flash answered her.

"And my parlor," Louise said, shuffling with a gritty sound over smashed window glass in the front room. "The ladies on the block, they come on Thursday afternoons for tea and cake, and we play canasta."

Louise hardly seemed to notice Anne turning, turning, recording every wall, ceiling and corner, every window view, and the splintered doorstep they stepped over when the picture taking was done.

7

"Dinner parties?" Daniel said to Tom at supper that night.

"Dad's been a hermit," Anne said to Tom in a teasing voice. "Ever since Mother died, really. He never wanted to entertain. He hid. You'd have thought he was wanted by the police."

"Parties are so much work," Daniel said.

"But I've got your Betty and my Mirabelle, and we can hire good help," Anne said.

Tom knew she was right: she had Mirabelle and Betty—had them as friends. She talked with them by the hour. Anne remembered the names of their sons and daughters, and which one was having a baby, or a bad cold, or bad luck.

"You two will have to help me with the guest lists," Anne told Daniel and Tom. "Tell which ones to invite first. You work with important people every day."

So the important people were invited, and they came to enjoy themselves and examine the two houses on the bluff with politely inquisitive eyes.

A cleaning woman watched Anne Hancock come into the Center for Senior Citizens. "Did you see her in the paper this weekend?" the woman said to the cook.

"Her fancy house," the cook said. "Way out on the river."

Anne held the door of the Center open for a shabby man with a cardboard box under his arm. The old and homeless came to the Center from their hidden nooks in the city, carrying all they had salvaged from a life. Some hid under their blankets in their room at the Center, strangers in a strange place. Others were sociable like Louise Downey, who went from room to room, carrying Anne's album of pictures to show everyone "My Home."

George Tredwell met Anne in the Center lobby. "Louise Downey said she had to go home last night after you left. You told us we had to take her, but we thought we'd wait until you came."

"Back home?" Anne cried. "She'll freeze." George's face showed her nothing. "I'll talk to her," Anne said.

"I'll wait here," George said.

"Come with me," Anne said, starting to the dining room, still wearing her hooded coat.

"I better not," George said, not meeting Anne's eyes.

"Louise knows you now, better than she knows me," Anne said. "You can help."

Anne found the old people gathered to eat breakfast. Louise sat at a table in the middle, Anne's album of photographs under her chair.

"Mrs. Downey?" Anne said, stopping beside Louise. Suddenly the book of photographs came sailing off the floor in Louise's knobby hands, and Louise rose from her seat, tottering, her hair standing on end, black eyes glittering, the few teeth in her mouth bared. "Bonfire's daughter!" she cried. "Get away from me!"

"Mrs. Downey–"

"Get away!" Louise shouted. "I don't want a Bonfire cent! I want to go home!"

Several dozen people in the dining room sat transfixed, their hands holding a fork, a spoon, a piece of toast. George had stayed in the hall.

Now Louise began to cry: a mournful howl in her throat. "Your father set fire to Clingman's warehouses!" she shouted. "He burned up my boy Joe! He broke my Bertie's heart!" Suddenly she slung the big album away from her with both hands—it barely missed Anne's legs, skidded across the floor and broke open. Large photos of a streaked wall, a star-cracked ceiling, a parlor with smashed windows slid from its sprung rings.

"How'd I know you was Bonfire's daughter?" Louise yelled, and it seemed to Anne that the big room rang and echoed *Bonfire. Bonfire's daughter.* "I don't want your damn pictures! Get away from me! I'm going back home." Louise sobbed in the dead silence. She glared at Anne. She spat at her, shouting over the bright smear of saliva on the floorboards: "Leave me alone!"

The room was full of staring faces. Anne saw, for a shocked second or two, that many faces were not surprised: Louise was yelling something they understood. Their old faces watched Anne Bonner leave, brushing past George in the hall. She went into the women's rest room and stood at the sink trembling, until she was able to splash her face with cold water and put on a calm expression. *Bonfire's daughter.*

George was in the lobby. "We'll have to see if we can get Louise into the Home for the Aged," Anne said to him. "She can't go back to that house of hers to sleep in rags."

George said nothing; he kept his old, red-veined eyes on the street outside the windows.

Anne looked at his expressionless face. "Have you heard stories like that about my father?"

"Yeah," George said.

"People believe them?"

"Yeah. They remember."

"That my father set fires? Killed people? When?"

"In 'twenty-nine. Clingman, he was Bonfire's competition. Had his warehouses by the river. Where the Bonner Building is now." George's voice was remote and dry, as if he were telling an old story everyone knew.

Anne waited, but George was silent.

Bonfire's daughter.

"I'll call the Home for the Aged," Anne said in a shaky voice to George's profile. "You can take her there."

Old people were coming into the lobby now. Anne turned her back on them, told George she'd call him later, and went out the front door. Cold morning wind whipped her coat around her legs and tried to take her hat with it. *People believe them. They remember.* She got in her car and drove to the library.

Stacks of the *Waterloo Courier* were yellowing on library shelves. Anne found the 1929 issues and turned them over, one by one, on a table. She had been four years old in 1929.

There it was in the November papers: *Clingman Warehouses Burn. Four men dead. Arson Suspected.*

Anne hunted through newspapers of the next month. No police had been dispatched to the fire at the Clingman warehouses. No fire engines had been sent.

Angry letters to the editor blamed Daniel: evidence against

"Bonfire's Daughter!" Louise cried. "Get away from me!".

him had been hidden...he had friends in high places...he wanted Clingman out of his way...the chief of police was Daniel Bonner's boyhood friend...Bonner was planning to building his warehouses on the very ashes.

Finally there was only a small article on a back page, reporting that there would be no further investigation. No witnesses had been found.

Anne's fingers were black with printer's ink. She sat by herself in the musty smell of old wood and dusty books, and remembered what she hadn't understood. Children in her school had set a fire in her locker once—she had never known why. They scrawled notes that said, "Your dad is a devil" and "Bonners is bad."

She had shown the notes to Clara. "They're just being mean," Clara said. "Pretend you don't notice."

Anne had tried to pretend she didn't notice, but she did. She had hated school for a long time. And she remembered that once she had walked with her father on a city street, and a stranger had shouted at him: "Murderer!" Her father had said, "He's drunk."

Your father set fire to Clingman's warehouses. He burned up my Joe. He broke my Bertie's heart.

Anne drove home. When she turned off the highway, there was her father's house, barely visible through bare trees.

She saw it as she had never seen it: it was hidden away, isolated on the river bluff, an island surrounded by trees and water.

She parked in Daniel's drive like a stranger, and stood by her car, feeling colder than the winter wind. Tom had worked in Waterloo long enough to have heard about the fire, and the people burned alive. He had married Bonfire's daughter.

When she opened Daniel's door, she brought the memory of Louise Downey's howl and George Tredwell's dry voice with her. This was her childhood home, she had thought. Now every chair and painting and statue seemed to watch her, like sly servants who had always known that she lived in Bonfire Bonner's house.

She stepped into her father's study. Daniel was at work in the greenhouse beyond the glass wall; she was invisible to him where she stood in the dimness behind reflection. He bent over a table there, enclosed in glass like a specimen: *Your father burned up my Joe.*

Anne watched her father for a long time. Why did Daniel stay by himself at parties, unless she or Tom stayed with him? He gave lavish gifts to Waterloo and Waterloo's charities, yet only a few people greeted him at a play or a concert. *He doesn't have any close friends—none who ever come to the house,* she remembered saying to Tom in London. *I suppose he's made enemies.*

Daniel stooped to turn on a greenhouse faucet, and the hose in his hands threw a silvery curtain of water over a fiery red *Sophronitis coccinea.* "Are you Bonfire Bonner?" she could ask him. She could ask Tom: "Am I 'Bonfire's daughter' to everyone we know? To you?"

Daniel turned as he heard the greenhouse door open. He smiled to see Anne come to him. She didn't smile. She put her arms around him and hid her face on his shoulder.

Tom came home at dark with a huge Christmas tree for their living room. "We've got the weekend to decorate it," he said, kissing Anne with lips still cold from winter wind. "Christmas cards?" he asked, picking up a pile of mail on a table.

He recognized Raina's writing on an envelope. She wrote on her card that the Hancocks were "her dear friends."

Tom tipped the card away from the light. Raina described "the guardians of tradition" who had insisted on Christmas trees on campus, and wrote: "such people feel they must guard the status quo." The "dear" and both "guards" were faintly underlined with the pressure of Raina's long fingernails.

The telephone rang, though it was dinnertime.

"You look tired," Anne said when Tom came back.

"I'll have to get a furnace working at the Schonfeld Apartments. And it wasn't a good day," Tom said. "I made a mistake—negotiated a lease, but I didn't make the tenant sign to pay the insurance. Daniel was disgusted."

Anne went to kiss him. "I imagine Dad's not easy to work for."

"Not easy," Tom said.

"Some people call him 'Bonfire Bonner.'" Anne stood close to Tom. Her clear blue eyes met his with a stern, straightforward look that suddenly set distance between them. "That's what they call him, isn't it? When I was four years old, Dad's competitor had warehouses on the river, and people were sure that Dad burned them down. His best friend was the police chief. I read old *Waterloo Couriers* in the library. It's all there."

"They never proved anybody did it."

"Men died," Anne said.

"Yes," Tom said.

"And you knew. When we married. You knew people still call him 'Bonfire,' and I was 'Bonfire's daughter.' You must have known."

"You weren't 'Bonfire's daughter' to me. You've got nothing to do—"

"And now you're working for him."

Tom held her by both arms and looked into her upturned face. "Who knows what happened more than twenty years ago?" Tom said. "They couldn't prove Daniel had anything to do with it. He's made enemies, but he's made a fortune, and he's giving it to us with both hands."

"But people *remember*."

"They'll forget."

"They remember. Old people at the Center remember. Louise Downey wants to go back to that awful house that you and I found her in—she threw her notebook of pictures at me! She spit at me! She said my father killed her son!"

Tom folded her in his arms as if to keep such words away from her. "Don't go to that place," he murmured.

"I'm not. I'm running away. The Center doesn't need me: they've got a full-time director now. I'm going to volunteer at Joyland Nursery School near the university. You know it—the university runs it for the married students' children. I start Monday." Her voice was muffled against Tom's shoulder. "I hope the school staff is too young to remember a Waterloo fire twenty years ago."

The Joyland Nursery School was an H-shape of Quonset huts in a fenced-in yard on a busy street. Half of one side was offices, and the crossbar was a kitchenette and teachers' lounge. The rest of the H formed three big playrooms, each with its bathroom of miniature sinks and toilets.

"Hi," the teacher for the three-year-olds said to Anne the first morning. "I'm Gwen French." She wasn't any older than Anne, but tall and thin. Sitting on the floor and yanking a small girl's boot on, Gwen was all sharp knees and elbows. "Am I glad to see you. Can you play the piano, by any chance?" Before Anne could say yes, Gwen yelled, "Don't take that chair out, Billy—not in the snow!" She brought her voice down an octave and said, "Our conversations are going to be like this, I hope you realize—put it back, Billy! The sleds are out there—go get one!"

"I can play the piano," Anne said. "Simple things."

"Good. We send the kids right out in the yard when they come in the morning," Gwen said. "There you go, Betsy." She watched the child push open the Quonset's door and face the winter wind. "They've been cooped up in a few rooms and told to be quiet while Daddy does university homework. These kids need *space*."

When twenty-five children came in from the cold, their noses were running, their mittens were wet, and their faces were red and cheerful. Gwen and Anne wiped noses and yanked stuck zippers, but the three-year-olds could undress themselves. "They learn," Gwen said. "Their mothers tell me, 'I can't believe it. She won't dress or undress herself at home.' I say, 'She *has* to do it here— that's the difference.' Get the kids into the bathroom, will you, and make sure they go? Tell the boys to put the seats down for the girls. Heaven forbid we should swell the ranks of the seat-up males."

Anne peered over the tops of the stalls at the matter-of-fact boys performing while girls watched, and matter-of-fact girls performing while boys watched. "Wash your hands, kids," Gwen called at the bathroom door. She checked hands and settled the children at tables in the big Quonset room, passing out paper and crayons.

Suddenly the classroom door slammed open and a three-year-old sprang in. He was thin and pale, with desperate eyes. The other children gave him one glance and went back to their crayons and paper. The boy, still dressed in snow pants and jacket, ran into the doll corner, curled himself in the big doll bed, shut his wild eyes, and sucked his thumb.

"That's Jesse," Gwen said, sitting beside Anne on a storage bench that ran the length of the room.

"What's wrong?"

"Who knows?" Gwen said. "I've talked to his mother, but she's as nervous as Jesse is. She acts like I'm booking her for a crime."

Jesse would not use clay or finger paint, though Anne knelt beside him and tried to persuade him. He would not build with blocks, or load the riding-trucks, or have juice and crackers. Children played around him, dressing dolls, undressing dolls; he lay without moving.

At "rest time" the big, long room was quiet, except for a child whispering to himself as he lay on his cotton mat, or humming a tune under his breath. Anne sat in the rocking chair and watched the little girl lying at her feet. She might have a daughter like that, Anne thought. Or perhaps a son, like the boy in the corner who sprawled on his stomach, running a toy car back and forth on the floor. For a moment her yearning played over them like an invisible light. Gwen had asked her if she had children, and Anne said, "No...not even one coming."

When it was time to go home, the children dressed for winter among heaps of boots, mittens, jackets, snow pants and hats. Jesse, still wearing his outdoor clothes, left with a baby-sitter. Now and then a father came for a child, but most children went home with their mothers—young, tired women who went into the cold again with a child trailing behind them, the wind trying to snatch the child's crayon drawing away.

As the winter days passed, Tom often asked Anne if she liked her work at the school. "You come home exhausted," Tom said late one night. "You'd be earning your salary, if they paid you one."

"Clay under my fingernails, dirt on my knees, finger paint on my shirt. I love it."

The children came to school swaddled in clothes, but they took off their coats and snowpants and hats and hung them in lockers—every one but Jesse. He hid himself in his winter clothes and would not take them off.

"He's so hot," Anne said to Gwen French one afternoon, her eyes on Jesse curled in the doll bed.

"Have you seen him when he goes to the bathroom? He's so bruised."

"Yes," Anne said.

"His father broke his mother's wrist last Friday. She finally told me about it last night after you left," Gwen said. "If she could take Jesse and get away from her husband, get far away, she could find a job. She's trained to be a pharmacist. But she doesn't have any money."

Anne knelt by Jesse. She didn't dare touch him, but she began to sing a song about opening a pigeon house and letting the pigeons fly away. She couldn't tell whether Jesse was listening, except that he pulled a doll blanket farther over his face.

But his mother listened to Anne, and cried. She sobbed her thanks and took Anne's money. "I probably won't ever see you again," she said, "but I'll never forget you."

Tom visited the nursery school one afternoon. Anne introduced him to the teachers, and he sat in a corner of Anne's room, watching her surrounded by three-year-olds. Children climbed on her lap, played with her hair, kissed her nose or her chin or her elbow—she was nuzzled and petted and stroked softly as if small hands were reading her in Braille. When she mixed soap flakes into poster paint to make it thick, a half-dozen hands were available to stir. She could only play the piano with a child on her lap; they took turns hugging her while the old upright piano, out of tune, pounded out marches and polkas, and shrill children's voices warbled around her.

"I've had to learn all these childhood jingles and songs and finger-play," Anne called to Tom as she pounded the keys. Listening to her, Tom remembered his mother singing those songs to him. "*It's raining, it's pouring, the old man is snoring…*" When Anne left the piano to sit on the floor, three-year-olds crowded close to her, hands in the air, shouting: "*Itty bitty spider went up the waterspout…*"

Nobody had ever sung those songs to Anne. She laughed with delight, her fingers twisting above her head. She blew Tom a kiss as she sang, and he blew a kiss back. "*This old man, he played one, he played knick-knack on his thumb…*"

Between school sessions, the teachers gathered at noon in the small "teachers' room" that was warm and close-smelling and stacked with boxes of crackers and cans of juice. They propped their feet on small chairs as they ate their sack lunches and teased Anne about being a bride.

"Isn't the first year something?" Marcy said to Anne. "Sam and I wouldn't have gotten out of bed even if there'd been a fire. My mother had fits. 'You're so pale,' she kept saying. 'You're thin as cardboard.' Of course I was. No sleep. When we got hungry we ran out for hamburgers and cokes and ate our meals in bed, naturally."

"Doing it everywhere," Rita said. "Kitchen table." Her fat chin jiggled when she laughed. "Halfway up the stairs."

"How about in the bathtub, with you wearing peanut butter, and him wearing grape jelly?" Gwen said.

Anne smiled and left the teachers' room to stand at the art cupboard. She sorted colored paper into piles, but what she saw was newlyweds in a London hotel room, and Tom in her arms, hour after hour. Tears came to her eyes. Tom was so tired now. He nodded over the evening paper, and fell asleep before he could say goodnight. He dutifully made love to her when the doctors' charts said he should.

The other teachers joined Anne. Rita said, "Were you Anne *Bonner*? *The* Bonner? Didn't I see those pictures of you in the paper when you got married?"

"A whole page." Marcy Bond said. "And they take pictures of your parties, don't they?"

Three pairs of eyes were fixed on Anne, whose hair was squashed flat on one side from a clown hat she had worn that morning. Her sneakers were caked with playground mud. She covered her chin with her fingers and said, "It's awful. The photographers follow you around and say, 'Smile—just one more picture...'"

The other teachers smiled then. When Rita and Marcy waited for the bus that night, Rita said to Marcy: "You'd never think Anne was anybody much, would you? I didn't, not when she came here."

"She was sure pretty in the paper last Sunday—all dressed up and having a dinner at her place."

"But she works the hardest of all of us. When Joey was sick this morning, she cleaned it up."

The bus came, and they climbed the steps. "I like her," Rita said.

The streets and sidewalks of Waterloo were rimmed with piles of soot-gray snow. The bus passed the Bonner Building, and two of the Bonner secretaries saw it go by from a third-story window. Edna Wilson watched it turn the corner and said, "I just want to scream."

"Me, too," Ruth Kline said, leaving the window to sit on the edge of her desk. "I sit there taking Bonner's dictation and I want to cut his throat. Poor Tom. Why doesn't he just get up and slug Bonner all the way across that fancy office of his?"

"Bonners's not just Tom's boss."

"Father-in-law," Ruth said with a groan. The two secretaries took their coats from the office closet. "Father-in-hell."

"Did you hear Daniel yesterday," Edna said, stuffing an arm in a coat sleeve.

"Yelling."

"I happen to have, right in my notes, that Tom had nothing to do with that ten-cent store moving out," Edna said.

"Bonner doesn't pay Tom what he's worth." Ruth yanked her coat collar up and glared at Edna. "Tom's doing all Harrison used to do—on top of handling rentals."

"But last week, did you hear Tom?" Edna said. "He asked Daniel for an evaluation of property values—said he wanted to buy into the business...wanted to pay for the house and land Daniel gave him. Daniel was too stunned to say anything, I guess, but he slapped Tom on the shoulder going out, like he admired him."

"He ought to," Ruth said. "Tom's bringing in new businesses, new stores..."

"Tom was happy when he came. And he's so nice."

"And so handsome."

"Can any man be too handsome?" Edna giggled as they pushed through the street door.

"Not for me" Ruth said.

In a few hours the lights of the Hancock house glittered in the early dark: Tom and Anne had invited guests. "A delicious dinner," Emily Snyder said to Tom as they left the table to drink coffee in the living room.

"Welcome home," Tom said. "How was the weather in Europe?"

"Rain. Aren't you and Anne going over before long? A second honeymoon?"

"My first look at Europe was magnificent. Like a dream," Tom said, and almost laughed: his cliché rang in his ears like somebody thumping a tin pot. "Like a dream? It was a shock." He remembered museum crowds laughing about art, arguing about art in foreign languages, standing transfixed before a statue, sitting to stare at a single canvas...he remembered lovers in a London hotel bed, so wedded to each other that one of the great cities of the world stood unnoticed outside their window...

"You two enjoyed Rome, I think, even if the traffic's impossible," Emily said, and Tom was in a Roman taxi again, kissing Anne and being kissed while the taxi careened down impossibly narrow streets, grazing pedestrians' hips and heels, dogs, parked cars, cafe chairs, to stop with a screech and jerk in the shadow of some immense pile of stone. "You talked about San Clemente when you came home," Emily said.

San Clemente.

Emily turned to talk to a friend, and Tom saw in his memory an immense church far above him, cool and dim, and Anne's soft voice, echoing there: "Twelfth century."

Tom had laid his palm on dusty stone and said, "Eight centuries ago."

"Not so old," Anne had answered, and led the way down a flight of stairs. Beneath the massive floors and pillars of a church eight centuries old were the floors and pillars of another church, deep in the earth. "This church is fourth century," Anne said.

Sixteen centuries old. Spotlights picked out fragments set in the walls: a statue's head...birds and flowers twined around a column.

"Still not so old," Anne had said, and they descended stairs to near darkness. Small lights seemed no more than glowworms there. "Now we're in the first century," Anne said. "In a family chapel where they worshipped Mithra." Hand in hand, they went between benches to an altar where a stone figure of Mithra stabbed a bull. "These were the houses of a town more than nineteen hundred years ago."

Dark, wet rooms held only one sound: a rush of water, hollow and lonely and constant. "That's water running to the Colosseum," Anne said. "People lived their lives in these rooms, made love, raised their children, with the sky above them and the sunshine coming through these windows. But cities burned, so they covered them up and built again, and again, and again, until this city was buried under all the others, sixty feet below the streets we've been walking this morning."

For that second or two Tom had felt the weight of the past above him; he'd breathed it in with the damp air and heard it rush past with the sound of buried water. He was in it; he felt it under his hands like wet stone.

Anne felt it too. They turned and ran as if centuries might cave in—they raced past Mithra's altar and his cloak full of stars, taking stairs two at a time like lovers out of a grave. Tom remembered how they had stood in Italian sunshine at last, blinking and solemn…

Emily Snyder turned back to Tom as her friend walked away. She said, "You're so lucky you can have another trip abroad with Anne."

"I'm still a pretty stupid tourist." Tom kept his tone light. "And I'm often clueless at home, too. I think Anne's afraid I'll see her as some kind of schoolteacher."

"She's more tactful than that."

Tom heard it: that faint amusement in Emily's voice at the boring young man and his schoolteacher bride. His face reddened. "Yes," he said. "Anne never complains, even though nowadays we hardly see each other. I'm at the office, early and late, and most weekends."

"Such a hard-working man?" Emily asked. "Earning your keep?"

"Daniel's got property all over town, and his Bonner Rubber and Supply business…the Foundation…his charities…"

"At least your trips abroad will be useful. When you're wearing your foundation-director hat, you'll fit in with the artists and writers and professors," Emily said. "You can chat about the 'Green Dining Room' at the Victoria and Albert, or the place where Keats died near the Spanish Steps…or 'Jenny kissed me when we met' in Chelsea…that sort of thing."

"I'll try."

"And Daniel's treating you well?" Emily held out her coffee cup to be filled again by a maid. "He's not asking you to run his supply company too?"

"No. He runs that. I think he's satisfied, now that I've brought three new businesses to Waterloo, and I've got contacts all over the city, contacts he doesn't bother to make. I've told him I want to buy into his business—be a partner, pay him back for our house and land as I'm able."

"Good for you!" Emily said. "More than good! Daniel respects a go-getter. How's Anne?"

They turned and ran as if centuries might cave in.

"She's..." Tom hesitated. "Somebody's told her about 'Bonfire.' She asked me if I knew she was 'Bonfire's daughter' when I married her. She hates lies. I had to say I did. She read old *Couriers* in the library." He glared at Emily. "She was four years old in 'twenty-nine! Why on earth should she care so much?"

Emily turned to watch Anne, who stood in a laughing group of her guests. "She's a better daughter than he ever deserved."

"She's with Daniel every weekend, working on the gardens," Tom said. "I'm at the office early, so they have breakfast together, and lunch before she goes to the nursery school. And I'm not home until nine or ten at night, so she goes to his house most evenings."

"She's with her father that much? Hours every day?"

"He's alone."

"So are you, evidently. And you have to manage all Daniel's business affairs while he spends all that time with Anne? Even on weekends?"

Tom drank his coffee and didn't answer.

"What can Anne be thinking of, treating you like that?"

"She's never had a loving father. She lost her mother."

"And you don't count?"

"Anne..." Tom hesitated. "She needs him. He's starting to say that she looks like her mother, and says he adored her mother, and that makes Anne so happy, even though there's no baby on the way yet. She works so hard at the nursery school, stays late to talk with some parent who's in trouble. Now she's set up a secret gift fund through the nursery school. She cares so much for people. Doesn't think of herself. I love her. I do. She came home yesterday upset because someone had died—an old woman she found sleeping in rags in a condemned house last winter."

Well-dressed people chatted and laughed around them. Daniel crossed the living room with a look their way. "Daniel's given you everything," Emily said. "Wife, beautiful house, a business to run."

"Yes," Tom said. "Everything."

"And you love Anne now." Tom heard Emily's emphasis on that *now*. "And you like Iowa."

"When I came here, it was like driving off a California freeway," Tom said. "You're in six lanes of traffic, you turn off on a ramp, and suddenly you're in a town where people are mowing their lawns or playing catch or carrying groceries home, as if freeways don't exist. You gear down. Notice details."

"So you're a settled Iowan now," Emily said. "And in May you can go abroad, and get away from your work for a while."

"Can't be away from the business more than a month or two, but I hope we can stay long enough to make Anne forget about not having babies," Tom said. "In the fall she'll go to the Mayo Clinic for more tests. We've followed all the directions the doctors can think of. The specialists can't find what's wrong."

Emily stood up. "At least you'll have her to yourself in Europe, and won't have to do Daniel's work for him." Her voice was as sharp as the glitter of her earrings. "Anne's a fool. She's got you and she spends all that time with her father? And you're supposed to like it?"

9

Tom and Anne left for England and the Continent. Emily Snyder worked in her garden one afternoon, then came indoors to mop her face and look at the day's mail. In a moment she stood in the kitchen doorway, a letter in her hand and a stunned look on her face.

"Trouble?" Clara Petersen asked, pushing her glasses up her nose to take a better look at Emily.

"Raina! Listen to this letter from Raina! You won't believe it—she's moving here!"

Emily read from Raina's letter: "'Just imagine, I'll be director of the Rolinger Gallery.'"

"Right here in town?" Clara said.

"Daniel's gallery." Emily read from the letter: "'I heard about the opening at the Rolinger and wrote to Daniel Bonner and got the job. It doesn't begin until fall, but I'm coming on Friday to get to know Waterloo and find an apartment. How wonderful to think I'll be so close to you. You've been like a mother to me.'"

"Well!" Clara said.

"It's not 'well,'" Emily said, her earrings sparkling as she scowled at Clara, then at the letter.

"But Anne has no idea. Neither does Daniel."

"Raina knows we'll never tell!" Emily said in an outraged voice.

They looked at each other without a word.

Daniel and Emily were waiting on the platform when Raina's train pulled in. Raina hugged Emily and shook

Daniel's hand. "My wonderful new job," Raina told him. "And it's your doing."

"Of course not," Daniel said. "You were the committee's first choice."

The next day Raina called Daniel to tell him she had found an apartment near the Rolinger. "Will you have money enough to live on until you begin work in the fall?" he asked, and didn't wait for a reply, but said, "I wonder if you'd care to work for me until then…I've always wanted to have someone catalog my collection of art pieces, and you're certainly qualified. You could work at my place; Tom and Anne are gone. Only the house cleaners come once a week—my housekeeper's away, caring for an invalid sister. I'll be glad to rent a car for you."

So Raina spent her mornings at the Gallery, but almost every noon she drove out of the city to turn down Daniel Bonner's long private road.

"Your house is so beautiful," she told him. "I've never seen an English country house, but yours is the way I imagine one might be: no neighbors, no city noise, no passers-by. Just the river's light playing on high ceilings…bird song…gardens…"

Daniel bought cameras to photograph his collection, and had one of his guest bedrooms made into a workroom for Raina. "You're tired," he often said at the end of the day. "Let's drive out of town to somewhere interesting for supper."

Daniel left his office early. Sometimes they talked for hours, roaming his woods and garden.

"Raina hardly ever drops in," Emily Snyder said to Clara Petersen.

"She's busy with her work at the Gallery, I suppose," Clara said. "And she's cataloging Daniel's art collection. You wrote Tom and Anne that she's living here?"

"I've written them in Venice," Emily said, frowning. "He's been warned."

Late sun filtered through the woods as Daniel parked in his drive one afternoon, home from the city. He paused at his front door. Patricia had found that door in England and had it shipped to Iowa; the age-worn oak grain was warm under his hand.

He heard Raina typing as he wandered through his house. He stopped at the door of Anne's old bedroom. A baby doll propped on Anne's bed looked back at him. Patricia had bought it for seven-year-old Anne. Its smooth pink face had a smile painted on it, but its eyes, lined with black under their stiff eyelashes, were too old for any baby.

He paced through his house...through his garden...back and forth, back and forth. After a while he found himself at his desk, reading a half-finished letter he was sending to Anne and Tom. He hadn't mentioned Raina.

Raina's typewriter kept up its steady, conscientious tapping: a devoted sound. He smiled at the thought. She gave him such skillful, inobtrusive respect. She dressed for him; he knew that. Men watched her.

It was late afternoon when he finished the letter. He went to a window to see the river flow past, scintillating like sequins in the sun, and walked from room to room again, looking at paintings on his walls. He opened closets to run his intent eyes over suits and shoes made to his measure.

He stood before his reflection in a full-length mirror.

Just before sunset he went through his garages to stand at the edge of the woods. Gravel paths tied his house to Anne's; he walked to the crossing of two paths where a great basswood had fallen at the edge of the woods years before. Its roots, high as a man, writhed in the air like a mass of snakes.

Sunlight dropped wide shafts through leaves; the river poured its brown current beneath the terraces. He started back to his house, breathing the forest's complex smell of hot grasses and thickets mixed with riverbank rot and mold.

"Daniel?" He heard Raina's call. He answered and she found him on the path. "The new photographs have come," she said, and opened an album to show him. "These records are so important. You have beautiful things. One-of-a-kind, priceless things."

"Yes," Daniel said. He was looking at Raina, not the photographs.

They drove to their favorite restaurant in a nearby town, and ate dinner by candlelight. "Anne and Tom are bound for the Yorkshire Dales," Daniel said. "They'll spend a week in Haworth. Anne writes that she's always been fascinated by the sad story of the Brontë sisters, and the unlucky lovers in *Wuthering Heights*."

How easy their conversation was as they drove home. How relaxed they had become. There were quiet pauses in their talk. Yet when their voices stopped another kind of conversation began.

"Come in for a nightcap before you go," Daniel said as he parked his car beside hers on the drive. Raina left her hat and gloves in his living room, and stood under his patio lantern, a woman so beautiful that a connoisseur might be tempted to circle her as if she were a statue, watching the planes of her body change.

They took their drinks down his stone steps, stairway by landing by stairway again, to a broad dock, a small table and chairs, twilight, and the river.

Raina's pale face glimmered, framed by her hair. Daniel took her glass and put it with his on the table, then reached for her to kiss her again and again. He was rough, but she didn't shrink from him; her arms went around his neck.

For a while they stayed by the river, murmuring and kissing, listening to waves lap the piers. An owl somewhere above them gave a soft call, as if it were crying through feathers.

When they climbed to his empty house, they looked at each other with serious faces. "Marry me," Daniel whispered in his living room, and again in his bed with its canopy of blue silk. "Marry me," he whispered again, and Raina said Yes, and answered him with her kisses, too, and her hands and her smooth body.

Daniel fell into deep sleep.

Blue silk sheets whispered faintly as naked Raina crept from bed. Half-hidden in the fall of her hair, she slid her dim reflection across Daniel's bedroom mirrors.

Moonlight through leaves flickered on the living room carpet. Brass and glass and polished wood caught that faint gleam. Raina laughed softly, pushed her heavy hair behind her shoulders and stretched out her hands. Turning slowly, she closed her fists in the air over and over, as if grasping one beautiful, shadowy thing after another: a bronze dolphin, a mahogany buffet, a stone nude, orchids clustered in a Chinese vase, a landscape in its glinting frame.

She wandered through room after room, stopping to light the blue flames of Daniel's kitchen stove and open his double refrigerator wide. It breathed mist at her: droplets on her skin. She slipped through a door to stand barefoot in the warm earth of a terrace bed watching the moonlit river.

When she went back in Daniel's house and crept through dark rooms, she was smiling.

Daniel lay asleep on his back. His extraordinary blue eyes were shut; he was an ordinary middle-aged man with his mouth open.

Raina crept into bed beside him, cool, smelling of midnight air, her feet trailing earth from his flowerbeds across satin sheets.

River fog rose to Daniel's house. At dawn his expanse of gardens shimmered with dew.

By nine o'clock Raina lay in a lawn chair and looked into beds of roses while Daniel asked, "Shall we set our wedding day?"

She didn't answer or look at him. To give her time, he went on to say that there was no hurry, except that he loved her. He'd marry her that day, if he could.

"We have so much in common," Raina said after a moment or two. "These last months..." she met his eyes, then looked quickly away. "We've been so close. And I think I knew from the beginning what it might lead to—didn't you?"

"Yes," Daniel said. "I wanted you from the moment I danced with you at Anne's wedding."

"Years ago?" She smiled at him. "It's such a wonderful thing for me. I've been so poor, and all alone."

"I've been alone," Daniel said. "And I've been dirt-poor. Desperation-poor. My father died when I was three, and my mother was a cook at a restaurant most of her life. The first thing I remember is a buttonhook pinching my legs when my mother fastened my high shoes. Every day I went with her to her job in a restaurant kitchen, and sat in a corner there for hours, quiet. I knew there wouldn't be any food for us if I didn't. No food. Absolutely nothing. I knew how that felt."

"Yes," Raina said.

"I came home from school to our one room, and read library books till Mother brought scraps she'd sneaked—even from the garbage cans," Daniel said. "We put it all in a pot and cooked it on our hot plate to kill the germs, and my mother said it was one of the oldest meals in the world, and was called 'Mulligan Stew.' 'We're so lucky,' she'd tell me. 'All around us there are people who don't have jobs. They're going to bed hungry.'"

Daniel smiled at Raina and she smiled back. "That stew was never the same twice," he said. "There might be ham, or a piece of fish, or a boiled egg, or a slice of lemon. I ate stew and read books with my mother, and in winter we read with our coats and blankets piled on top of us."

"In the summer we couldn't sleep," Raina said. "Except on our fire escape."

"We put water on our skin and our clothes," Daniel said. "Sat there and fried in that little stove of a room." His blue eyes were on the roses in his garden. "My mother had been a teacher."

"My mother died before I worked my way through college," Raina said. "And my father...is he still alive somewhere? Who knows? All my life I dreamed of having a family. Just an ordinary father-and-mother family." She sighed. "But what about Anne and Tom? I'll be Anne's stepmother."

"Let's go to England and tell them," he said. "I can get you a passport fast. We'll pack up and take passage from New York next week, maybe on the *Ile de France*?"

"England." Raina's eyes widened.

"Haworth."

"Haworth," Raina echoed. She watched him from the shade of her big hat that was a wonderful affair of yellow straw, brimful of silk poppies. Its glow spread an oriental gold across her cheekbones above her red-poppy mouth.

"A Renoir," Daniel said to her. "You're definitely a Renoir this morning."

They looked at the garden for a while in silence. A rose-scented breeze caught a corner of Raina's skirt, and a few of the sheer pleats stirred, then cascaded to touch the patio bricks. Raina turned so that her huge hat hid Daniel, but she felt he was watching her now, a woman framed in his still eyes like a portrait: a Renoir.

10

Tom sat with Anne at a small table, so close to a Venetian canal that water lapped almost at their feet. They had finished their cheese and fruit, and were drinking coffee in a palace's blue shade; ogee curves framed the palace's dim rooms. Reflected light from the canal played on ceilings there. A stone platform was green with moss.

Children shouted in a courtyard. Tom breathed air that held the scent of roses, rotting wood and strong coffee. A gondola slid by like a curled black leaf on the water, its crooked oarlock creaking. The palace's stone lace was doubled in the shaken water. It had often seemed to Tom, traveling through such riches, that he and Anne were like the small, incidental figures in paintings by Canaletto or Rubens or Fragonard: a tiny couple gazing at one monumental scene after another.

He had never dreamed of such pleasures. He lounged in his chair, perfectly happy, and thought what a charming companion Anne was. She so seldom put herself first, or put him out, but she could be firm, and very clever, and there was a beauty he was conscious of, more and more. People came close to look into her deep blue eyes: her feelings glowed there under her long lashes. Her full upper lip gave her mouth a delicious shape, and her body was pretty: men noticed it.

She was wearing a wide white hat. He watched light from the water play over her face beneath the brim, glints coming and going like his sleepy admiration. She was happy and showed it, and that made her prettier still.

"News from home?" he asked lazily. They had found mail

waiting at their Venetian hotel, and Anne had opened a letter.

"Good news." Anne looked up and smiled. "Dad's gallery has been looking for a new director—well, they've found one, a friend of yours."

Tom watched a gondolier row by, his load of fish glinting silver in the sun. Their dead eyes contemplated Tom. "A friend?" he said, only half listening.

"A friend from California. Raina Weigel," Anne said, tucking the first page of Emily's letter behind the second. Intent on her reading, she didn't see Tom's eyes widen; he sat up. "She came to our wedding with Emily, remember? You told me her name was from Shaw's *Arms and the Man*." She smiled. "Or *The Chocolate Soldier*? She's in Waterloo already. She's found an apartment, and starts work in the fall."

Tom stared at Venice with eyes as blank as those of the fish that were passing him on the water, though nothing around him had changed. The sun shone. The gondola was still in sight. Anne had not even finished her letter.

June was hot as Tom and Anne traveled back through Italy and France, then hired a car in London and started north. Soon Yorkshire spread its gray stone and green summer fields as far as Anne and Tom could see.

"I couldn't have imagined taking this kind of trip ten years ago," Tom said. "My idea of travel was..." he shook his head, gripped the wheel of their rented car and looked at the car roof for a moment as if appealing to heaven. "Can you imagine? Certainly not exploring Literary England. Wandering through museums? Seeing the cathedral towns?"

"You love it," Anne said. Tom glanced at her contented face. Breeze from an open car window blew her brown hair across her cheek; she pushed the hair back and watched Yorkshire with tranquil eyes.

Haworth was a rock-walled town, deep gray even in the afternoon sun, and crowned with the Reverend Brontë's church tower. Near the church was the *Black Bull* inn. As Anne and Tom finished unpacking in a room there, a telegram was brought to their door.

"It's from Dad," Anne's tone had shock in it. "He says, 'Raina and I will drive to Haworth and meet you June 13.'"

"Raina?" Tom said. "Here?"

"Coming with Dad," Anne said. "Today."

Tom took the telegram from her and read it. "Why?" he said.

"We'd better reserve their rooms before we window shop," Anne said. Tom followed her down a narrow staircase. *Raina.*

They went to the desk through a barroom that smelled of stale cigarette smoke and popcorn. When the rooms had been reserved, Tom and Anne left the *Black Bull* to walk down Haworth's cobbled street in the late afternoon sunshine. The way was so narrow and steep that cars crept uphill or down.

"Why are they coming here?" Anne said. She had circled her black hat with a scarf; the ends of it flickered like blue chiffon flames in the sunshine. "To tell us that they plan to marry?"

Tom halted at a shop window, staring at a row of male manikins in leather coats.

"How can it be anything else?" Anne said. "Dad wouldn't bring an unmarried young woman over here otherwise." She looked into the window glass to see Tom's expression. "And Raina wouldn't come, would she?"

Tom pressed his lips together, but said nothing.

"From what Emily's told me," Anne said, "Raina's very proud and independent. She's worked so hard and come so far. But you knew her at Berkeley. Emily said you met Raina at her house."

"I knew her," Tom said, and the old meaning of "knew" flashed into his head and made his three words true words. He found other words to hide in: "She was engaged to a rich fellow then."

"What happened?"

"He...preferred men," Tom said.

Anne gave a small commiserating sound. They looked at the shop window in silence for a moment. "You'd have a stepmother," Tom said.

"Dad must be at least twenty years older than she is."

"More than twenty," Tom said.

"That tan jacket's very nice," Anne said in a preoccupied tone. Tom looked at the jacket in the shop window as if he hadn't noticed it. "You might try it on," she said. "If it fits, you'll have it to remind you."

"Of what?"

"Of the day the four of us were together in Brontë country," Anne said.

They stepped into the strong-smelling little shop. "I'd like to try the tan coat in the window," Tom said to an old man almost invisible in the dark back corner.

"We certainly haven't had a single warning," Anne said. "If that's what they're doing. If they're going to marry."

Tom caught the tinge of mournful surprise in Anne's voice. Her father had done this without her, almost behind her back...except that she had guessed. He put on the coat and turned slowly before a mirror that was half hidden in racks of studded leather. His gray eyes stared into their reflection and through it to something else, until they focused again on what was there, and he turned to Anne.

"There's no question about that coat, at least," Anne said. "It will certainly do."

Tom paid for the coat. Carrying the parcel into the sun, he looked down the narrow, rough street before him.

A woman wiping glasses in a teashop saw Tom and Anne go by. She picked up another glass and leaned to look at a car stopping in the street. A young woman climbed from the car, her brown hair hanging far down her back under a straw hat. "Look at that," the waitress said, and the other waitress came to look. "Maybe she's a film star."

They watched Tom and Anne hurry across the street to talk to the film star and an older man at the wheel.

"Isn't that black-haired young man a dream?" the other waitress said, squinting into the light.

"He's married to that girl in the black hat with the blue on it, I think. They're staying at the *Bull*."

"Too bad. He's lovely."

Sunset laid red patches of light over Haworth's cobblestones. Lanterns above the shops began to glow.

"Haworth's a sort of dream town, don't you think?" Anne said to Daniel and Raina as the four sat down to dinner in the *Black Bull*. "A tourist's dream, maybe. It must be a nightmare to the townspeople in winter with the wind howling in from the moors."

Raina had said very little since she'd arrived with Daniel. She was eating almost nothing. Daniel's eyes were often on her, but she rarely looked at anyone but Anne.

"Tomorrow we can walk to Wuthering Heights and picnic, if you want to. If it's good weather," Anne said.

"Anne's in love with Yorkshire," Tom said, and for a moment all three of them smiled at Anne, as if relieved to find something so easy to do.

"The *Black Bull*'s no luxury hotel," Daniel told Raina.

"Branwell Brontë drank himself to death in here," Anne said. "And we're as close to the Brontë parsonage as we can get." She glanced through the window at a streetlight beginning to glow. Daylight was fading as souvenir shops on the square locked their doors. Brontës were buried at the foot of a pillar in the church. Lovers of their books had left bunches of heather there; the bouquets withered in the dark.

"I think the two of you may have guessed why Raina and I came," Daniel said as they drank their coffee. "To ask your blessing. That's the old phrase, isn't it? She's promised to marry me, and I think she's a bit worried about being a stepmother and stepmother-in-law. It doesn't worry me." He took Raina's hand in his.

Raina looked up in time to see Tom's eyes over his coffee cup. "I..." She faltered, then went on. "I thought we should tell you first."

Anne lifted her chin and put a hand on their joined ones. "I hope you'll both be very happy," she said, smiling.

Tom stood up to smile and shake Daniel's hand as they left their table. "Congratulations," he said.

"Shall we walk for a while?" Anne asked. "Talk about the wedding?"

They came from the *Black Bull* to see lights shining here and there, but the stone walls of Haworth seemed to soak up darkness, making night blacker still.

The four stood on the cobblestones, discussing dates and places. "You can marry in early August?" Anne said. "Why not? If the four of us can get passage home in a week or two, there'll be time for your honeymoon before Raina's job begins in October." Tom remembered the Anne of that morning, riding so contentedly through Yorkshire. It was another Anne whose voice echoed now from Haworth's dark walls.

When the others turned back to the hotel and bed, Raina seemed reluctant to follow them through the *Black Bull*'s noisy bar and up the narrow stairs.

"You're tired after such a trip," Anne said, standing outside Raina's door. "Train, then days at sea, then miles in a car..."

"How can I be?" Raina said. "I slept through half of our drive from Liverpool. The minute I get in a car, I go to sleep. I've always been that way. Daniel teases me."

Raina said goodnight, and shut the door of her room behind her. She turned on every lamp. The drapes were pulled across the window; she sat on her bed and faced them, knowing what was just beyond the thin cloth. That afternoon she had tried not to look, but the window drew her back and back.

Ugh! At the foot of her bedroom wall—not even a strip of grass between—the churchyard gravestones began. Some of them looked like cradles with flat slabs standing at head and foot. Others were boxes with huge, flat lids. Corpses were lying not twelve feet from her bed.

Dead bodies. She had seen a horrible one as a child: a corpse dug up by the police in a trash-filled lot. After that she had nightmares, and she would shrink from touching the pages of books that had pictures of skeletons, or Egyptian mummies with their caved-in noses and brown-skinned skulls.

Here and there a grave lid was cracked open or pushed ajar. She had watched late afternoon shadow strike across angles and corners, turning moss to soft green fur, picking out letters in centuries-old names. When she leaned over her windowsill, she could almost have touched the nearest ones, or looked into the dark under their skewed lids.

And beyond the grave boxes there had been what looked like a crowd coming downhill in hazy sunset light. The shoulders of some of the figures tipped this way or that as they walked; some wore hoods; some had peaked caps or round hats or what looked like plumes. Lit from behind, that mass of descending tombstones had all faced forward, and the haze around them seemed to be the dust they raised in their downhill march. Were they coming closer and closer past the cracked-open boxes?

She had pulled her curtains shut then, even though it was only afternoon.

Now the tombstones were still making their footless way downhill in the dark. They might even seem closer now...a step or two, facing her window...

Raina undressed in the light, put on her gown in the light, brushed her hair in the light. She heard Daniel talking with Anne in his room next door, so she climbed in bed while their voices still murmured through her wall.

But the voices stopped. She heard Anne go to her own room. Daniel shut his door. Raina covered her head with a pillow. Stone boxes beneath her window stood with their lids ajar, and she lay in a bed that seemed as small as a grave. The tombstones were coming downhill through shadows and moonlight...

Along the *Black Bull*'s narrow corridor, another room looked out on the graveyard. Tom and Anne had gone to bed there, and lay talking in the dark. "See how much your father cares about you?" Tom asked, stroking Anne's cheek. "He's come all the way from Iowa to tell you he plans to marry." He tightened his arms around Anne, and made love to her in their new, shaken world.

They were drifting toward sleep when Tom began to talk. He told Anne about Emily's house in San Francisco, and how much it meant to him to be in such a home, because he was living on almost nothing. His Aunt Emily fed him and sympathized: he was balancing a sales clerk job and a full schedule of classes. She'd invited other students to her home so he could have friends. "I've told you some of this," he said. "I was lonely."

It seemed to him that he was speaking into darkness that was blacker than the night around him. "Then Emily invited Raina," he said, "and when I met her for the first time I thought she liked me, but she was dating Quentin Bradford." His voice sounded thick with feeling and fear. "We fell in love."

Tom was sweating with the strain; his forehead was wet. He said, "Raina asked me never to tell, but her plan to marry Daniel changes everything. I don't want to live near her. I don't want her close to me. You can talk to your father. I can't." There was only blackness and silence around Tom now. "Stop him. Do it for me."

Suddenly he cried out and sat up to fling sheet and blankets off, and grabbed Anne almost tight enough to hurt her. "Don't listen to me! Don't listen!" he cried.

"What?" Anne's eyes were open; he could see how sleepy they were in the faint glow from a cemetery light. "What?" she repeated.

"Selfish—stupid—cruel—"

"What?" Anne said again.

"I...was talking to you," Tom said.

"You were?" Anne said. Tom's hands were holding her arms so tightly that they hurt her.

"Didn't you hear me?"

Anne pulled at his fingers until he let go. "Hear what?" Her voice was foggy. "Were you dreaming?"

Tom hid his face in his hands for a moment. "I dreamed I was talking. It was a bad dream. Kiss me..."

Owls hunted in the graveyard's damp air. The wind was rising; it struck a shop sign that rattled and swung. Solitary footsteps, clicking along the graveyard path, echoed in the *Black Bull*'s halls where an old door creaked open, creaked shut.

Another door creaked.

Daniel was warm and fast asleep when Raina climbed into his bed. He woke with a start to give one little grunt of pleasure, and folded her in his arms, then caught his breath at the tigerish way she loved, like a Spanish dancer with her white teeth showing, entering a man's embrace as if someone had dared her to love him, as if it were dangerous.

She lay in a bed that seemed as small as a grave. The tombstones were coming downhill through shadows and moonlight.

11

The sun rose in a blue sky the next morning, so the two couples drove to the end of a country road, then left the car and walked on a moor path to Top Withins.

"Here we are," Anne said as they came over a hill. "They think this might have been 'Wuthering Heights.' What's left of it." The house stood roofless, its walls enclosing a few rocks and tall grass.

They stood silent in the silence of the moors. Cloud shadow dappled the land like watercolors touched to wet paper, flooding color with deeper color. The path they had taken looped over the nearest rise and was gone.

"I want some pictures of this," Daniel said. Tom put the lunch sacks in the shade by the door and went with him, his camera around his neck. Anne and Raina watched them climb the slope above the ruined house. Raina's long hair blew over her face in the morning moor wind; she pushed it behind her ears.

"You've certainly made Dad happy," Anne said, smiling at Raina. "He seems years younger than he was when we left him in Iowa."

How huge the sky seemed, full of windblown clouds. "It must be a shock to you," Raina said in a low voice. "You don't think it's a mistake?"

The moors surrounded them with silence and the slow roll of the land: greens shading into gray. "How could it ever be a mistake?" Anne's eyes were wide and very blue. "If you love each other."

"But I'll be your *stepmother*," Raina said.

"Why not? The four of us together." Anne opened her arms

to the men on a slope above them, the moors under shadows of clouds, a constant flow of wind over the ruined house. "Can't we be a family? Four close friends?"

"Strike a pose, you two," Daniel called. He and Tom were aiming their cameras; Anne and Raina heard the faint shutter clicks. Film caught their thoughtful, preoccupied faces. "Lunch," Tom called, skidding and sliding down the slope through dusty bracken.

The wind was strong; they went through a low stone doorway, spread a blanket on grass, and unpacked their lunch: roast chicken, tomatoes, bread, cheese, wine and chocolate cake.

Anne watched Raina lift her heavy hair with both hands, and show her long, shapely legs as she sat doubled up on a stone... almost as if she were putting herself on display, perhaps? A little game a woman loves, teasing the man she'll marry, making his eyes sparkle? Raina could make any man's eyes do that.

They finished the last of their wine. Wind blew through a ruined house. They talked of traces of lives spent in that place: the stone mouth of a hearth...gaping windows open to clouds that were slowly blotting out the blue sky. "Looks like our nice weather's ending," Daniel said.

They packed up the remains of their picnic, and left the ruin for the path that was hardly wide enough for two. Anne said to Raina, "I'll walk with Dad for a little while, if you don't mind," and Raina echoed the change they all felt when she smiled and said, "I'll let you."

For a few moments father and daughter walked in silence. Then Anne said, "You're happy, I think."

Daniel looked over the moors with his blue, blue eyes. "You like her?" he said.

"She's so beautiful, of course." Anne smiled at him. "You've always appreciated beautiful things. And I think she has courage. Emily told me once about Raina's hard life—she worked and went to college late and went on to get her degree..."

"I talked with Emily before I proposed," Daniel said. "She knew Raina's mother...knew her background. She told me that Raina was engaged to some man in San Francisco."

Anne followed Daniel through a small gate. Stone walls meandered down a slope and away, disappearing far off like a thick, knotted gray rope.

Daniel looked back to see Raina and Tom come over a distant

slope. Tom was carrying a long weed he'd snapped off, switching it against grass at the path's edge.

Raina's eyes were on Tom. "I thought of you so often in California," she said to him. "Our little closet-room. I rented it again, lived in it for the last year."

"I can't believe you're doing—"

"You and I were so poor! Sharing a hamburger at that little place on Telegraph Avenue...and remember the eucalyptus grove? The smell of the trees?" Raina had tears in her eyes.

"Don't," Tom said.

"I'm only doing what you did," she said. "Marrying."

"Don't."

"I love Daniel."

"I love Anne," Tom said. He gave her a grim look. "Daniel Bonner's not someone you fool with. He's clubbed and clawed his way to the top, and he's hated by plenty of people. You only cross him once. He tolerates me, but I'm careful."

"All that money."

Tom said, "If you marry him, we'll live next door to each other."

"And he'll be supporting us," Raina said with a dry little laugh.

"No. He won't." Tom's voice was sharp. "I work with him. For good money."

"But that's what it comes to."

"It's what he's proud of." Tom scowled at the path before him. "It's what he likes."

"You hate it," Raina said.

"No. He's given me a job and a home it would have taken me years to get, if I ever could have climbed that high. If I were rich and had a daughter, I'd do exactly what he's done for her, and love doing it."

"I haven't any choice," Raina said softly, watching Tom's profile against the darkening moor. "I'll have the kind of job I've only dreamed of—I can hardly believe it! And I'll be a good wife for Daniel, and never be poor again. Never."

"We have to tell them," Tom said. "I can't stand—"

"Yes, you can," Raina said in a flat voice. "What's so awful about it? If they see us liking each other, it's only natural. I'll be your stepmother-in-law. If we live next door to each other for the rest of our lives, what could be better? We have a right to it. We can look out for each other."

"The rain's coming," Daniel cried from the path ahead.

Raina and Tom walked faster, and came closer to Daniel and Anne. "You know what kind of life I've had so far," Raina said so softly that only Tom could hear. "You'd never ruin my chances."

Their car waited over the next slope. The fresh, sharp smell of rain swept over them as they began to run.

Anne had said, "Have an early August wedding." Tom and Anne and Raina and Daniel put England behind them and hurried home.

Less than two months was hardly time enough—the four of them planned, discussed, prepared. At last the August day arrived, a beautiful day of gardens still in flower, and hardly a hint of summer's end.

Wedding presents had been delivered to Emily Snyder's house since early morning, and were still arriving.

"Your clothes are packed?" Emily said, as she came to Raina's bedroom with Clara and an armload of gifts.

"Yes. Such beautiful clothes," Raina said. "Daniel wanted me to have this, wanted me to have that…"

"He'll show you off in Paris," Clara said.

"And Rome. And London." Raina bounced on her bed like a child, then began to unwrap wedding presents.

Silver. Glass. And the last package, a small package.

Emily bent closer to look in the box Raina opened. A stuffed toy soldier lay in tissue paper there. His eyes were black beads beneath his helmet.

"Who could have sent that?" Emily said.

"There's no card," Raina said, looking through the tissue and the wrapping paper.

"Some kind of joke? Wishing you a baby boy?" Emily said.

The toy soldier disappeared under a sweater Raina stripped off. "I'll take my shower," she said, and carried the toy and sweater into the bathroom and shut the door. While Clara and Emily laid her wedding dress on her bed, Raina held the toy soldier and cried.

The toy soldier went into one of her suitcases. Clara and Emily brought her white camisole, sheer stockings and satin slippers. They dropped her shimmering gown over her head, and buttoned the long row of satin-covered buttons at her back. "Such a lovely bride," Clara said as the three rode in a limousine to the church. "Simply lovely," she repeated as she helped Emily arrange Raina's veil and train on the chapel carpet.

Emily didn't answer, except with one look, but her filigree earrings quivered.

Anne arrived, the train of her matron-of-honor dress trailing behind her, and stopped before Raina. "So beautiful!" she cried. "The most beautiful bride!" Raina's pungent perfume surrounded her. Mirrors caught the icy white of satin, and Daniel's huge diamond on Raina's hand scintillated in late summer light. She had braided and coiled her heavy mass of hair under her veil's thin cloud, and held a cascade of white orchids before her.

"Isn't she beautiful?" Anne asked Emily and Clara. They agreed that she was.

The church was full. Daniel had given the organ to the church; its powerful bass traveled through wood, flesh, metal and stone: a profound shudder, universal as the air. Slight things trembled: the baby's breath shivering on its green hairs in Anne's bouquet...ferns in the baskets of roses...pearls dangling from Raina's ears.

Tom and Daniel, waiting in their tuxedos by the altar, watched Raina as she came, until at last Tom, Daniel, Raina and Anne stood before the minister. The bride's gold ring traveled from Tom's hand to Daniel's hand, from Daniel's hand to Raina's.

"Disgusting," Alice Ryesdal said, watching the bride and groom dance in the ballroom of Grover Place.

"It's nothing new. Daniel's got the money and Raina's got the looks," Mary Clellan said.

"She's got Bonfire Bonner, that's what she's got. And how old is he—fifty-six?"

"He looks ten years older," Mary said. "And he's certainly not well, if you ask me."

"Bob Henly says Daniel's no fun to do business with," Joyce Bettingdorf said, "but Tom's really taking over. Before long, Tom'll run the whole show while Daniel stays home and raises orchids—that's what Bob thinks."

"Anne's a dear."

"Nobody's ever said she wasn't." The three women regarded Anne with thoughtful eyes as she waltzed with Tom. The music stopped. When it began once more, Daniel had Anne in his arms.

Tom was dancing with Raina. "Look at that," Mary said. "What a couple they make."

Many eyes were watching Tom and Raina.

Raina whispered, "I keep thinking: if we had only…"

"Don't," Tom said, twirling her around in her rustling white.

Mary eyed Raina's huge, ruffled skirt that billowed as Raina waltzed. "She's his mother-in-law."

"Stepmother-in-law," Alice said. "Disgusting."

"Interesting," Mary said.

They watched Tom give Raina back to Daniel, and take Emily Snyder out on the floor. "Emily's engineered it all," Joyce said to Mary. "Both Bonner weddings."

"I wish Emily could find my Russell a rich wife," Mary said.

"He's still playing in that band?"

"He's a painter now," Mary said. "I think."

"Emily's always got gorgeous clothes. And so proud of herself," Joyce said.

The three women watched Emily Snyder dance with Tom, her filigree earrings sparkling, a smile on her face.

Emily was smiling, but what she was saying was, "I'm sorry… I'm so sorry."

"It's not your fault," Tom said. They revolved to a stately waltz.

"When you were so settled and happy…"

Emily's words followed Tom through the long evening. When he drove home with Anne after midnight, the moon had gone down, and the private road was dark as they passed Daniel's house… Raina's house.

Tom wandered through his living room and den, the patio room, the halls and his big bedroom. "Come to bed," Anne called after a while, but he prowled his home.

Anne came in her nightgown and slippers to find him. "It's late. You're wandering back and forth as if you think something's out there waiting to get in."

"Paris!" Raina cried when Daniel brought her there. "Paris!"

She kicked off her shoes to dance in the gardens of the Tuileries.

She pulled Daniel up flights of stairs to see what Paris looked like from the top of Notre Dame. "It's a dream. I'm dreaming," she cried, and made him laugh, and then whispered, holding him tight above the lights of Paris: "I love you, truly. I'm happy for the first time in my life, and I want to make you happy, too."

Raina kicked off her shoes to dance in the gardens of the Tuileries.

"You do," Daniel murmured. "I'm impatient as a kid of twenty. Can't wait for the dark. You make love the way the French chefs cook. Zest!"

Raina wasn't shy; her hair's brown silk seemed covering enough for her, and yet she made love with her eyes closed. "You're a miracle, something I don't deserve," Daniel said, and made her open her brown eyes that were so dark they were almost black. They could sparkle like a child's eyes, then glow like the eyes of a fierce lover.

She was as changeable as Paris weather. She could be an elegant young woman in a Paris gallery, watching the shopman unwrap an ancient bowl, startling the man with her knowledge, saying, "Crystal, I presume, overlaid with gilt." And then, so quickly, she could whisper to Daniel in another shop: "We'll have a baby, shall we? The two of us? A son for you?" And then, so quickly under the eyes of a clerk, she became a cool, rather bored, exquisite bride: Daniel's Bonner's most recent acquisition.

Daniel had been the awed newcomer to Europe once, following Patricia. Now he watched Raina's delight. "All my life I've seen pictures of masterpieces," she cried. "Now I'm surrounded by the real things. I can't believe it, even though I can see the actual brush strokes are there, or the real stone or wood or bronze or bits of glass." In London, she roamed the National Gallery for hours. "A child in a candy store," Daniel said, sitting down with a sigh before Rembrandt's portraits.

"Yes, yes, yes," Raina said, settling close to him. "And the ballet, and the opera, and the plays and concerts. I'm too happy. I'm in heaven with you."

September was ending, but it was still warm in Italy; Daniel took Raina there. Rooms in the richest hotels had high, ornate ceilings and cool terrazzo floors; their shutters opened above flower stalls and vegetable markets—a feast of colors and smells overlaid by the cries of children, shouts, snatches of music, and the warbling of birds caged above the cobblestones. If Raina leaned on a windowsill there, her long hair catching a red sheen in the sun, men who passed did more than look: they shouted their admiration; they blew kisses.

Daniel saw and heard them. He laced his fingers in Raina's fingers, kept her close as they walked a crowded street, and met male glances with a cold blue eye.

It was October when Daniel brought Raina home to his house on the river bluff. He carried her over his threshold to the cheers of Anne and Tom. While they drank champagne, Anne said that marriage must agree with Raina: she was prettier than ever.

"It's the clothes." Raina gave Daniel an adoring glance. "My new husband doesn't seem to mind if I buy a whole new wardrobe for winter. Daniel says, 'You'll be a gallery director. You have to set the style.' There's no husband so wonderful in the whole world." Raina looked at Tom and laughed. "Present company excepted, of course. But only Anne would know about that."

Daniel's eyes followed Raina. He stood with his arm around her as they said goodnight to Anne and Tom. "Beautiful," he murmured when she lay in his blue silk bed again. Her arms were around him. Her eyes were shut.

Morning sun shone through falling leaves when Daniel woke. He had a cup of coffee in his breakfast room, then shut himself in his study. His deep voice rose and fell as he talked to his broker in New York.

Raina woke late and naked in his blue-curtained bed. Stretching and yawning, she wrapped herself in the silk sheet and stared around her. Her eyes were full of tears.

When she sat up to look at the huge, rich room, beyond it was another richness of autumn gardens and forest trees. She rubbed her wet eyes, rolled out of bed, and stood naked at a window. Nothing watched her but a lone bird and a mass of dying chrysanthemums.

In a few minutes she said, "It's a dream." Nobody could have told skinny Raina Weigel as she cleaned nightclub tables and swept up cigarette stubs that someday she would sleep in this bedroom, and find her beautiful clothes in the closets, and step into a shower with gold faucets and soap bars shaped like cherub faces.

She had never owned such stacks of towels on a marble shelf, or opened such a vanity table of glass and mirrors. She had never had such a choice of soft robes, satin slippers...

All mine, Raina whispered. She trailed her blue robe through her rich rooms saying to herself, *All mine*.

But where was Daniel? She hunted through the house. Where was he?

She found him. He had left his study and joined Anne in his greenhouse. Father and daughter were intent on the orchids; they didn't even look up as she opened the glass door. When they finally noticed her, their eyes had the polite but preoccupied look of workmen interrupted by an amateur. They stopped their examination of the orchids to answer her questions, but when she left them in the heavy scents of the greenhouse, their conversation closed over her departure like the seamless closing of waves over a dropped stone.

By the time Raina finished her breakfast coffee, Anne and Daniel were out in the gardens. Raina watched through the kitchen window as Anne trotted to and fro in a shapeless hat, jeans, sneakers and a too-big shirt. She had a good figure, but who could see it? She ought to have her hair styled; it straggled under her hat, limp. And why didn't she ever wear the right makeup?

Look at Daniel. His jeans bagged in the seat like an old man's pants. Father and daughter dug and chopped and scraped and crawled.

Before Raina began her work at the Rolinger Gallery, Anne had time to tell Raina how the two houses were run. "All the work of our housekeepers, Mirabelle White and Betty Jacobs, and our gardener-handyman, Bill Hanson, is done in the morning. When the noon meal is over and supper's left ready for us, our help disappear for the day, unless we make special plans. Dad and I enjoy this system, and I hope you will, too—from noon on, we have the houses to ourselves."

Raina learned the habits of Betty Jacobs, her housekeeper, and the cleaning schedule, the planning of meals, the routine of laundry, bill paying and shopping. She made love to Daniel whenever he liked, listened to his beloved classical music, and soon began to entertain important people at his house.

When her new job at the Rolinger was official, Raina was no stranger there: she had spent long hours in the summer and autumn learning how it was financed and run. She told Daniel that she planned to make the Rolinger Gallery the finest gallery in the middle west.

And yet, so often, she found herself walking from one window of her house to another, her eyes on the gravel path to the house next door. She spent hours on her hair, her makeup, her clothes. When Tom and Anne came to dinner, or she went to their house, she was conscious of only one person in the room. And she felt Tom's answering awareness traveling to her, a connection as invisible as a spider web the light has not caught.

12

Tom and Raina, so naturally and so often, were left together that autumn. Daniel and Anne drove out of town for garden supplies, or spent long days in the greenhouse. "Why don't you and Raina go to that gallery show she wants to see?" Anne might ask Tom, and Tom—what could he say? He sat beside Raina in restaurants. They rode in cars together, their bodies touching.

He slipped her coat from her shoulders at a play and she said, "Thank you," watching Daniel and Anne, who had stopped to talk to a couple in the theater aisle. Seats around Tom and Raina were empty, so Raina could say: "The Bonners have certainly made you into their Renaissance man. How did they do it? Leave art books open on coffee tables? Play their classical music until you could tell a symphony from a concerto? My God—how long have you and Anne been reading books to each other in the evenings?"

"It's a necessity for my Foundation job—being a 'Renaissance man,'" Tom said. "And I like it. Anne reads well. I'm tired at night; I shut my eyes and the books come alive. But we haven't done much of that lately."

"You go to plays. You go to concerts. You go to operas." Raina said. "It's a miracle. You discuss them afterward. You're interesting to talk to, not just to..." she let her voice trail off. "What a handsome, dull business major you were. You thought steak and beer and football games were the limits of the known world."

"I've learned," Tom said. "They've both worked hard on me, especially Anne. Not everyone will give you a gift like that."

Daniel and Anne joined them in their theater row. Tom leaned away from Raina in the seat beside him, and took Anne's hand.

Anne and Daniel worked in the Hancock gardens one warm autumn day; Raina saw them as she sat at Tom's desk, a pile of Gallery accounts before her. She had gone out to watch the two of them for a little while. When she went back in the house, they never missed her: they were kneeling close together in the mud, cutting off dead delphinium stalks.

She stuffed her papers in a briefcase, sighed, and watched father and daughter carry heavy bins of mulch, laughing as they struggled to dump them on the flowerbeds. She had often wanted to say: "Don't you hire Bill Hanson to do this kind of dirty work?" but she never had. She knew they would say, "But we enjoy it!"

In a little while she heard Anne kick off her boots on the patio. "Raina?" Anne called, and came to the living room barefooted to sit with Raina on a couch.

Raina held a brass-framed picture. "Is that Daniel and Patricia?" she asked, showing it to Anne. "I found it in a drawer. What's that in the background?"

"That's Mom and Dad on their honeymoon," Anne said. "Look at those hairstyles. They went out west and hiked in the mountains, and somebody took their picture in front of that rock face. It really was a 'rock face.'" Above the smiling couple the cliff was split, and the split made a broad, dead-white streak like a missing nose. Holes stared from each side of it: deep eyes.

"Daniel's never told me how he met Patricia," Raina said.

"He was home from the navy after World War One, and she caught her heel in a street grating and fell into his arms."

"On purpose?"

Anne laughed. "She'd never say. She took him home to meet her father, and Grandpa Sadler said that Daniel Bonner knew more about what was in the Sadler Supply catalog than anybody he had working for him—even if Daniel *had* grown up on Wasserman Street. And Daniel always claimed Mother made him a new person."

Raina set the photograph on a table. "How did you meet Tom?"

"At Emily Snyder's house. She says she invited us with matrimony in mind, and I believe it. That's the kind of thing she would do."

"Yes," Raina said. "That's the kind of thing. And I imagine you took one look at Tom and knew what you wanted."

"But would he want me? That was the question," Anne said.

"I can't believe he hesitated very long," Raina said.

"I'm so in love with him," Anne said. "Just the way you're in love with Daniel." She glanced at the photograph. "You and I both lost our mothers."

"My mother was…difficult," Raina said. "After my father left, she changed completely. She almost went crazy. I'd come home from high school and she'd say my father had called her, and was coming home. The first few times she did that, we cleaned our room and dressed up." Raina looked away, and her long hair hid her face.

"How sad," Anne said. "How hard for you."

"She was dead by the time I went to college."

Anne hugged Raina. Raina said, "Sometimes I wonder if my mother and father might have stayed together if I hadn't been there."

"It wasn't your fault. How could it be?" Anne said.

Raina shrugged and said nothing.

"I remember Mother, after all the years," Anne said. "She was beautiful, like you, but she had blonde hair, not brown. I think she was surprised to have a plain daughter."

"Not plain," Raina said. "But someday we could talk about makeup—they've invented some wonderful things." Anne saw Raina's eyes travel over her for a moment, objective and calculating.

"I guess Tom…likes me the way I am," Anne said. The small catch in her words didn't change Raina's expression.

"Yes," Raina said, "I expect he does."

On a December morning before dawn Anne woke to the beat of rain on the floor-to-ceiling windows. It turned to sleet.

Listening to winter moving in, Anne began to cry. Tom woke and put his arms around her.

"I was dreaming of babies again," she said.

"Take one of the sleeping pills Dr. Hess gave you." Tom climbed from bed to find them, and brought a glass of water.

Anne took the pill and tried to stop crying. "I'm scared of today. Today the doctors might tell us there's no use and we might as well give up hope." She burrowed under pillows and sheet.

Tom turned off the light. He could feel her sobs like heartbeats throbbing in the mattress. "Don't cry." He found her in her damp dark and kept her tight against him, whispering into her hair: "Don't cry."

Tom fell asleep with Anne in his arms, but Anne lay awake, staring at the bed's dim canopy above. There had been tests for her, tests for Tom. When she'd married and thought of babies, she hadn't thought of thermometers and charts, and then white-coated doctors and gleaming machines. Love words had turned into words ending in "scopic" and "gram" and "etrial" and "opsy." And making love? She and Tom had to perform to the calendar and the clock.

The doctors had explained kindly to her that if she couldn't conceive a child, she could still live a perfectly normal life. Her health was splendid, they said.

But perhaps there was something they could do. Anne woke with that hope. She tried to be cheerful at breakfast. The wind had died down and sleet was no longer falling, but farm fields were glazed with ice as she drove to Rochester again with Tom. Waiting rooms at the Mayo Clinic were, as usual, full of patient, serious people. At last Tom and Anne heard their names called.

Three doctors met with them in a small examination room. "We're sorry," one of them said to Anne when they were seated. "It seems that Tom is fine. Nothing wrong there. And you're in perfect health. The only problem seems to be that you won't be able to conceive."

Another doctor said kindly to her, "You're young and healthy. You and Tom can adopt a child."

"But there's no hope for me?" Anne said.

"We don't believe there is."

"You should certainly consider adoption," another doctor said.

Anne and Tom went back to the waiting room and the wide hall beyond. Anne stopped in the empty hall. "I just can't have children," she said to Tom. "That's absolutely all that's wrong with me." Tears ran down her face; she didn't feel them on her cheeks. "I look like a woman. I act like one. I'm perfectly healthy. I'll live to be an old...f-fake."

Tom took her hands. "It doesn't matter," he said softly.

"It does—it does—it does—" Anne turned away down the hall, almost running. All Tom could do was follow.

Corn-stubble fields lined the highway as they drove home. Anne watched rows of brown, broken-backed stalks under a gray evening sky and was grateful for the season; it couldn't hurt her like spring and summer would.

"We could adopt a baby," Anne said.

"Let's wait."

"Why?" Anne said.

"I knew a couple in California who'd tried for years to have a family. We all felt sorry for them—they wanted it so much. They'd tried for almost ten years, and then—a baby!"

"But the doctors seem so sure…"

"Doctors can be wrong. And we're young yet." Tom took her hand as he drove. "I want your baby."

"And I want yours," Anne said, kissing his hand and trying to smile.

They drove to the Bonner house and Raina met them at the door. "What did you find out?" she asked, following Anne into Anne's old bedroom. "What did the doctors say?"

Anne laid her coat on the bed. "I can't have babies." Her voice was dull and flat.

"I'm so sorry." Raina put her arms around Anne.

"We're trying to learn to wait, and keep hoping for a miracle," Anne said. "Tom says doctors are fooled sometimes."

Raina let Anne go. She said, "Well. Would it help if you had a little half-brother or half-sister?" Anne heard the pride in Raina's voice. "I've brought one back from France," Raina said. "Or was it Italy?"

Anne said nothing.

"I wanted to tell you first of all," Raina went on, smiling. "Even before I told Daniel. I've been to the doctor today, too."

Anne had a stunned look, as if she had just been awakened. "A baby?"

"Early next June," Raina said. "I'll continue with my plans for the Gallery, of course, but I won't be able to do some of the things I wanted—"

"A baby," Anne said again, her voice lifting with an effort. "How wonderful! A baby in our family."

"And I had a thought," Raina said. "To cheer you up. Wouldn't it be fun to go to Chicago? Just the two of us?" Anne followed her into the master bedroom.

Raina sat on a bench and opened her vanity counter to show

piles of lipsticks, rouge jars, mascara and eye shadow cases, brushes, perfume bottles—a jumble, smeared with face powder. She dug in one corner, fished out a lipstick without its top, and said, "Let's go buy pretty things." Raina's eyes sparkled.

"Well, I'm not sure…"

"You seem a little tired these days," Raina said. She stood up to look at herself in the mirror. "You need some attention. That's what you need. I know a wonderful salon in Chicago. Let's go in and buy you a complete makeover: hair, face, everything. Nothing cheers a woman up like looking pretty."

Raina sat down again and looked at herself in the mirror. When Anne said nothing, Raina took Anne's silence for agreement. "Let's go next week," Raina said.

Winter weather met Raina and Anne in Chicago when they took a taxi from the station to the beauty salon. They left the snow and biting wind for a warm, multicolored sea of cosmetics and fragrances. Women sat in pink chairs, gazing into mirrors while pink-coated, pretty young women moved around them, stroking, combing, brushing, rubbing, penciling and painting.

In a few minutes Anne was at the center of just such pink attention. "She wants to look absolutely stunning," Raina told two attentive young operators. "Hair. Face. Everything."

The women told Anne she had "such eyes," and naturally long lashes. Lovely cheekbones. Her hair was washed and rinsed and cut and squinted at, discussed, sleeked close to her head, fluffed out a bit, then rolled tightly in papers on rollers. The smell was strong as they clamped each curler to a high machine, until she was tethered tight, and wondered what would happen if there were a fire.

When her poor hair was unwound from curlers, it hung in skinny corkscrews around her face. Hard combs raked her scalp. Busy fingers wound tight pin curls and covered them with a pink net. The hair dryer hid half her face and wrapped her in steady sound for a long time; Anne finished leafing through a pile of magazines she'd never seen. They were crammed with photographs of perfectly dressed, perfectly beautiful women.

Finally, soft brushes fluffed her dried hair around her head. "Close-fitting and elegant, like a helmet," an operator cooed as she waved Anne's hair at top and sides, then finished her off with a fringe of curls. "So you can wear those cunning Lilly Dache hats."

You've seen them? Little caps or bands or crescents pinned to the very back of the head. Ravishing!"

"How do you like it?" they asked Anne, handing her a mirror, while Raina nodded enthusiastically.

Anne looked at one side, then the other. "There isn't much of it," Anne said.

"That's the idea," purred one of the young women in pink. "You want to have elegant, slim hair with the spring sheath skirts. Tiny jackets. Isn't it an 'elegant' season?" she asked Raina.

"Absolutely," Raina said. She met Anne's eyes in the mirror and smiled. "Absolutely elegant."

"Now, how about the face?" an operator asked. "Pretty, but a bit pale?" They talked to Raina as if Anne sat before them like a portrait to be repainted.

The portrait in the mirror before Anne took on its new face slowly. Six hands were busy; three voices flattered and exclaimed.

Finally the last woman in pink stepped back, smiling. Raina smiled, too. "How do you like your new self?" she asked Anne.

"Not so new," Anne said, looking at herself in the mirror. "Tom will know me." When she looked at Raina, her dark-rimmed and fringed eyes glimmered, blue as steel. "It's fun to take all this trouble now and then," she said. "But Tom likes me just the way I am."

"Wait and see what he says when he meets us at the station," Raina said.

They had an "elegant" luncheon, shopped for clothes, had dinner high above the city and went to a play. Anne was in the fashion now and very pretty; Raina saw it in the eyes that turned to follow Anne as she walked by.

"Do you need some help with your makeup and hair?" Raina asked the next morning as they dressed to take the train home. "Until you're used to it?"

"Oh, no. Thanks," Anne said. "I memorized the directions for the ton of bottles and tubes and jars and brushes and pencils I'm taking home. It's fun to paint on a face for special occasions, but Tom won't like it for everyday."

When they reached Waterloo, Tom was waiting on the Waterloo platform. Anne wore no makeup but her usual lipstick. Her hair, blown by the wind on the runway, was hardly close-fitting and "slim."

"Beautiful!" Tom said, hugging Anne tight. "Back from the big city and so beautiful."

"It was Raina's idea," Anne said.

Raina opened her mouth to explain, but Tom wasn't looking at her. Anne's eyes held his, and they had lights in them; they lingered on his mouth, on his shoulders, on the curve of his cheek.

13

Month after month Anne watched Raina's figure change. Anne's father was as happy as she had ever seen him: he threw back his head and laughed often, and his cold blue eyes were warm when they followed Raina.

Raina was beautiful even in her expensive maternity clothes, but she was impatient and fretful. Most of her dreams for the Rolinger had to wait, she told Anne. How could a pregnant woman trundle around finding important artists? She had so many plans. June would never come.

But June came. Daniel was as nervous as any young father when Raina's pains began. He sent for an ambulance and rode with her to the hospital.

Daniel Steven Bonner arrived a few hours later, to Daniel's delight. "He's a fine fellow almost big enough to play football," Daniel said.

They called the baby "Stevie." He had the blue eyes of the Bonners, and a yell, Raina said, like a hog caller.

Anne couldn't stay away from her new half-brother. "Lie down and rest," she told Raina when she brought the baby home, "I'll see why he's crying."

In a few weeks Raina said, "I've got to get back to the Gallery. Work's piling up on my desk. We can get a nurse for the baby."

"Could Betty be a live-in housekeeper at your house for a while?" Anne said. "She was the oldest girl in a family of seven—she'd be a good nurse for Stevie. Maybe she could use the extra money."

Betty moved into the Bonner housekeeper's apartment. Raina went back into the world, her head full of plans. She had spent the awkward months of pregnancy studying her small gallery: it was hers, hers, hers. Now she was able to travel, and she did, hunting down artists whose work she had seen elsewhere.

"Are you satisfied with your gallery?" she asked them. "I have the money to give you a reception you can't imagine, and help with your résumé. I'll guarantee you a show a year, and your work on continuous display."

Raina had flair; artists felt it: a sure sense of who would be famous and what would sell. By the time Stevie was a year old, artists were seeking Raina out, lured by Daniel's money and her increasing reputation. Collectors and interior decorators were drawn to the Rolinger by the new and the weird: an African mask above a Barcelona chair, chrome end-tables, and Marin's watercolors that were almost as transparent as light itself.

Raina hung prints of Pollock's drip-and-spatter paintings between swirling crowd scenes of Thomas Hart Benton and the plump farmlands of Grant Wood. When gallery-goers were shocked at Pollock, Raina said, "Pollock and Wood and Benton—they've got Midwestern roots. They're famous. They're ours." The young and rich loved her gallery: the rice paper-and-wire table lamps in wild shapes, the Danish modern furniture, and the aura of the east and west coasts that hovered there.

As months passed and Stevie took his first steps, Raina was sometimes at the Gallery all night, hanging a new show. One day she came to the Bonner Building at noon to go out to lunch with Daniel, but he couldn't get away. If Daniel was busy, she said, she'd go with Tom—why not?

They drove to a restaurant in Cedar Falls. "Taking your mother-in-law to lunch," Raina said, and laughed at Tom as she followed the waiter to a table. When they had ordered coffee and opened their menus, Raina said, "Here we are together: the Second Bests."

Tom gave her a look over his menu.

"Go on," Raina said. "Admit it."

Tom didn't answer; he gave the waiter their orders. They sat in silence until huge salads and hot pecan rolls were put before them.

"I'm wrong," Raina said. "We're not Seconds. We're Thirds. I forgot Stevie. He outranks us both."

"He ought to outrank us," Tom said. "He's a Bonner. We're not."

"You're on the job early every workday, aren't you?" Raina asked, picking up her fork and tasting her shrimp salad. "You work early and you stay late. He's given you three big jobs—Bonner Supply, his town properties to run, and the Bonner Foundation. Nobody else would do all that. Three men might—with three fat paychecks. You sign for him and decide for him and speak for him, and he stays home and plays with Anne and Stevie."

Tom said nothing.

"Daniel's devoted to Anne nowadays," Raina said. "Have you noticed? He told me last week that he's tired of going to work. He's going to indulge himself, he says. I guess being with Stevie and Anne is his indulgence."

The fork in Tom's hand trembled, but he said in a level voice: "At least Anne has Daniel's attention now."

"Emily said Daniel wouldn't have anything to do with Anne for years, but that's certainly changed." Raina gave Tom a bitter look. "You might put yourself in my place and think about where I stand. My case is even worse than yours. Anne's so perfectly sweet. So perfectly kind. You saw how she acted while I was pregnant. Now she's at my house more than ever, because Stevie's there. She's so helpful. She's so thoughtful."

"She is," Tom said.

"And now it seems that the Bonners are planning to stay on their river bluff in their velvet-lined cocoons with Stevie, day after day. You're exhausted. I can tell, even if Anne can't."

Tom looked up. Several men were watching Raina as she leaned toward him, smiling, a beautiful woman on show.

"Stevie's toddling everywhere now," Anne said to Daniel as he ate breakfast on a summer morning. "I came early today to talk to you. Stevie has to be watched every minute. It's too much for your housekeeper to do, I think. If it's all right with you, I'll stop going to the nursery school and be with Stevie instead."

"Whatever you want to do," Daniel said.

"I'm helping Betty can the tomatoes this morning," Anne said, and went to the kitchen.

Raina stopped at the kitchen door in a while; she looked cool and fashionable in her ice-blue linen suit and hat. Anne stood alone at the stove in a rumpled housedress, her face pink with steam from the canning. "Why don't you let Betty do that?" Raina said. "What do I have a housekeeper for?"

"Betty's got so much to do—I don't mind," Anne said.

As Raina left for town, Betty Jacobs came to the kitchen to pour herself some coffee. She sat down at the table with a sigh, a thin woman with hair halfway between gray and blonde. "Going to be a hot day," she said to Anne, and gave her dry little chuckle. "I remember one awful August when my whole family slept on sheets on the living room floor, with one little fan blowing on us. What year was that? Do you remember? Was it 'thirty-nine?"

"If it was, I was about four years old, and probably thought sleeping on floors was fun." Anne sat down across from Betty and smiled. "Maybe we should have a cold lunch."

"Something hot, too," Betty said. "It's better for your insides in hot weather."

"Stevie's awake," Anne said, and went down the hall. Daniel was talking on the phone in his study. She brought Stevie to the kitchen, and he sat in her arms, a half-awake two-year-old. Raina's new refrigerator hummed in a kitchen corner, and bird song came through the open door. The scent of fresh coffee mixed with the steam of the canning.

Anne kissed the top of Stevie's head. "I'm going to stop going to the nursery school," she said to Betty. "I'll come here for breakfast and take care of Stevie while you work."

"Mrs. Bonner told me she feels better about leaving him when you're here." Betty gave the little sniff she gave when she disapproved of something, but couldn't say so.

Anne took Stevie to his room, and Bill Hanson came in from the gardens. "I told you what was going to happen, and it has," Betty said to him.

"What?" Bill sat at the kitchen table.

"Stevie's got his world figured out, all right," Betty said.

"He's talking," Bill said. "Pretty soon he'll be talking non-stop. You watch. Just like a garden hose going full blast."

"It's *what* he's saying, not how much." Betty cleared a breakfast plate with a self-righteous scrape and dropped it in soapsuds. "Guess what Stevie called Anne yesterday, right in front of Raina."

"'*Momma*'?" Bill said. "Well, that's what Anne is, isn't she? Who else is he going to call that?"

"Anne's trying to get him to stop."

Bill snorted. "That kid's smart."

After lunch Anne drove through Waterloo to the nursery school that waited in hot grass under hot sun.

"We're all cranky in this heat," Gwen French said to Anne. "Let's put a sprinkler in the yard and let the kids run through it in their underpants. They've got extra ones here."

The three-year-olds ran back and forth through the silvery fountain, gasping as the cold water hit them, shrieking with laughter as mud spurted between their toes. Anne and Gwen sat on chairs in the shade. After a while Anne said, "I'm afraid I can't do my volunteer work any more."

"Oh, no!" Gwen cried.

"I wanted to tell you first. I love it here. I'd stay forever, if I could."

"We can't get along without you."

"I'll keep the 'secret fund' going to help the parents when they need it. The three of you can see the money goes to the right places."

"You're pregnant. That's what it is," Gwen said.

"No," Anne said. "Wish I were. But there a strong reason why I can't: it's Stevie." Anne gave Gwen an uneasy look. "My father's busy, and there's no one to watch Stevie. A two-year-old gets into everything and anything."

"Raina can't watch him? She's his mother."

'The Gallery's her baby," Anne said. "She's going to make it the best gallery in Iowa, or die." Anne sighed. "I'm the only 'volunteer worker' in the family, and I can't bear to see Stevie left like that."

"When'll you go?"

"As soon as I can. I don't want a fuss. You'll have to find another volunteer."

"Not even a goodbye party? We could—Oh, look at that—" Gwen leaped from her chair. There were twenty-five wet and naked children running wild in the yard. Their underpants were patches of white on the grass. Beyond them, people passing on the heavily-traveled street pointed from bus and car windows and grinned.

Gwen caught Betsy and got her into somebody's underpants. Anne did the same for Jimmy. The rest of the children squealed and ran, delighted with the game of tag. If they were caught and put into underpants, they were naked again in seconds, and running away.

Naked children ran wild under the lawn sprinkler, their underpants scattered on the grass.

The fountain of water doused Anne and Gwen as they chased back and forth. "Go inside and I'll bring them," Anne yelled, shutting the water off, her dripping hair plastered to her head.

Gwen shut a growing group of children in the classroom as Anne caught the rest, one by one, and carried them in. "Look at us!" Anne said, putting the last child down and blocking the door to the play yard. Wet teachers and wet, naked children giggled and grinned at each other.

"You see?" Gwen said. "See how I'll miss you?"

"I won't forget," Anne said. Her eyes traveled from child to child. "I wish I didn't have to leave."

Anne woke each day at dawn. While Tom slept, she dressed and hurried through the still-dim gardens. No one was awake at her father's house except Stevie. He was waiting for her in the kitchen, and they breakfasted with Betty while Daniel and Raina slept.

One September morning Anne and Stevie went downstairs to the river and Daniel's shady dock. Stones and roots and grass tussocks broke the water's flow and formed pools under the willows for water striders and whirligig beetles.

Stevie sat with Anne on the dock edge, their feet in the cool water. "My brother," Anne whispered. She bent her head to kiss him, tightened her arms around him, and watched water striders running over the invisible skin of a pool. The striders raced each other in the morning sun as if the pool were a solid floor, but each step they took dropped magnified circles through the water: black coins that swarmed on the mud below.

River breeze stirred the gardens. As morning sun grew stronger, flower scents rose on the air. When blue jays screamed outside Tom's window, he woke alone in the master bedroom.

Tom drank some coffee, shaved, dressed and found Raina on the driveway when he opened his garage door. It was a hot morning; she had been jogging, and wore shorts and a halter-top.

"I can't believe how hard you have to work," Raina said without a hello or a smile. "I'm amazed at how little Daniel does now. He's stopped coming to town in the mornings and some of the afternoons, hasn't he?"

Tom said nothing. She came closer and then, since he didn't move, put a hand along each side of his face. Her mouth was only inches from his. "You can be free," she whispered. He could see himself in her wide, dark eyes. "You aren't tied to Daniel Bonner for life. Neither am I. We have reputations in our fields now. We can find jobs anywhere."

She turned her face so that their lips, only an inch or two apart, were on the brink of a kiss—then smiled and ran off along his driveway, her long hair rippling down her back like a dark banner.

All day the sun beat on the big houses. In the late afternoon the heat reached even Daniel's shaded patio where he lay in a hammock.

Anne brought Stevie into the shade and put him in his father's lap. "He needs to cool off," she said to Daniel. She had never touched a baby before Stevie arrived, but now she had learned exactly how diapers must be pinned, how spit-up milk smelled, what a year-old child's various cries meant. She knew how hard a two-year-old strained to learn: Stevie was tense and grave with the effort, and fell asleep exhausted by it.

Stevie looked up at his father's middle-aged face, bushy eyebrows and graying hair with eyes as blue as Daniel's. Anne sat beside them to read the evening newspaper.

They heard Raina's car in the drive. In a minute or two she came to the patio, sat in a chair and sighed.

"Tired?" Anne asked, bringing her a glass of wine.

"I've had an interior decorator underfoot all day: Mavis Maxwell," Raina said. "Awful. I grit my teeth and watch Mavis change the picture frames to match her imported wallpaper."

"Who's her customer?" Daniel asked.

"The new vice president of Figlers. He's got to have an office with 'the best originals' in it, of course, and the same for his new house. This means 'the newest thing,' starting with an original Norman Rockwell for the baby's room and working up to 'something very east coast.'" Raina sighed.

"What's 'very east coast'?" Anne asked.

"He's got a wrought-iron stairway the whole height of the house, and I put the 'Marilyn' up there. Looks as if it's made of silver."

"I liked that piece," Anne said.

"Which one?" Daniel asked.

"Remember that famous picture of Marilyn Monroe—the one with her dress blowing up to show her legs?"

"Ah, yes, now I remember that piece," Daniel said. "Marilyn's dress, copied full-sized in steel mesh, but it's empty. Just a silvery cage: Marilyn's gone."

Raina finished her wine. "You aren't dressed," she said to Daniel.

Daniel raised one of his bushy eyebrows and shook his head. "I've been dizzy most of the day," he said. "If I go to that ball and fall flat, people will think I'm drunk."

Raina felt his forehead and behind his ears and looked worried. "I want you to see a doctor about it." She turned to Anne. "He won't go when I tell him he should. See if you can get him there."

"I'll talk to him tonight. I told him I'd stay home with him, keep an eye on him," Anne said.

Raina stared at Anne. "You're not going? When you have that beautiful dress?"

Anne smiled. "You'll have to do the beauty bit for us tonight. You'll be wonderful, and I wish we could see it. But Tom's going. He can pick you up and bring you home. He has to make a speech about the Foundation's youth program and drum up money from the moneyed. You'd better dress. I'll call Tom, and then watch over these two and see that they get their suppers."

Raina stood for a moment looking at the three of them: father, daughter, two-year-old.

14

The Junior League Ball was always held at Grover Place, an immense brick house built in Victorian days. The city had grown around it and made it a public building with a vast ballroom in red and ivory, gilt and mirrors.

Raina Bonner stood by herself at a ballroom doorway. No one would think it odd to see her alone: Daniel seldom went out. She saw Emily Snyder watching her from the balcony above. Raina smiled at Emily, but never shifted her pose, like a fashion model in her apricot-colored silk and diamonds. Then Tom crossed the ballroom to Raina, making his way through waltzing couples, his gray eyes on her. Raina went into his arms.

Eyes followed Tom and Raina: Emily saw that. Like some advertisement for liquor or perfume or a tropical cruise, they whirled on the honey-colored floor. Emily watched them, then went downstairs.

At last Raina settled on a scarlet loveseat while Tom went for champagne. "Aren't Anne and Daniel coming?" Emily asked, gathering her skirt in both hands to sit beside Raina.

"Daniel's been dizzy all day. Nothing serious, but he wanted to stay home, so Anne stayed with him." Raina was flushed and breathless; her eyes shone.

Emily said, "I see."

Something in Emily's voice made Raina straighten her back and tug at her long white gloves as if she were readying herself for some task. "It's what Anne and Daniel love, being together at home," she said. "They're so perfectly happy. They're with each other every day, and if they don't enjoy dressing up and going out in society, Tom and I can do it for them."

"If Daniel's too sick to come..."

"He's a little dizzy, that's all. I wouldn't have left him otherwise."

"But Anne was worried?"

Raina leaned toward Emily, her beautiful face tinged with the pink-orange of her gown. "You know Anne. You know how she worries. She's afraid of these spells Daniel has."

"And you're not?"

A strange look in Raina's eyes seemed to intensify. "No. Anne does the being-afraid for me. She does it for me with her father. She does it me with my son." Raina shrugged her smooth, bare shoulders. "So to Daniel I'm in third place—after Anne and Stevie. You must have noticed. You were my mother's dearest friend, so we can talk to each other like this, and you'll have to admit that I'm... third." Her lovely eyes narrowed. "It's a fact."

Emily stared at Raina. "Anne's so in love with Tom."

"But she's not here, is she? That's a fact, too. So the final fact is that I'm here with Tom, and without Daniel. And why shouldn't Tom and I be together, after all the years we've known each other?"

Emily's mouth opened a little. Then she shut it tight, and stared at self-possessed Raina, who sat smoothing her long white gloves.

"And Tom is second in Anne's life, obviously—or perhaps even third," Raina said. "Daniel's given Anne everything: he's even given her the baby she wanted, and Tom has to watch."

Emily found she was holding her breath.

"So Tom and I are in the same corner, really," Raina said.

Emily stared at her.

Raina laughed, meeting Emily's stare with a sparkle in her eyes. "If Tom and I weren't in Bonfire Bonner's corner, living in luxury, where would we be?"

"You've given Daniel...you've given all of us...good value for the money..." Emily said, and smiled, but Raina caught the tone in her voice that added: *so far*.

"I'm glad you think so," Raina said, and added something with the tone of her voice, too. It ran under her words like water running under thin ice. "You brought us all together, didn't you?"

Emily found she could not say a word.

"It was a wonderful chance for us all," Raina went on. "And now that Daniel has his son, how could my life be any better...

as long as I have any decent sort of freedom?" Now her voice had a playful tone, but Emily didn't think she was playing. "Because I'm with Tom in this corner where Daniel's put us, you'll admit. And that corner is—a corner." She shrugged her bare shoulders. "Don't worry. If Tom and I leave our pleasant corner now and then, we know our way back."

"You ought to be perfectly happy," Emily managed to say. "Just as you are."

"Oh, I am," Raina said, looking beyond Emily's shoulder to Tom, returning to her. "You'll never, ever hear me complain."

The next afternoon Tom stood at a window of his master bedroom. The cottage garden's white and green was fading at summer's end. He went down the hall to watch the river from one of the "children's rooms." No one called them that any more.

Tom sighed. It was Saturday and he was home, for once, but Anne was with her father and Stevie, no doubt; she'd been gone since early morning. Earlier in the week, he'd left work early to take Anne and Stevie to a traveling zoo. The three-year-old's brown hair and blue eyes had made one stranger tell the boy, "You look like your mother," and smile at Anne and Tom, who were, it seemed obvious, the proud young parents.

Tom went into his living room that was bright with late summer sunshine, just as it had been when Daniel had showed them their new house, and Anne cried, *Dad...Dad...it's all here, everything, just as we planned it.*

Tom thought of his parents' little bungalow. It had been like all the others on the block: ruffled curtains at the small windows, ruffled doilies on the small chairs, narrow spaces between their walls and the next house. Even the sunlight of their days had been narrow, running from east to west from a front walk to a back alley. His parents had died together on a wide expressway, but they were buried in a row of graves almost as close together as piano keys.

Tom listened to the quiet of late Saturday afternoon. The house was empty. He poured himself another drink. He'd be drunk before long. He was exhausted. And after supper he'd have to report to Daniel.

He stopped before a framed Picasso print on his bedroom wall, and winced to imagine what Tom Hancock would have said, once upon a time, about Picasso's button-eyed self portrait with the green face and shredded clothes. And the Bonners had seen Tom Hancock as the know-nothing he had been.

Picasso's button eyes stared at "the Bonner Renaissance man."

We're not Seconds. We're Thirds. Daniel has two Eves in his Eden, and a son. Stevie outranks us both. Do you like it?

Tom caught sight of himself in his bedroom mirror: a furious, half-drunk face. He put a hand on either side of that reflection and said, "Stop it. You've got everything you ever wanted."

He turned his back on the mirror, but the prints of his hands stayed. Anne wouldn't come home until dark…long after dark.

Suddenly he heard a door open and shut. Anne must be home—

It was Raina: barefoot Raina in a man's shirt and shorts, with her hair down her back in one long, glossy braid. She had worn it that way at Berkeley, but never in Iowa.

He remembered. She saw it in his eyes, and she laughed. "You used to play with my hair, remember? You always wanted to make me a Lady Godiva."

"Yes."

She stopped smiling. "So tell me," she said. "What else can we do?"

He was silent, seeing her face. While her words were still in his ears, he found she was right, and felt as if he had stepped through a wall he'd thought was solid.

She followed him into the living room and watched him mix drinks. They stood side by side at a window, glasses in hand, their eyes narrowed against daylight dropping in the west. The sun's long rays were split into shining knives and spears by river trees.

"Daniel and Anne have built a nest for us," Raina said. "Step by step. Twig by twig. When we walked that path at Wuthering Heights, we were scared, weren't we—terrified at what we were going to try? But now they've brought us together so comfortably in this nest they've made for us…so safe…lined with such soft, soft money."

"They trust us."

"Oh!" Raina cried. "I feel so free! Don't you? It's our Berkeley days again, but not poor! Rich!"

They stood together watching the last glimmer of the sun.

"The two of them—don't they expect us to take care of each other?" Raina said. "Don't you and I meet for lunch, and go to gallery openings, plays, meetings...even out of town? They like to think, don't they, that you do these things for me, and I do these things for you?"

"You're reckless," Tom said.

"You knew I would come. Sometime. Didn't you?"

He didn't answer, and she laughed.

"Yes," she said. "And I've been away from home *all day*," she cried. "I've been gone and come back *three times*. Anne was always there. Now, ten minutes ago, they took Stevie for a ride. They left a note."

Tom said nothing, but rattled the ice in his glass.

Raina said, "When did you last see her?"

"Yesterday night," Tom said.

"She didn't tell you where she was going this morning?"

"I didn't ask."

"On one of your scarce free weekends? You didn't ask?" Raina made a small, helpless gesture with her hands, palms out.

"No."

"This morning I ate breakfast with Daniel," Raina said. "There Anne was, as usual. So I decided to experiment, and stayed away from home all day. All my free day." Her voice rose. "Where do they think I go? Is it my house? Is it my child?"

Tom turned away. "We've always known how they are," he said. "And they trust us, don't they?"

"I'll stay here till Anne comes home." Raina glared around a living room turning darker with the darkening woods.

"What will you tell Daniel?" Tom said.

"That I've been with you all day."

"All day?"

"It's what they want, isn't it? We're a foursome, and obviously *interchangeable*—so Daniel can be company for her, and you can be company for me." Her tone was matter-of-fact. "So we take them as they are."

Tom looked around him. Whiskey made his head spin.

"I suppose she'll come home sometime," Raina said.

"And I tell her you've been here?"

Raina's beautiful face was very close. She smiled.

But Tom left her where she was and walked unsteadily through dimming shafts of light to throw himself among pillows on a couch. He gave Raina an infuriated look. "I don't understand them. That's what I told Emily."

"Emily?" Raina said. "She doesn't understand it at all." She joined him on the couch, and took a picture from the table beside them: a snapshot of newly-married Daniel and Patricia under a Colorado rock-face, smiling from their frame. "We're the only ones who do."

"Daniel's got Anne."

"Daniel's got two wives and you've got none," Raina said, putting the picture on the table again. "Look at you: living alone. You don't even have a child. And I'm living alone, too." Raina's arms and shoulders were bare; the perfume she always wore seemed to surround him. "They don't need us. They've got each other and Stevie. They're perfectly happy with each other. How many people would marry them and put up with that? They're perfectly, perfectly happy!"

Tom stared at Raina and the room and the darkening view of the river trees through a haze of anger so thick that he couldn't speak. He was drunk. He was very drunk.

"But we'll put up with it," Raina said. "We can see what they're doing and be sorry for them, and make sure they're never ever hurt."

Tom's eyes would hardly focus on the room or Raina. "He cuts me out."

"They're happy," Raina said. "Completely." All at once she was in his arms, and all of her was so familiar to him: her mouth, her perfume, her slippery hair under his hands, her breasts–amorous, secret—they were two students again in a tiny, hidden room, missing classes, missing meals, finding everything they wanted among piled books, clothes flung off—

"Completely," she murmured, making it a love word, and with no more words they ran to scatter their clothes on the blue rug of the "children's room" under a row of stained-glass angels.

When the gardens were turning blue with dusk, Anne came home. She found Tom and Raina in the living room, and Raina entertained them with an impersonation of two businessmen touring her gallery. The three of them laughed. Raina said: "But I didn't make fun of them while they were saying, *How can it cost that much?* and *My kid could paint like that when he was two*. I want the Gallery to succeed. I owe my job to Daniel. I'm so beholden to him."

Anne didn't see the look on Tom's face; she was tucking her

T-shirt into her jeans. "Dad's so proud of you," she said to Raina. "He should be. I told him so today."

Raina smiled at Anne, who stood by herself, her jeans muddy from the garden, her blue eyes on Tom's face, then Raina's. "I'll see you two at supper," Raina said.

When Raina went home, Anne cried, "I'm so happy!" and whirled in her living room, throwing her arms out as if embracing everything she could see.

"Our life's going so well!" she said. "I can help Raina with Stevie while she's putting in such long hours at the Gallery."

Tom watched Anne do a joyful little dance step around the living-room furniture. "You're really the head of Dad's business now, aren't you?" she said. "You've climbed to the top already. And Dad's a different person since Stevie's come. He was laughing in the garden today."

"Yes," Tom said.

"It's perfect," Anne said, throwing her arms around Tom. "Every one of us has what they want most. We're so lucky."

"Yes," Tom said, and kissed her, and watched her go into the garden. He'd had too much to drink; he started down the hall, but stopped at the door of a room where stained-glass angels hovered in the windows, dusk darkening their wings. A perfume came to him with their faint light—

Raina's scent of lost California days still hung in that air.

He shoved the angel windows open and closed the door of the "children's room." For a few moments, Tom stood alone in his fine house, his back against a door. When he opened it, night air moved through the room. Raina's scent was gone.

Daniel's paths and terraces were lantern-lit the next night, and his doors were open to show groups of chattering people.

Anne and Tom walked through the woods from their house, and paused on the patio for a moment, looking through the windows at Daniel's guests: the wealthy, the politicians, the businessmen—middle-aged, well-dressed, powerful and dull.

Then they saw Daniel through the glass: Daniel Bonner entertaining in his expensive house—a man as wealthy, middle-aged and powerful as any in the room. He had his arm around Raina.

Raina never looked Tom's way as he came in, but she knew gray eyes were on her. She slipped out of Daniel's grasp and joined

The stained glass angel windows dropped rainbows on scattered clothes.

a group of men at the wide fireplace. The celadon bowl on the mantel was exactly the green of her dress.

Anne had gone to Stevie's room; in a few moments she appeared with the little boy. Raina saw her at once, and came to take Stevie from Anne.

Eyes followed the charming mother, the pretty child. Raina's glance met Tom's, and he thought she took on a glow, a subtle, added sheen. Then Raina gave a light laugh, slipped through the charmed circle, and took another glass of champagne from a waiter.

Wasn't she Raina Bonner, the lady of the house—beautiful, wealthy, powerful, bringing powerful people to her husband's home?

No. Tom watched Anne. She had given Stevie to Raina, and now she was standing at Daniel's front door, welcoming his guests with kind questions about their families. If they were newcomers, he heard her introduce them to strangers with flattering introductions.

Anne. Tom watched her, minute by minute, sipping his drink. Who took care of Daniel's child? Who planned his meals and ran his house while Raina was a gallery director? *Daniel's got two wives, and you've got none.*

Daniel's guests laughed and chattered in Daniel's handsome rooms. When had the Hancocks entertained like this? And who had persuaded Daniel to open his house to city leaders—people he hadn't invited to dinner for years? Not Raina; she was too busy at her Rollinger Gallery. Had Raina sent invitations? Decided on the china and silver? Arranged flowers in every room? Daniel's house sparkled and shone. Had Raina spent hours with the two housekeepers planning the food, laughing and drinking coffee with them in the kitchens? No.

Tom watched men run their eyes over Daniel's wife, then smile at Daniel's daughter. Men came close to Anne. She had a way of speaking to one person only, and that person grew animated and eloquent for her—Tom saw it. Guests would remember this evening with pleasure, singled out by Anne Hancock, Daniel Bonner's daughter.

Tom stood by himself along a wall. Who, he asked himself, were Raina Weigel and Tom Hancock? Day after day and night after night, the two of them were displayed, expensively dressed and smiling: "Raina Bonner, Daniel's Window Dresser"... "Tom

Hancock, Daniel's Shop Clerk." The window dresser and clerk were values: they were checks endorsed, year after year.

The crowd mingled and chattered. Every room of Daniel's house was lit. Tom and Raina played there together, so close to each other. Raina's gestures were for Tom: she pushed back her hair so that he, watching across a table, saw a jade earring touch her white neck like a kiss.

Her glance never quite reached him through a lattice of thick lashes, but she turned her water glass, little by little, until he could see the red print of her lipstick on the rim.

How easy it was for Tom and Raina to meet, for they were in Waterloo every weekday. They told Daniel and Anne that they planned to "work late," but at night they met at their cars in the parking ramp and drove in Raina's car to the Gallery's parking lot.

The Rollinger was lit by nothing but a few small lights in the exhibition rooms. They slipped in a back door and had Raina's office to themselves. Raina had closed the window curtains before she left work: heavy linen drapes appliquéd with rows of tigers on a purple-black ground. The same linen covered the couch: tigers prowled beneath naked lovers there in a candle's faint light.

15

October sent dry leaves scudding across city streets. One chilly afternoon Edna Wilson and Ruth Kline sat at their desks in the Bonner office. They paused in their typing and exchanged glances as Daniel's shouts and Tom's loud, short answers filled an office behind a closed door. In a few moments, the men left the office without a word and clattered downstairs to the street.

Ruth sighed. "Why doesn't Daniel just stay home and let Tom run everything? It's Tom's business now, I'd say. Daniel calls himself 'the silent partner.'"

"But he's not silent," Edna said. "He always butts in."

"Daniel wants to be top dog, and he isn't. He hasn't got a bark left. Tom knows everybody who matters in town, and Anne's throwing parties for them."

Out on the street, Daniel and Tom went separate ways. Daniel stepped into his car at the curb, slammed the door and drove away. Tom went to the parking ramp and took the stairs two at a time.

Raina stood on the top stair, watching Tom's angry face as he climbed to her. She smiled. "Daniel came to the office? I thought he would. Aren't you glad he's not driving you home?"

"He's off to Des Moines," Tom said.

"For the whole afternoon!" Raina unlocked her car in the parking ramp and was in Tom's arms before they shut the car doors. "We'll have hours to ourselves in your 'angel room.' The housekeepers will have gone home by now, and Anne's taken Stevie to Aunt Emily's for lunch and the afternoon."

Tom scowled at her as she drove down the ramp levels, pulled into traffic and drove toward the highway home. "It's dangerous."

"We've been in danger for weeks—isn't it dangerous 'working late'—sneaking to the couch in my office when the Gallery's closed..."

"You take too many chances."

"I've told you—today they're all *gone*," Raina said. "And I know you want it as much as I do—you love me more than you love Anne. Haven't we found that out?"

"No," Tom said.

"As much."

"I'm playing a game with you," Tom said. "You're playing a game with me."

"You're playing a game with Daniel." Raina laughed. "Taking his woman."

"Yes."

Raina laughed, her dark eyes narrowed. "Revenge?"

"If we're honest."

"You like the *danger*. We'll be on his turf in fifteen minutes—in our 'angel room' he built." She laughed again. "You enjoy knowing Daniel's a gangster at heart: Bonfire Bonner. Don't you?"

"I don't want to think about my reasons," Tom said.

When Raina turned off the highway to Daniel's private drive, she said, "Nobody home" as they went by Daniel's house.

But Daniel's big house wasn't empty: it was echoing with Stevie's fretful cries. Anne never saw Raina and Tom drive past: she was calling Emily. "Daniel's off to Des Moines," she said, "and Tom and Raina are at work for the day. I was ready to leave for your place, but Stevie wouldn't eat a bite of lunch, and he's got a temperature."

"Poor fellow," Emily said.

"Yes," Anne said. "So we can't come, I'm afraid. I'll let you know how he is."

"You might try half an aspirin," Emily said.

"I'll do that," Anne said. "Goodbye." She went to lift sobbing Stevie from his crib. He only wanted to sit on her lap and be rocked.

At last he slept. Should she give him half an aspirin when he woke?

She put him to bed and looked for aspirin in Daniel's cupboards, but couldn't find any. She'd go to her house for some while Stevie was sleeping.

Tom and Raina hid her car in Tom's garage. The housekeepers and gardener were gone for the day. They kissed in the empty rooms. "This is where we belong," Raina whispered as they closed the door to the 'angel room' behind them and locked it. "Naughty children."

The heavy carpet was their deep blue bed. "You're worse than drugs or whiskey," Tom murmured after a while. "You make me feel twenty years old again."

Nothing interrupted them: a lawn beyond the angel windows muffled Anne's footsteps as she came from Daniel's house to hers.

Anne crossed the patio. She took the carpeted hall to her bedroom.

Voices stopped her outside a shut door. "*Lovely!*" she heard Raina cry. "*Someday I'll be with you like this for the rest of my life.*"

Tom's eyes were shut under the stained glass angels. How handsome he was, his chest rising and falling with his quick breath. Then he scowled at Raina. "For years Anne's gardened with Daniel. Or worked in that greenhouse with him."

"It's as if you're a visitor they've made very comfortable," Raina said, twining a long, polished-red fingernail in Tom's hair. "They want you to be happy. They're polite and thoughtful. Then suddenly you find they've taken a step away into their own precious life, and you're not in it."

Leaf shadows darkened the blue rug in the children's room. Tom said, "And then you had Stevie."

"Since she can't have children of her own," Raina said in a contented voice.

"Anne's almost given up going out in the world at all."

"She says she's best at baby-sitting."

"That's not her best. She knows it." Tom sat up. "She worked at the Center, and then the nursery school. She's a diplomat. She could talk Russia into raising the Iron Curtain. The worst people do their best for her."

"She's a fool," Raina said.

"She's smart. She may seem soft and sweet—"

"She chooses Daniel when she could have you," Raina said. "She's a fool. And Daniel's got everything now, except me."

Anne stepped softly away from the door of the "angel room,"

staring at nothing, feeling nothing. She found a bottle of aspirin in her bathroom cupboard. She crept along the hall and hesitated…stopped again at a closed door…

"But he doesn't suspect a thing!" Raina said, laughing. "How could he? Remember how careful I was, writing notes to you and Anne after your wedding—with all the 'guards' in them to remind you of our toy palace guard who never says a word? I've put him in a drawer with my frilly underwear, just where he belongs." She giggled.

Anne shut her eyes as she heard Tom's voice. "You take too many chances," he said.

"Having a secret like this? Beating somebody who thinks he's in control?" Raina said. "I make Daniel feel young again. And I'm good at it. I want to do it for him. Look what he's done for me. It's perfect. Anne has what she wants, and so does Daniel, and now I have what I want, and so do you. And next week we'll go to the Drayton Point conference together…you—Director of the Bonner Foundation—and me, Head of the Rolinger Gallery. Two nights together! Two whole nights!"

There was no one outside the "children's room" door now.

Tom lifted a handful of Raina's hair from the blue carpet and held it against his cheek. It had a heavy smell, not unpleasant but pungent.

"It's heaven here in the 'angel room,'" Raina said after a while. She pinned Tom under her and shut their two faces in the curtain of her hair. "I'm so happy."

"You're so careless," Tom said.

Raina gathered her long hair out of her way, and lay with her cheek on Tom's bare chest. "Just be happy," she said. "Why feel guilty and spoil it? Haven't we worked hard? Your awful jobs at Berkeley. My awful jobs from high school on. Rich people don't know."

"Daniel's been poor," Tom said.

"He's forgotten how it feels," Raina said. She gazed through the angel windows at blue sky and clouds. "Do you notice how his eyes look sometimes? As if he's hidden somewhere in there."

"Yes," Tom said.

They lay in each other's arms, listening to crows in the river trees.

"Four years," Raina said after a while. "I've lived in Iowa four years. And you've stood it for nine."

"I don't think I could get up to California speed again," Tom said. "I've slowed down to this—big sky, big fields, big storms, deep snow, deep quiet. I can't say what. I like it."

"You're weird," Raina said. "It's the *Midwest*."

"So you do without first-rate exhibitions? Plays? Good orchestras? Foreign films? Dances? Festivals? Famous names?"

"No," Raina said.

The crows rose in one black crowd and flew away. Tom said, "Daniel's hated in this town. You can't imagine how much he's hated."

"With all his money?" Raina smoothed the faint lines in Tom's forehead and ran her fingers through his hair.

"You don't manage his affairs like I do, and hear what I hear," Tom said.

"He picks on you. Don't think we don't hear you both yelling!" Raina said. "Last night you two shut yourselves in his study and shouted about 'the Courtridge Property' and increasing the riverfront rentals, and went on to call some lawyer and some accountant and—finally–called each other names! We'd have had to be deaf not to hear you. But Anne won't say a word. She wants Daniel to love her."

"He's Bonfire Bonner, and he's getting old."

"Getting old and getting richer," Raina said. "And he says he's thinking of taking the four of us to Italy."

"Maybe I'm in one of those notebooks you filled with Daniel's collections," Tom said. "Maybe what he paid for me is typed under my picture."

Raina kissed the bony line down the center of Tom's chest. "If you're in those books, you're the most precious thing he owns." She had a teasing look in her eye, as if she knew Tom would say that Daniel's chief prize was his wife.

"It's Anne," Tom said. "She's one of a kind, and he's got her."

Raina lifted her head to look at Tom. Then she said, "And I've got you. And we're going to have a whole weekend at Drayton Point—just imagine!" She kissed him, but he was staring at the ceiling as if he were seeing its smooth whiteness for the first time.

Anne ran across gardens and into the woods to Daniel's house. Her mouth was wide open, but she made no sound. Her hands were pressed to her ears.

When she opened Daniel's door, Anne saw again a house that had kept secrets from her...Raina's furniture, Raina's pictures, Raina's pillows on the couches...they seemed to smirk at her—sly servants who had always known what she'd never guessed.

She found Stevie in bed asleep, his cheeks red and his breathing deep and slow. His forehead wasn't hot. She shouldn't wake him...

She gave a single sob and crawled into Stevie's big closet. Stevie's teddy bears, stuffed dogs, and cowboy dolls lay in a heap in the corner. Sudden hate scalded her like a pot boiling over on a stove. The toys watched her with steady button eyes. If she pulled off their heads, tore their fat bellies open, pulled out their stuffing...

When she burrowed under the pile of toys, hate left her for sudden icy fear. Daniel. The thought froze her heart, like a footstep in Daniel's silent house. If Daniel...

How could she look in their eyes, ever again? How could she eat with them, talk to them...sleep with...

She'd run away. No one would miss her.

Crouched in a closet that had always been her hideaway place, Anne hugged the toys. Her father had wished her dead. Clara had found her in that closet hugging her dolls.

On her wedding morning her satin dress had hung there in green light from the gardens...

She chooses Daniel when she could have you.

Run away.

"Anne?" It was Stevie's sleepy, fretful voice. She crawled from the closet. When he turned over, he saw her sitting at the foot of his bed. Anne gave a deep sigh, and straightened her back as if she were shouldering a heavy load for a long journey.

"Can we go out on the grass and lie on our story blanket when the stars come out?" he asked. "Can we?"

"We'll wait a few days until your cold goes away."

"But tell me a story anyway," Stevie said. "Right now. Make up a story, like you always do—maybe a prince fighting for a princess again, like last night?"

Anne got up to wander around the room. She said, "Maybe it might be the other way around."

"A princess fighting for a prince?" Stevie sat up. "Princesses don't do that, do they?" He watched her stop at a window to see her house through the trees. "They just sit around in palaces or towers or something."

"Not this time," Anne said. "I think my story is going to be about a princess nobody likes, and she's going to fight."

"Nobody likes her? Not even her mother and father?"

"They don't like her much," Anne said. "She isn't very good looking. They're disappointed—they wanted a pretty, charming princess."

"Am I charming?"

Anne came to hug him. "You are very, very charming. A Prince Charming, in fact."

"Mother doesn't think so."

"What?" Anne pulled back and stared at him.

"She doesn't," Stevie said. "I'm always getting dirty, and I like bugs and things."

"That's just because you're a boy!" Anne said. "You'll grow up to look like your mother, and you know how beautiful she is. Does your mother ever say you're *not* charming?"

"No."

"Of course not! You are!" Anne cried.

Anne crawled under the sheet with Stevie and was quiet for so long that Stevie thought she'd gone to sleep. He poked her and said, "Go on."

"Yes," Anne said. "Yes. I have to. Let's see: the princess in my story is called 'Princess Mary,' and she isn't charming, and she knows it—she's even heard people say so. She believes it, you see, and she curls up inside herself, and seems cold to everybody, so of course they don't like her. Not even her mother and father. She wants them to love her, but they send her to the kitchen to eat, and she thinks they wish she were dead."

"Do they?"

"It certainly seems like it. But her father the king is very rich, of course, so one day a prince comes to the palace looking for a princess to marry. He's a poor prince, so he needs a rich princess. He asks for Mary's hand. The prince is handsome, and Princess Mary loves him at first sight."

"So they get married? But where's the fighting?"

Anne didn't answer for a while; she sat up and looked out his bedroom window at the road. As she watched, Raina drove by, going to the highway. Tom was with her.

"Anne?" Stevie said.

Anne didn't answer.

"Go on!" he said.

Anne turned to look at him. "Yes. I will. There's another princess who wants this prince. She's very, very beautiful, but she's very, very poor."

"So the prince marries the beautiful princess instead?"

"Princess Mary is afraid he will."

"So she kills the beautiful princess!"

"No—her father's the king, and he kills anyone he doesn't like, but she doesn't want to do that."

"Her father can kill the princess for her!"

"But that would end the story, wouldn't it? No...Princess Mary is very sad and lonely and hopeless. She wanders here and there in her father's palace gardens, and what do you think she finds?"

"Magic!" Stevie cried, wiggling in excitement. "It's always magic!"

"It's a Secret Garden, all walled away and hidden," Anne whispered. "And there's an old gardener there, called Ben Weatherstaff."

"A wizard!" Stevie piled pillows around himself and bounced up and down.

"He is. And Mary tells him she's lonely and no one likes her and she's going to lose her prince. And he says he can help her."

"And he does, doesn't he?"

"He gives her something very special to win her prince and send the beautiful princess away."

"A magic key?"

"No."

"A magic box?"

"No."

"A magic wand, then."

"No."

"What's he give her?" Stevie yawned and put his head on Anne's shoulder. He didn't see the tears in her eyes.

"What do you think she needs the most?" Anne said.

"*I* don't know," Stevie said in a cross voice. "It's your story!"

"It is. You're right," Anne said. "Well, Princess Mary's not a very pleasant kind of person. The prince wants her money, but she thinks he wants the pretty princess more. "

"Well..." Stevie frowned. "You said she was going to have magic."

Anne turned her back on the window. "Weatherstaff gives her

magic. It's a magic *smile*."

"Just a smile?"

"Just a smile. Weatherstaff tells Mary that she's going to have a magic smile. It won't be a real, honest-to-goodness smile, of course. She'll have to pretend she's not worried or afraid. But it'll be magic. When people see it, they'll do what she wants them to do."

"Magic?"

"So Mary pretends she's happy and smiles. The prince chooses her. She gets what she wants most. People will do whatever she wants them to."

"You said there'd be fights," Stevie said. "I don't think that's a very good story."

"Neither do I, but it's all I've got," Anne said. "I can't think of anything else."

The autumn wind howled at the corner of the house and blew rustling leaves against the windows.

"Tell about when you were little," Stevie said.

He waited, but she only sat watching the leaves blow past. Finally she said, "Well…did I ever tell you how Mr. Hanson helped me catch moths with syrup?"

"How?"

"Mr. Hanson was our gardener then, too. He's always been so good to me. And one afternoon when I was six years old, he said, 'See that sheet lightning? We'll have a thunderstorm after you're in bed and asleep. How about some sugaring before it comes? Go ask your mama if you can come sugaring with me.'

"So I went and found my mother reading a magazine in the living room—your very living room, you know. I remember her sitting there with the light of the lamp on her hair. She said I could go."

"Her picture's up there," Stevie said. "On my wall."

"That's right. And Mr. Hanson said to me, 'Lots of beautiful things are just waiting for dark out there, and the lightning gets 'em stirred up.' We went into the kitchen and he said to our housekeeper Clara (she works for Aunt Emily now, you know) 'Give us some sugar, any old sugar. Doesn't matter, long as it's sweet. You got any rum?' Clara just scowled at him and said, 'Rum!'

"'Got to have rum,' Mr. Hanson said. 'Got to have beer.' The beer smelled like medicine. We mixed it with some rum and a whole paper bag of sugar, and Clara said, 'Ugh!'"

Stevie laughed.

"'We don't drink it,' Mr. Hanson told her, and he said to me: 'Now, missy, you take the flashlight and I've got the pail and brush. It's getting dark enough.'

"So I followed him, and smelled the rum and beer in his pail all the way into the woods. Mr. Hanson picked out a few trees he said were 'likely,' and he painted the syrup on their bark while I held the flashlight. Then we waited, sitting on a fallen tree and slapping at mosquitoes. We waited and waited—ages, it seemed to me. But finally Mr. Hanson said, 'Let's go look.' And there was our sugar syrup smeared on the gray bark of an ash tree, with three silvery-white moths on the syrup! The sweetness was so sweet that it caught them—we'd made them come out of the dark! 'We don't kill 'em and collect 'em, like some fools do,' Mr. Hanson whispered to me."

"Could you do it again, so I could see it?" Stevie said.

Anne said. "Maybe I can."

16

One autumn noon Anne came for lunch at Emily Snyder's house.

In a few moments, Emily felt uneasy: Anne seemed, in some strange way, different.

What was it? Emily smiled and chatted, but from the cheese soufflé to the raspberry tarts, Emily felt that Anne had come for some particular reason.

Clara took the last tray of dishes into the kitchen. The door swung shut behind her.

Emily fiddled with a crumb of piecrust on the linen cloth and admired subtle makeup that made Anne's eyes an even deeper blue, fringed by the same long lashes that Daniel had. Anne's hair was shorter now, and fashionably cut. "The four of you go everywhere together; it's so lovely to see," Emily said. "You and Daniel were nearly becoming hermits. You've changed your hairstyle and makeup and clothes. So becoming. That dress you wore to the Benefit..."

Anne wasn't smiling. "I was one of the main attractions there, wasn't I?"

"Tom certainly thought so," Emily said. "And he was right. You're an asset to the community, and you ought to be seen more often."

"I was seen," Anne said. "It was quite a scene."

"The crowning?" Emily said. "But you made a lovely Black Hawk Queen."

"Too bad I wasn't wearing a bathing suit and they didn't have a runway," Anne said in a peculiar tone. "But I imagine that Raina told Tom: 'Put Anne in the public eye. She'll be pleased.'" They walked into Emily's garden room, to her solarium's green plants and white wicker chairs.

An autumn shower ran down the windows. "Raina has a wonderful sense of fashion," Anne said as they sat down. "When I went with her to Chicago, she 'made me over,' I think she called it. She said, 'There's nothing I wouldn't do for you.' Wherever I am, nowadays, Raina's there, like a..." Anne searched for a word.

Emily felt something entering the room, ominous, like a whiff of smoke. She heard herself chattering, as if words were fresh air. "Raina and Tom are both so clever with people."

"Oh, yes," Anne said. "Raina and Tom carry Daniel and me along, working together. Dad and I don't have many of our old times now: our stuffy days of greenhouse work and playing games with Stevie. Sometimes..." Anne turned in her chair to look through the window. "Sometimes Dad wonders, I think, why he and I have to keep on this way with Tom and Raina, like four horses in harness, you know, wearing the newest saddles and bridles and tassels and bells. And it worries me: that he wonders why the four of us must suddenly be seen together constantly in society. He doesn't let me see him wondering; he hides it. I don't think he does that because he loves me. He doesn't."

Emily was spellbound now. She sat without a word to say.

"Tom and Raina are, evidently, trying very hard to keep the four of us in harness," Anne said. "I am, too."

"Yes, of course," Emily managed to say.

"I've always wanted us to be close. A close family, the five of us. You know that," Anne said, "but..." She suddenly met Emily's fascinated eyes. "I never imagined that it needed to be worked at day and night. I didn't complain. Did you ever notice that I complained?"

"Never," Emily said.

"I was happy," Anne said. "Or at least I thought I was. Now it seems that I am supposed to be happy in just that same way forever."

"I hope you *will* be happy," Emily said.

"Tom and Raina are invited to a weekend conference at Drayton Place next month," Anne said. "You'd simply expect that they'd attend a conference of gallery directors, wouldn't you? But I had to insist that they go, and I had such a strange impression that they were afraid—afraid to go unless I insisted!" Anne turned away from Emily to watch the rain glisten on the windows. "Lately I often feel that they're so anxious to please me that they'll do anything I ask. That's the way I make them do anything. Everything. I'm supposed to stay happy." Anne turned back to Emily, and suddenly there were tears in Anne's eyes; Emily saw them shine. "I love my father and Tom and Raina and Stevie, and so I will *stay happy*," Anne said. "I can stand it."

"You make them do everything you want?" Emily said in a disbelieving voice. "They're afraid not to? Why—I can't imagine it…afraid of you? You're sure?"

"They wouldn't be working so hard to keep me happy—unless they know something that would make me very unhappy indeed."

The two women sat near the rain-streaked glass, staring at each other.

Finally Anne said, "I'm telling you all this because I feel, I really feel, that you know what I'm talking about."

"Have you talked to Tom?"

"I've never said a word," Anne said. "But he knows me. And I know him. So I feel how afraid he is. He's kind. I love him."

Emily turned suddenly to take Anne's face in both her hands. "I always thought you were sweet, and kind…"

"*Stupid*, you mean," Anne said, staring at her.

"No. Never. You always had something about you—I've felt it, but I've never known what to call it. And now I see. You're—"

"Then help me," Anne said.

Emily let her go. "Help you?"

A strange young woman got up from her chair and said words that made the young woman stranger still, and almost…Emily tried to think of a word to describe it later to Clara…almost menacing.

"I've come to ask you for help, because I've felt for weeks that you wouldn't be surprised at anything I've said today, and I was right," Anne said. "You've seen exactly what I've seen. In fact, you've been aware of it, I think, for years."

"For *years*? But the five of you are—"

"Yes," Anne said in a voice Emily had never heard her use. "A perfect, happy family. I've used those words often, haven't I?"

For a moment it was so quiet they heard rain strike the solarium glass.

"So now, since you're so much a part of the family and know so much about every one of us…" Again Emily heard Anne's new, strange voice. "I'm asking: will you help me?"

"Of course," Emily said, blindly getting up to follow as Anne went to find her coat in the front hall. "Of course I'll do anything—"

"Will you be a kind of touchstone for my father?" Anne said. She shrugged on her coat. "Show him you think we're all happy? I don't have to tell you what kind of a man he is. How important it is that *he's* happy."

She opened Emily's front door. "So will you show him how much you doubt that anyone is...unhappy?"

Emily stood at her open door, staring at Anne.

"Even though you're not telling the truth. You've had so much practice in that sort of thing," Anne said. "I've already—though I didn't suspect it—taken lessons from you."

Anne hurried down Emily's walk in the rain and drove home.

Clara had gone out. Emily was alone.

Emily talked to herself in room after room of her empty house.

She yelled.

She hammered her fists on a kitchen table, slammed a door, lay face down on a bed, then got up to talk to herself again.

Drayton Point had been an imposing and dignified Iowa house in late Victorian days, built of brick and native limestone by a president of the Union Pacific Railroad. But the following generations of Draytons had favored one style after another: Second Empire, Queen Anne, Greek Revival, Italian Revival. The house had spread north and south: gingerbread verandas and arched porte cocheres below mansard roofs with a widow's walk and a soaring tower flying the Iowa flag. Then the great birthday cake had been frosted with cake-icing colors: strawberry-pink walls, pistachio-green wooden lace, and vanilla stonework at corners and eaves.

"Doesn't this house make you hungry, just looking at it?" Raina asked Tom as they drove down the long, serpentine drive. "It's like a big dessert. Can't we break off a corner for lunch, like Hansel and Gretel at the witch's house?"

George Drayton was the latest of the family line: a substantial supporter of midwestern arts. He met Tom and Raina at his door. "Delighted," he kept saying as he eyed Raina and led them over polished floors under high ceilings. "Delighted." They climbed a stair that spiraled like a shell.

Their rooms adjoined. When George left them, Tom unpacked, then stood at his window, thinking of Anne. The day before, he'd found her on her knees in their garden chopping blindly at rain-packed dirt, a trowel held in both her hands as if she were stabbing with a knife. Tears ran down her face. She'd wiped them away and left a smear of mud on her cheek. "It's the cold wind," she'd said.

Tom heard a key turn in a lock. The connecting door to Raina's room opened, and Raina came in. She was laughing as she said: "The key's on my side! They think you can protect yourself, but they're wrong." She slid her hands under his suit coat, but he pulled away.

"All week I've called your office and called your office," Raina said. "What's the matter? We've been so careful. You're scared of Daniel?"

"We're due downstairs for lunch," Tom said.

Leaves blew across the gardens below; a man raked a flowerbed at the corner of a Japanese teahouse. Cars drew up at the front door, and guests unpacked suitcases in rows of high-ceilinged bedrooms.

Raina went down the winding stairs with Tom, feeling the promise of Tom's lips and hands on her. He'd make love to her all night long: he knew they were safe here.

She thought of the Victorian women who had worn their cocoons of whalebone corsets and billowing bloomers in this house. Their lovers must have had to unwrap them, layer by layer. Afterward, had they called their maids—hurry, hurry—to wrap, button, comb and lace them, until they were serene and cool again, descending those stairs?

Tom was beside her. Eyes turned their way.

Eyes followed them as they went into the conservatory after lunch. "Maybe this isn't real," Raina said as they sat down in sunshine. "Maybe it's a trick of the light."

"Not real?" Tom said.

"I used to say that to myself at the Rolinger, too," Raina said. "One minute I was a window dresser in California, crawling on my hands and knees among male mannequins, yelled at by this fat department head who said things like: *If I would have been smart, I would have fired him*...and *I convinced her to go*...and *I was laying on the bed*...and *Where's it at?*"

Raina grinned at Tom and said, "Really! And the next minute I was head of a gallery. I was listened to on all possible topics.

I could write grant proposals and get the money." She sighed. "Now I feel that way again. How could I be any happier, unless I could marry you?"

A gallery owner and a museum director passed the door of the conservatory, glanced in, and smiled at Raina and Tom. "She's his mother-in-law," the director said in a low voice.

"Incredible," the gallery owner said.

And it was "incredible." Raina often used that word as the weekend passed. They attended panel discussions on "The Conservation of Art" and "The State of the Arts in America" and "The Under-Served: Bringing Art to the People." Afterward they hurried to lock their doors and shed their clothes.

"What are Daniel Bonner and Anne Hancock thinking of?" Raina whispered, propped on pillows in bed.

She dropped a row of kisses in the hair of Tom's chest. "Sending their spouses off to live together for days at a time?" She giggled. "It's incredible. Anyone who's ever been to these conferences knows what the secondary activity at such meetings is—or is it the primary one?"

Tom didn't answer. "Sex," Raina whispered against Tom's bare shoulder. "So what do your wife and my husband think we're made of? What would the women here think of me...of you...if we didn't—"

"Daniel and Anne trust us," Tom said. He buried his face for a moment in Raina's pillow, his lips so close to her ear that she heard him finish his thought: "How very old-fashioned."

"Old-fashioned?" Raina sat up to pour cups of their four-o'clock tea, delivered to their doors. "No. It's just convenient. Comfortable."

She handed him a cup. "All four of us have what we want most, except you," she said. "You don't have a child, and you never will."

"No," Tom said.

"But you deserve one," Raina said. She looked over her cup at his serious face. "So Daniel's next child is coming next April. And the baby will be yours."

Tom spilled his tea as he pushed himself back on pillows to face her. "My..."

"Your own son, or daughter," Raina said.

"You told me you were being careful!"

Raina laughed. "Careful to have your baby, not his."

She put her cup and saucer on a table and slid flat in the bed, her face framed by her long brown hair. "I don't love Daniel. I want to put your child in your arms. I'll hand him to you and say, 'Isn't he the most beautiful baby you ever saw?' and you'll say, 'Yes. He is.'"

Tom watched Raina climb naked and proud from his bed.

She dressed for dinner in a blue dress that skimmed her body like rippling water. There was a child under that warm silk.

He went down to dinner with her, descending the curving pink stairway.

"Venus stepping from her pink shell," a good-looking man said to Raina, the crystal chandelier glittering in his eyes.

"Watch out for my son, then: the one with the bow and arrow," Raina said, and laughed at him.

Dinner was an ornate affair at Drayton Point. On the last night of the conference, Raina talked to the men on both sides of her at the table, but she watched Tom.

When at last the others started up to bed, Raina and Tom didn't follow them; they sat talking in the gold and green parlor until the great Victorian house grew silent around them. After another hour, servants came to turn out almost every light.

Climbing the curving stairs with Tom at last, Raina took his hand and then, without warning, took Tom in her arms and kissed him in the hallway. Tom pushed her away with an angry look and shut himself in his room.

Raina sighed, shutting her door. As she undressed, she still saw that look of his. She shouldn't have kissed him out in the hall, but no one was watching, no one would know.

Naked in her bed in a moment or two, Raina listened to the silent house, the tick of her bedside clock. Minutes passed, and lengthened to a half hour. Suddenly she jumped from bed, put on a robe, and hurried to the door between rooms. She'd locked Tom out, poor man. She'd forgotten to turn the key.

The key was gone. The door was locked; she tried it.

"Tom?" she called softly through the keyhole. "They've locked the door. Midwestern morals. Now what?"

There was no answer. Tom was probably in his bathroom. She sat on the rug by the door and shivered a little. In a few minutes she crawled to the door again, and called "Tom?" again through the keyhole.

She put her eye to the hole and could see nothing. Crawling to drag a lamp from a nearby table, she shone its light into the keyhole. In the depths of the lock was the shining brass end of the key.

The key was on Tom's side. She put the lamp back, and was glad to crawl into her bed again. She had hardly closed her eyes the night before: Tom had been with her until dawn. It had been Berkeley again…those vanished hours making love to Tom in her little Berkeley room that was nothing but a broom closet. Students had gossiped and yelled and fought in the hall outside her door… traffic had honked and roared in the street…

Tom would come. The key was on his side. She closed her eyes and drifted into a dream. At last she dreamed that she heard a bell ringing, and woke to the alarm on her bedside table. She was alone in her bed in the morning light.

Tom was at breakfast when she went downstairs. They packed afterwards, and thanked their hosts, said goodbye to others who were leaving, and went into the bright mid-morning sun.

"Are you angry?" Raina said to Tom as they drove down the long, winding drive.

"You're reckless," Tom said.

"Kissing you? Nobody saw us."

"You've been flirting with me all weekend. Obviously. People aren't blind."

"You're afraid of Daniel? You think he'll listen to gossip? Look what he has to lose if he ever makes a fuss—people will laugh at a man who can't keep a young wife, won't they?"

Tom said nothing as he turned on the highway.

"And he'll lose Stevie and the next baby—your baby—I'll win custody. And just think what it will do to Anne, if he cares about her at all."

"You don't fool with him," Tom said.

"Daniel's terrified of publicity," Raina said. "He'll do anything to keep this family from getting dragged into any public spotlight. His past has to stay past."

Tom said nothing. She glanced at Tom's stern profile. "Besides, he loves me," she said. "He's proud of how I run the gallery, and entertain his friends." She laughed and laced her long fingers together. "And aren't I having another Bonner baby?"

She looked through the keyhole and saw the shining brass end of a key.

17

At eight that evening Anne showered, surrounded by empty rooms and silence, then dressed in a new nightgown, and brushed her clean, shining hair,.
She sprayed herself with perfume Tom liked. What would Tom think when he came back from Drayton Point and found she was ready for bed at nine?

Anne, startled, looked at herself in the mirror. How often had Tom found his wife at home at nine in the evening? Her look intensified, as if she were looking at miles before her. At last she turned from side to side, examining herself. Raina was the beautiful one. "Very pretty," Raina had said to Anne the week before, looking at Anne's gown for the Thanksgiving Gala.

She heard Tom's key in their front-door lock.

In a moment or two he was in their bedroom doorway. "You're home," he said.

Anne met his eyes in the mirror.

He was afraid. For a second she saw it. She had dressed especially for him. She was waiting for him in their own house at nine o'clock at night.

Tom shed his clothes without a word. The quickness, the silence, the wildness was as unfamiliar as if they were two strangers in a dangerous place who could not speak each other's language.

He made love to her as if she were someone else, and Anne answered him, but in seconds they were the lovers they remembered: they were newlyweds in London again, too hungry for each other to know the rest of the world was there.

At last Anne was back in the world, panting. Her blood still beat in her ears, and every inch of her seemed to be on fire. Anne stared at the white canopy above their bed and listened to Tom tell her how he loved her, he loved her, he loved only her. He made love to her again…

At last he fell asleep.

Light from the hall showed her Tom's clothes in a heap beside her new nightgown. His suitcase stood just inside the door.

She drifted into sleep, only to wake before first light to find Tom's lips on her, his hands on her, his voice whispering against her bare skin. And again she met his new strangeness and answered it: a near violence, a love-language they both had remembered.

Their bedroom grew light with dawn. She watched Tom's sleeping face, then drew away from him. Had he been with her? Or pretended she was someone else?

She left Tom asleep in their bed, dressed without a sound, and went to Daniel's house through a forest shrouded with mist.

Daniel was at the breakfast table when Anne joined him, holding Stevie. Daniel said good morning, but his blue eyes were intent on his newspaper as Raina came in. "You're up early," Raina said to Anne.

Daniel passed Anne a plate of croissants. "Mary Clellan dropped in yesterday afternoon."

"One of your old flames," Raina said, teasing him.

"And she claims the four of us are the talk of the town."

Anne felt, for a heartbeat, a twinge of fear.

"She wondered if I knew what a marvel we are to our friends," Daniel said.

"Marvel?" Raina said. "Who?"

"Anne and Tom and you and me. We're incredible, Mary says. It's a mystery to them, the way we avoid driving each other crazy," Daniel said. "Now we're all going to Italy together. How do the four of us do it?"

Anne felt as if her calm face were made of wood.

Raina's long hair swung against her crimson robe, and every curve of her face, turned faintly pink by that rosy red, was beautiful. When Raina's eyes met Anne's, there was a moment's glint before her eyes fell. Anne recognized that look. Tom had worn it the night before: it was a look that struck and glanced off, afraid to stay.

After breakfast, Anne and Daniel went downstairs to the river with Stevie, and sat on chairs along the dock. Stevie walked a little way along the riverbank and found a caterpillar on an overhanging branch. It reared on its back legs, exploring in air, trying to find a new leaf, a new road, but there was nothing around it but empty space.

"I wanted to talk to you today," Anne said to Daniel. "Here, where no one's listening." She picked up an autumn leaf and held it to the sun. "I'm the only one who can say certain things to you because you're fond of Tom and Raina, so they wouldn't risk making you angry, but I..." she shrugged.

The leaf spun on its stem in her hand, as real as the suffering in her quiet voice.

Daniel said, "Anne..."

"It's all right," she said. "You've always felt that way, and I know how you feel, but you've been so good to me anyway, and given me so much. It's all right. But it's not all right for Tom. At first you treated him like a son. It was wonderful. I knew you'd always wanted a son instead of me. Now I think you're jealous of him: he's made a place for himself, and you couldn't. He's respected and liked, but..." Her voice was low and hesitant. "We'll always be the Bonfire Bonners."

Anne felt her last two words split the air between them like two heavy blows. But Daniel heard them in silence, without a look.

Stevie squatted on the riverbank, poking flowing water with a stick. Daniel, elbows on knees, stared at swift water from beneath his heavy eyebrows. "Tom told you to talk to me."

"No. Never. He can't imagine I'd say such things. But he needs help, and he can't tell you. You've been mistreating him. He's doing too many jobs. I've heard you criticizing him, dictating, bossing. If you want to retire and stay home, that's fine, but it seems to me that you might suggest that Tom get a good assistant, then leave him alone. We're a family, aren't we?" She smiled at him. "You and I can't enjoy ourselves at home while Raina and Tom work, unless we make sure they're enjoying themselves, too."

Daniel stared at her. "You've got guts, I'll say that. All right."

Anne didn't answer; she only nodded and turned away to climb the stairs to his house, a pretty young woman, straight-backed and graceful.

When Anne had bathed Stevie that night, she fed him, put him to bed, and walked home. Tom's study lamp shone through the front-yard trees: he sat at his desk. She went in to kiss him. "You're looking tired so much of the time," she said. "Day after day. Dad asks you to do too much, and he's mean."

Tom looked at the pen in his hand and said nothing.

"He's mean," Anne said in an angry voice. "And you never complain."

"No," Tom said. "He's given us so much."

"You're the one who pays for it." Anne left Tom and walked up and down. "You do it for all of us, especially me."

Tom was bone-tired. He sighed. The columns of figures before him blurred. "Yes," he said.

"So I talked with Dad today," Anne said. "He's angry, but I told him the truth. I told him..." Anne's voice was trembling a little. "I told him I thought he was jealous of you."

"You what?" Tom met her eyes.

"I told him he'd been mean lately. I said he envies you because the people you work with like you. And trust you."

"My God," Tom murmured.

"I asked him to give you an assistant: somebody to take half the load, since he's not going to the office much. He probably won't talk to me for a while, but I was used to that once, and I can be again. He's going to suggest you hire an assistant."

Anne was silent for a moment or two, looking into Tom's face. She smiled. "I'm the only one of us who could say such things to him," she said. "I should have done it before. I can tell Dad what I think because he doesn't care as much for me. I'm the one who has the least to lose."

Tom jumped up and took her in his arms. She wasn't crying. She held him close, her face hidden against him.

Daniel and Raina entertained the next evening. Anne went to her father's house early to help; Tom followed her just before dark, taking the graveled path to Daniel's house, his tuxedo as black as the shadows under the forest's autumn canopy. That red, yellow and gold would grow thin and fall before long, but the river never changed, running as promised beyond the trees.

He took that image with him into Daniel's huge living room. Raina was there, beautiful in an emerald-green gown.

But Tom watched Anne. When Daniel played the host, the

guests met Daniel not quite halfway; there was always a little space around the tall man whose eyes were so cold and blue. But glances of the guests followed Anne with pleasure; people talked with her, laughed with her, crowded around her. Anne's face shone with what seemed such simple and friendly regard.

Tom watched Anne cross the narrow no-man's-land around her father. She smiled at the world from Daniel's side, as if there was no barrier.

Emily Snyder joined Tom in a doorway and sipped her champagne. She saw Anne put one arm around Daniel. "Look at her," Emily said in a low voice. "She works so hard for Daniel. And he's found out she's worth loving. It's about time."

"He hasn't," Tom said. "I don't think he ever will."

Emily stared at Tom. "But she loves him. She'd do anything in the world to make him love her."

"Not anything," Tom said. "Not quite."

November rain descended during the next week, but the Hancocks entertained on two rainy evenings, and their house was brightly lit above its gardens and river-bluff terraces at nightfall.

By the second evening Anne was sure of a familiar, uncomfortable sensation. What was it? Smiling and talking with her guests, she tested the feeling, and found it was a heavy weight she had carried before: gracefully, persistently, she was being *displayed* by Raina.

Raina seemed determined that no one should miss any of Anne Hancock's talents. "Anne has done so much exhaustive research on the Van Roche painting Daniel gave to the museum on her wedding day," Raina said to a Des Moines art patron and a museum director at the table.

The specialists had been talking of Eisenhower and Nixon; now they gave Anne their polite, slightly indulgent attention. Anne, astonished, was obliged to tell what she had found in an afternoon or two in the library. She managed to do it swiftly, laughed about her "amateur expertise," and asked the museum director intelligent questions about his new native-American acquisitions.

"Anne's dinners are always superb," Raina said as she left the dining room. The guests nearby agreed at once. Anne accepted the praise as gracefully as she could.

Hour by hour, Raina's compliments followed Anne so deftly, so persistently. "Anne's so good at this kind of party," Raina said to guests as they were leaving.

"I was just saying how pretty you and Anne are," a university professor told Raina in the front hall. "Did you and Anne decide together to wear the same shade of blue?"

"Anne and I are like sisters," Raina said. "We probably chose the same color without knowing it. We have the same tastes."

Daniel had gone to the kitchen to compliment Anne's cook on the dinner; he heard Raina's words as he started back along the hall to the front door.

"They have the same tastes *in bed*, too," said a plump gentleman in a low voice to another man. "We saw *that* at Drayton Point." No one but Daniel could hear them as he stopped short in the dark hall.

The other man's answer came clearly to Daniel: "Tom Hancock," he said softly, and laughed.

Raina turned in time to catch the two men grinning at her. Then Daniel joined the two men, his face expressionless.

The guests left by ones and twos. Daniel, Raina, Tom and Anne put on coats and said goodbye to their guests on the drive. When they were gone, Daniel turned to Anne. "I don't think," he said, "that the four of us can go to Italy next month."

Anne, standing between Tom and Raina, braced herself slightly, that was all. She kept her voice light. "Why not?" she said.

"You know we've always talked about the five of us as a family," Daniel said.

"Of course we are," Anne said. "Always."

"Of course," Daniel said.

Anne said, "You don't want to go?" Her smile was only a little strained. "It wouldn't be for long." Tom and Raina seemed turned to stone, they were so still.

Daniel gave a sound that might have been a laugh and reached for Raina. He held her tight against him and said, "Raina can tell you why we can't go. Why our family of five is going to change."

Tom, Anne and Raina were caught for an instant in icy, absolute silence. Then Raina gave a choked sound that turned into a laugh, and hid her face against Daniel's black wool shoulder. "I'm having a baby in five months," she murmured. "Next April."

For a few seconds no one spoke. Then Anne stammered, "How...wonderful." Tom said, "Congratulations." Daniel and Raina said nothing at all.

Then everyone recovered. Their light, bright voices joined in plans, and set up faint echoes among forest trees.

"Time to go home," Daniel said at last, and turned away down the dim forest road with Raina. Tom and Anne, together on their front walk, watched them go. Anne was glad of the dark. She was trembling in the November wind.

Tom pulled her to him and kissed her, his arms tight around her, but she kept her arms at her sides. "We're not going to Italy," he said. "Disappointed?"

"No," Anne said, and was rigid under his lips and his hands. "Dad loves Raina. You can see how much. He won't go to Italy without her."

"You're shivering," Tom said. "Come to bed."

Before Christmas the air was thick with heavy, clotted snow that whirled on the wind over creek beds, or roads cut through a hill. Anne lifted her face to the wet flakes as she cross-country skied on a path near the river, leaving her trails beside those of the rabbits and white-tailed deer. She skied for hours, glad to get away, trying to think.

But she didn't want to think, couldn't think...she skied as if in a dream, and came home cold and red-cheeked to feel the hot currents pass between her and Tom all evening long. That heat shot across the rooms of the two houses like streamers of lightning; couldn't Daniel and Raina feel it?

Yet why was it—so suddenly, after years—there?

Sometimes Anne laughed as she skied, a joyful sound in the empty winter woods. Night was coming: another night of lovemaking. She remembered every look Tom had given her across the table, across the firelight, across the conversation—an intent look, waiting for that the moment when they would be alone in their empty house...

Sometimes, seeing that love in Tom's eyes, Anne smiled to herself. Sometimes Raina, waiting for the baby through that long winter, saw that smile of Anne's. One evening, as they watched a play on television, Raina noticed Anne gazing quite happily at one of the saddest scenes.

"You're smiling," Raina said to Anne as a commercial came on.

Anne had learned that Raina never liked to see a smile unless she was sure the smile was not at her expense: she would investigate.

"You're happy?" Raina asked, investigating.

"How could I be anything but happy?" Anne said. "With Tom and Dad and you and Stevie, and the new baby coming?"

There was nothing Raina could discover in Anne's face but pleasure.

18

Emily Snyder sat by her fire with Tom, her eyes wide, her mouth open, and her filigree earrings quivering. "You fools," she cried at last. "You *fools*!"

"I'm pretty sure Daniel knows," Tom said. "Anne, too."

"The Bonners! Look what they've done for you and Raina! The two of you could *never* have climbed so fast so far by yourselves–"

"Raina thinks they won't do anything. They'll never want publicity and gossip."

"But you knew what Raina was like," Emily said sharply. "Better than anyone."

"Who knows what she'll do?" Tom threw himself back on the couch. Emily was suddenly thankful that she wasn't Anne or Raina or any young woman within range of that face of his, that body of his.

"The wonderful one is Anne," Tom said. "She's trying to keep the five of us together. She's the only one who's thinking of somebody beside herself. She's been cheated, and lied to, and she must believe that her father thinks she's spineless—if she knows. Or else he thinks she's too dumb to know what's going on. She can't have a baby and she sees this one coming. She must suspect it might be mine, and still she—" he shrugged his shoulders.

"Loves you?"

"Yes," Tom said in a low voice. "God knows why." He covered his face with his hands. "And I love her." His voice was muffled. "Raina's not worth loving."

"But she's having your child."

"Yes." Tom's face was still covered. "I could blame it on Anne and Daniel. Raina does. They shut us out, she says. Threw us together. But you said I'm a fool and I *am* a fool, one of the oldest kind of fools in history. I've broken Anne's heart."

"I think you're a lucky fool," Emily said. "Awfully lucky, if you've still got Anne." She bit her lip. "But watch out for Daniel Bonner."

Early one April morning Daniel drove Raina to the hospital before it was light. James William Bonner opened his eyes on the world at noon.

"Another big Bonner boy," Raina said when the five Bonners brought "Jamie" home the next week. The family settled in Daniel's living room with their coffee while Stevie played on the rug.

Daniel looked at Jamie in his arms. "This fellow's got such dark hair. The darkest hair of any baby in the hospital nursery. A nurse told me they called him Clark Gable."

After a pause Anne said, "Don't newborn babies often have dark hair?"

Jamie began to cry; Raina took him from Daniel. She was slim again. Her silk suit seemed to bring the fashionable outside world into the nursery as she carried the baby there.

Anne followed Raina, and stopped by Jamie's crib to look at a photograph of her mother on the wall: a pretty young woman in a 'twenties bob and dark lipstick. Raina said, "Your mother might have been Stevie and Jamie's mother, if she hadn't died so young."

Tom came to the nursery doorway.

"Tom," Raina said, and put the baby in his arms. Anne couldn't see Raina's face, but Raina's voice was oddly solemn. "Isn't he the most beautiful baby you ever saw?"

Tom wasn't looking at Raina, though she stood so close to him. "Yes," Tom said in a low voice. "He is." The little boy looked into Tom's eyes, and Tom, for a moment, laid his hand on the baby's dark head.

Raina took Jamie back, as if the three words from Tom had been what she wanted. She put the baby in his crib.

Anne bent over Jamie where he lay in the folds of a dark blanket. "What's this? I haven't seen this before. Look—Jamie's got his own palace guard." She took a small toy soldier from the crib. He was splendid in his red, black and gold.

Anne bent over Jamie's crib. "Look—Jamie's got his own palace guard!"

"Anne?" Daniel stood in the nursery doorway. "Jamie's nurse called. She can't come. Could you babysit for us while we go to the concert? Raina hates to bring in strangers."

Tom said, "I'll stay here with Anne. You can give me those figures you've worked up, and I'll read them over."

Daniel and Raina drove away after supper. Anne put Stevie to bed, read him a story, and settled in a study chair with a book. Tom sat near her at Daniel's desk, rows of figures before him, tapping his pencil on his teeth. They heard Jamie cry.

"I'll check," Anne said. She went down the hall to the nursery, and caught Raina's faint, flowery scent still in the air.

Jamie was wet. She changed him, then held him close. Her mother watched her from the brass frame on the wall.

Tears came to Anne's eyes. "Are you my brother?" she whispered to the baby in her arms. "Who are you?" Jamie's small face nuzzled her neck.

When she put Jamie in his crib, the soft nursery light seemed to show her something...she picked Jamie up again to look into his eyes.

By the time she tucked him in, Jamie was asleep.

Anne went back to Daniel's study to sit in her chair and look at her book. When Tom looked up, she was reading. When his eyes were on his papers again, she watched him: the planes of his cheeks, the shape of his eyes.

The house was filled with a Bach fugue's interwoven richness. Tom bent his dark head over a desk where Raina had scattered pages of a Gallery brochure.

Anne put down her book after a while and went to Jamie's room. The music had died away. Anne rocked in a rocking chair beside the crib and waited for a quarter hour...a half hour...

She hadn't said a word. Not yet. When Tom called, "Anne?" from the study and started down the hall, Anne still had time to decide: to say much, or nothing. She still had time when Tom stood in the nursery doorway. Tom was smiling, and she could smile, too, while Raina's faint scent still hung in the air, and Jamie slept in the lamplight.

But Tom's expression changed. He stopped by a table after one look at Anne's still face.

Anne said nothing. She went to Jamie and lifted him from his crib where the toy palace guardsman stood at attention. Every movement of hers was slow and deliberate; she kissed the little boy's cheek, as loving as a mother with her child, and never looked at Tom. Finally she said softly, "I love Jamie. I love Stevie. I couldn't bear—ever—to lose them."

Tom said nothing. The silence in the room deepened.

"You underestimated me," Anne said.

"Yes," Tom said. "I underestimated you. I'm still doing it."

Anne hid her face against Jamie for a moment. If she wanted to go into Tom's arms with Jamie, she didn't. She said nothing.

Again there was silence. The baby made soft sucking sounds in Anne's arms, and she felt a response in her womb; her nipples stung. Tom said, "You...haven't told anyone?" He didn't have answers. He was asking questions.

Anne was not answering them. She said: "Neither of you wanted to hurt Dad and me. You tried very hard not to hurt us—you worked together, and that's how I knew. Now I've found out that you and Raina have been...friends...for a long time."

Again the room was very still. At last Tom said, "Would you have married me? If you'd known?"

He was not begging or denying. She felt his helplessness. She had once seemed helpless to him and Raina.

"I'd have married you. I love you," she said. "But would I have wanted—ever—my father to marry..." Anne's voice trailed off; then her face flushed with her sudden, strong feeling. "Jamie's yours."

Again Tom did not deny or beg. His voice had respect in it when he said, "You'd never have told me that you knew he was?"

"Maybe not." Anne met his eyes. "I would have thought about it. To see what difference it made. I think I would have wanted to show you that I know. That I'm not..." She stopped.

"What?" Tom said.

"What I was. What you thought I was."

Tom seemed so calm that Anne felt, for a moment, that he might be brazen: admitting nothing, denying nothing, telling her nothing.

Then he made a small, despairing sound, as if he couldn't talk, as if silence was all he had left. Anne came close to him, Jamie in her arms; they were the image of a family: father, mother, child.

"Does..." Tom stopped at Daniel's name; he couldn't say it. "Does anyone else know?"

He hardly recognized Anne as she looked at him and, suddenly, gave him a look he had never seen on her face. "Oh, I think you would probably know if he does."

"I only know what you tell me." Tom's voice had a serious ring, as if he were making a promise. "I wouldn't ask anyone else."

Now sounds came from the front of the house: a door was unlocked; there was a call. It was Raina's voice: "We're home."

Anne put sleeping Jamie in his crib. When Raina, beautiful and beautifully dressed, stood at the nursery door, she looked from Anne to Tom and back again, but their faces told her as little as the face of the young woman in a brass frame on the wall.

"You're so upset," Clara said to Emily. "All the time."

"I've got to warn Anne," Emily said. "I simply can't sleep, can't rest. If anything happened I'd never forgive myself."

Emily drove to the Bonner house. When Anne opened Daniel's door, she had Jamie in her arms. "Come in," she said, kissing Emily. "No one's here but the baby and me."

"Of course not," Emily said in a sharp voice, following Anne to the kitchen. "You're always here, aren't you? Who else holds these two families together? Raina? Tom? Daniel?" Her short laugh was sharp, too. "I had to come."

Anne said nothing. Emily looked at her as if she were admiring that silence of hers. "You haven't anyone, have you?" Emily said. "You're alone. You don't think you can have any real friends. You're Bonfire's daughter."

Anne's eyes were very blue, fixed on Emily. "I'm Tom Hancock's wife."

"Yes," said Emily. "But there's Daniel. He's sitting in the middle of your life. He wants to grow old in this fortress of his, doesn't he, with you and the babies to enjoy and his gardens and greenhouse to putter in?"

"I don't know what he wants," Anne said, her eyes on tea she was measuring out.

"He doesn't want *anybody* in his way," Emily said. "He never has, especially in matters involving women. Some people thought Daniel paid to have somebody burn Bob Clingman's warehouses because of business competition. But it wasn't business—it was Rachel Harriman. Did anyone ever tell you that?"

"No," Anne said.

"Daniel married your mother, but he didn't want to give up Rachel. He'd set her up in an apartment in Waterloo," Emily said.

"But Bob Clingman took her away from Daniel. Daniel didn't like to lose a woman to somebody else—especially his business competitor. Bob Clingman married her. Daniel went after revenge. He wanted to make sure Rachel would have a pretty poor life with Bob, so he wiped Bob out. Burned him out, to be exact."

"I don't know my father," Anne said in a low voice. "I never have."

"*You're* not in his way," Emily said. "He thinks you're simple and sweet. If you don't know him, he doesn't know you."

"I told him to get an assistant for Tom," Anne said in the same low voice. "I told him he was jealous of Tom—jealous because Tom is so well-liked in town. I told him I was the only one who could beg for Tom because I didn't have anything to lose."

"*Oh, my,*" was all Emily could say. "*My, my.*"

Jamie gave a gurgle and waved his arms. "Baby boy," Anne cooed. "Tom's beautiful baby boy." Her eyes met Emily's over the baby's fuzzy head. "A little boy I never thought I'd see," she said. "Right here in my arms."

"Oh, my dear," Emily cried, jumping up to put her arms around Anne and the baby. "Be careful. That's what I came to say."

The dance floor was crowded at the Junior League Ball. Sally McDonald and Alice Ryesdal sat beneath gilded mirrors at Grover Place watching the couples whirl by. "Anne Hancock's striking, isn't she?" Sally said. "She used to have nice clothes, of course, with Daniel's money, but now she's..."

"As good-looking as Raina?" Alice asked.

Sally gave a light laugh. "You didn't think so once."

"But now I do," Alice said. "Anne's fashionable now, and pretty, and she's younger than Raina." The two of them watched Anne Hancock dance by with Tom, her dress brushing Alice's toe as she passed. "She's got a special glow. Marriage agrees with her, obviously."

"How old is she?" Sally asked.

"How long has she been married? Almost seven years."

"Then she's thirty-one. And Raina's..."

Alice frowned, thinking. "Her Stevie is four now, and her Jamie's newborn. So she's thirty-six."

"She's sitting with Daniel in the corner over there."

Alice frowned again. "He's sixty-one."

They watched dancers stop as the music stopped. Tom took

Raina out on the floor, and a young lawyer danced with Anne.

Daniel and Emily Snyder passed them, revolving to a waltz.

"I do enjoy dancing," Emily said to Daniel, "even at my advanced age."

"You?" Daniel smiled. "You're hardly fifty. I'm far in advance of young ladies like you." His eyes were on Tom and Raina.

Raina's black skirt frothed around Tom's black trouser legs as they whirled; she was all in black except for a wide white frill beneath her high-piled hair.

"I never can find you alone," Raina said to Tom in a tortured voice. She smiled as they passed Emily and Daniel. "Not for lunch, ever. And if I call your office…"

"I have lunch with Anne," Tom said.

Raina's eyes flashed. "Anne's so perfectly friendly, so perfectly kind, so—"

"Yes," Tom said. "She is."

"Does she know?" There was desperation in Raina's tone.

"Of course not," Tom said. "She's transparent. You've always said so. 'Colorless,' I think you called her."

"We were so careful," Raina said. "Now you've got your son." She had tears in her eyes. "And I'm smothered in Anne's perfect little life."

Tom said nothing. He wasn't looking at her.

"You and I were absolutely alone at the Denver convention," Raina said. "For a whole week. In adjoining rooms! And you left me alone—what have I done?"

Tom smiled at Emily as they passed her again, and said, "Nothing's changed."

"It has. Daniel looks at me sometimes—"

"Anne's the only hope we have," Tom said. "You'd better be careful. Anne's working on him, trying to show him we're a big, happy family. But Jamie's mine. Anybody can see that by now. God." Tom had a pleasant expression on his face as he danced, but there was agony in his voice. "I could blame the two of them, but I don't."

Light from the chandeliers flashed in Raina's diamond earrings. "We'll leave them. What can they do? We'll have our own life, more children—"

"I was a fool."

"A fool to love me?" Raina said, smiling at Tom as if they were in the midst of a pleasant chat. Her body followed his so that they seemed two halves of a black and white whole.

"Yes," Tom said.

Raina had no expression on her face now; it was a beautiful mask at Tom's shoulder. "A fool to have your own son?" she said.

"We've hurt them."

"They've got each other. That's all they ever wanted," she said.

"They trusted us. Anne forgives us. But Daniel?" Tom left Raina beside Emily as the music ended, and took Anne into the cool garden.

Raina was left to sit beside Emily. They talked of their usual Sunday evening suppers at the Bonner house. Emily asked her about Jamie and Stevie. Raina described her new Richard Somerson show at the Gallery. She sat poised and smiling, her gloved hands in her lap.

"You must be so happy," Emily said with a slight tentative tone in her voice.

Raina smoothed her gloves and stood up, looking beyond Emily's shoulder to Daniel. His cold blue eyes were on her. "Oh, I am," she told Emily, and joined Daniel, her back straight, her diamonds sparkling under the high chandeliers. They walked into the garden.

The small lights of hanging lanterns dappled lawns and flowerbeds, and a breeze carried music from the ballroom. Tom and Anne walked hand in hand, and Tom said, "Emily told me you were growing more beautiful every day, and she's right."

Anne gave a contented little laugh. "It's because you love me."

Tom put her arm around Anne and pressed her close to him as they walked. Her dress glittered with scattered beads. A fountain's sparkling waters rose in their path. Tom's head was down; he seemed almost afraid to look at her.

Anne stopped by the fountain. She wanted to hold Tom's face in her hands and kiss him and be kissed, her scarlet against his black, and whisper: *I've watched Raina. You're not telling her anything, ever. Torturing her. And showing me in every possible way...* But she said nothing, only stood with him to watch the play of light on water.

19

Summer surrounded the two houses on the bluff with deep woodland shade. Late one Saturday afternoon Anne, Tom and Stevie walked on woodland paths lined with the heart-shaped leaves of wild ginger and the mottled gray and green of waterleaf. A woodpecker hammered above their heads; birds called.

They took their usual route. Stevie's legs were short, so they strolled through woods and down the highway.

Afternoon breeze crossed miles of farmland to cool Anne's bare legs and arms. Foxtail-barley at road-edge stirred in that breeze, and she snatched a stalk as she passed; the tail was as soft as feathers. A red-winged blackbird flew to a telephone line. The air smelled of clover.

Tom and Stevie left the road to explore a bird's nest on a low branch, and Anne saw for the hundredth time how the two of them were bound together. Tom loved Stevie. Stevie followed Tom everywhere.

The three of them kept up an easy pace. Before long they topped a last rise and saw the farm's towering, silver-blue grain bins. Jack Tice's house, ringed with its porches, was yellow with late sun: a house for a farm family, snug in its windbreak of walnuts and oaks.

They took Jack's lane past his mailbox and a row of wagon wheels painted white.

The feed screw was running. A corncrib was full of dusty air.

"Maybe Jack's in the Quonset," Tom said, and they walked to a big hut and looked in. Farming tools were crammed in open drawers and hung from nails. No one was there. The scent of hot cornfields blew in with a breeze, and joined odors of old wood and hay. A tractor droned in the fields; a few flies buzzed among dust motes in sunlight.

"I'll find him," Stevie said, and ran off.

Anne held Tom in her arms and looked into his eyes. "I see what you're doing," she said.

"What am I doing?"

"You're pretending. Telling Raina that I don't know. Leaving her alone."

"Yes."

She stared at him. "Men frighten me. Even you."

Tom didn't meet her eyes.

"She's miserable," Anne said. "And my father…"

"What about him?"

They stood looking at each other in the warm silence of the barn. "Don't I show Dad that Raina's my best friend?" Anne's wide eyes stared at Tom. "Don't I make him see that, all the time?"

"I've watched you," Tom said.

"Doesn't he see that you and I are more in love than we've ever been?" Anne cried. "We're *six together*, a family. He *has* to see how much you and I love the boys. As if they were really ours." They held each other tight, throwing a single long shadow across the straw-scattered floor.

Stevie came back. "I can't find him," he said.

Anne sighed. "We'd better go home. Tom and I have to get ready for our dinner party."

Stevie rode home on Tom's shoulders. When they left the fields and highway behind, the woods on the river bluff were deep green with coming night.

Tom stopped Anne on the woodland path by the uprooted basswood tree. "We'll be together. Always," he said, kissing her, and Stevie leaned from Tom's shoulder to kiss her too.

Together. Anne said that word over and over as she showered and dressed. By the time she stood at the bedroom mirror, ready for the evening, her fears seemed lost behind her in a dark wood. She held a pair of earrings in her hand and looked in her mirror. The woman who faced her there in the glass, fastening her long topaz earrings, had wide and shining eyes. A man was courting her.

Tom came from his shower. "Beautiful," he said.

Anne threw her head back until her topaz earrings swung and shone. She watched her handsome husband dress.

When he stood before her in black and white—black hair, black wool, white shirt— Tom went to open their bedroom door for her, then halted, his hand on the knob. The woman at the mirror stood where she was.

Suddenly Tom locked the door and had her in his arms, pinned under his kisses and his hands.

"There are twenty-five people—" Anne was silenced by a kiss.

"Then who'll miss us?" Tom whispered. The doorbell chimed and the maid answered it; there was the distant sound of animated voices. "They've got plenty of drinks and food—who'll miss us?" Tom murmured against Anne's bare shoulder. Anne tried to answer, but could only manage a series of 0's and Mm's that were buried in a pillow.

The doorbell chimed, and chimed again. "And they won't miss us after dessert, either," Tom said to Anne in a little while. Ah...how he looked, standing above her, his gray eyes wicked. "Meet me back here!"

The Hancocks joined their guests a little late. No one noticed: the room was full of chatter. When dinner was announced, Anne took her place at one end of the long dinner table; Tom took his place at the other.

"I've got the prettiest woman in the room to talk to," a bank president said to Anne, who was unfastening an earring from her ear, an old one with a screw back. Where was the other earring? Anne thanked the bank president, and two women beside him gave her appraising glances: her face was flushed a little and her eyes shone. *Meet me back here after dessert.*

"You keep so busy with worthwhile things," a woman said to Anne as the soup was served. "What are you doing now?"

Anne opened her mouth to reply and caught a single glance from the other end of the table, but managed to say that she volunteered at several places when she was needed. She was able to pick up, after some confusion of mind, the right spoon beside her plate, but tried not to look at Tom again.

Dinner guests discussed Eisenhower's Highway Act. Anne's face showed nothing more than polite interest; her body glowed beneath her unwrinkled gown.

A maid took Anne's soup dish away. "I read your piece on Senator McCarthy," Anne said to the *Courier* columnist beside her. "You're just back from Washington?" While he talked she remembered that in childhood she had hidden in closets, or meadow grass. She had always hidden in clothes: they were a kind of disguise. Now at last, knowing what she knew, she could sit at her dinner table and hide herself in nothing but a quiet face, a relaxed body, and attentive eyes that showed nothing at all.

And then, after dessert, when coffee was served in the living room and people talked in groups, satisfied with good food and drink…and again, when the house had grown empty and still…

Had she dreamed the evening before? Anne woke the next morning to ask herself that question. Tom lay asleep in her arms—was it a dream? But a topaz earring under a chair winked at her with a golden eye.

The Rollinger Gallery had a new wing. Raina had spent months on every detail, and by the winter of 1956 it was complete except for the landscaping. Raina opened it for Emily, Daniel, Tom and Anne on a Monday in early December.

"Your whole gallery to ourselves," Emily Snyder said to Raina. "How pleasant." She looked from the gallery's windows to see Tom and Daniel walking along the newly cut flowerbeds in the December sunshine.

Daniel turned to face Tom and said, "The more you give, the more they'll take."

"I've listened to the tenants in a couple of our buildings," Tom said. "They'll freeze this winter."

"Fix the sidewalks? Put in new roofs and furnaces? Throw money away?" Daniel glared at Tom.

Tom looked up to see Raina watching him from the gallery window. She smiled her daredevil smile, then turned to say to Anne and Emily: "I'm so glad you can see the new Rolinger before anyone else does."

"What on earth," Emily said, stopping before a painting. Her eyes often had a glazed look when she visited Raina's gallery. She peered at a naked, winged figure laid on canvas in violent strokes of thick paint. He was as red as if he had been skinned, and he rode sharp bolts of lightning bareback, his bow drawn, his arrow aimed at the viewer.

"George Avenel's new work. His oils are selling very well," Raina said.

"The painter you told us about? From Michigan?" Anne said.

Raina nodded.

"The General of Hot Desire," Emily read from a card on the wall, then stepped back, then farther back, as if the painting were a hazard, apt to explode. The scarlet bowman grimaced at her, and his arrow seemed about to pin her to the wall.

"Avenel told me the title's taken from a Shakespearean sonnet," Raina said. "That's Cupid. Eros. The god of love."

"Love?" Emily said in a perplexed tone. She gave a last vague look around the gallery. "I believe I'll go out to hear the men discuss the landscaping. That's more in my line." She went through glass doors to join Tom and Daniel on the lawn. Raina and Anne were left in the company of a scarlet Love riding bareback on lightning.

For a moment they simply looked at each other, then Raina said, "While we're by ourselves for a moment, there's a question I've been wanting to ask you."

Raina's tone was odd. "Yes?" Anne said.

Raina hesitated. Behind her the scarlet bowman showed his sharp white teeth. "I've felt lately that there might be something that's come between us... something I've done without meaning to," Raina said.

Anne looked as if she were at a loss; Raina saw it. She put her arm through Anne's and drew her across the room to the gallery's wide windows.

Anne waited for Raina to speak, but Raina only looked through the glass, making Anne follow her glance to where Daniel stood by himself, staring with narrowed eyes into a cold December wind.

Raina raised her chin and turned to Anne. "He's fond of me," she said.

They stood watching Daniel; then Raina walked away as if a point had been made. She turned back and said, "That's why I can't stand it if you and I aren't friends."

"But we are," Anne said.

"You're worried. You don't talk with me the way we used to talk. Is there anything I've done wrong? Anything I've done to hurt you?" Raina's tone was not humble or apologetic.

"What *could* you do to hurt me?" Anne asked with wide eyes.

"I don't know!" Raina cried. "I haven't the least idea. How could I?"

"You couldn't," Anne said.

Raina looked her in the eye. "You're sure?"

"Absolutely," Anne said, and knew Tom had lied, as she was lying now. They were together.

"Then I'm glad I've been so honest with you," Raina said. "I like to be honest. It's a weakness of mine."

"I've always thought that you were my true friend," Anne said, and had to put her arms around Raina when Raina put her arms around her.

The glass doors of the Gallery opened behind them. Tom, Daniel and Emily halted there.

The next second or two everyone pretended they were not pretending to have seen nothing. Raina let Anne go and said, "Now that you've toured my new gallery, we can close the place up and have dinner."

Anne felt a spasm of pity as she followed Raina from the gallery: Raina had to know what no one would tell her. Anne had been trapped in that cage once.

The Riverside Restaurant had pink and black rooms, lotus-topped columns and black mirrors. When they had ordered dinner, Emily said to Tom and Anne: "It's nice the two of you are taking your trip together next week. Business and pleasure."

"We'll be in New York, then Chicago," Anne said, her hand in Tom's.

"We'll see as much as we can, when I'm not listening to the usual convention speeches," Tom said. His shoulder pressed Anne's; they leaned together, smiling at Emily, Raina and Daniel.

"If Dad and Raina were going too, that would make it perfect," Anne said to Emily.

"It's leaving the children," Daniel said, sounding the note of the worried father.

"No, it's repotting the orchids," Raina said in the tone of a teasing wife.

"The four of you will have years to travel together," Emily said.

"And we will," Anne said, putting her head on Tom's shoulder for a moment. Daniel watched them both. The reflection of winter sun on the river below lit sparks in his blue eyes.

Raina slipped her hand in Daniel's.

Tom spent long days in the Bonner Building. Work seemed to grow on his desk each night, multiplying in the dark, even though he had an assistant now. The assistant kept strict work hours, and left at five sharp. Tom sat at his desk long after closing time, night after night.

"Tom Hancock slaves—he does! Practically lives in his office." Tom's secretary leaned back in her desk chair one gray December noon to scowl at Daniel's secretary. "He's gone early today, but most times he stays here I don't know how long. You know he does. He's running the whole place, if you ask me—he sure knows more about the business than Bonner."

"He smiled a lot more when he first came...how long has he been here?" Daniel's secretary tapped her fingers with her pencil. "Started in 'forty-seven, didn't he? Before he got married? Nine years."

"He's taking his wife to New York and Chicago next week."

The women began to type when they heard the outer door open. Daniel came in without a word. He signed a few papers on his desk before he left. Tom's secretary looked from the window in a few moments, and saw Daniel on the street below, turning the Fifth Street corner. "He's walking off," she said. "Not getting in his car."

This was the old part of town near the river. Daniel crossed the small front yard of an apartment block. When he thumbed a bell and said "Dan" to a small grid, the door let him in.

"Come on up," a woman's voice called from the landing above. "Come right on up!" He could see her in a moment or two: a plump, dark-haired, no-longer-young woman whose black eyes were lit with concern as he climbed. "You're not feeling good?" She came down to meet him and took his arm as they climbed to the second floor.

"I'm all right," Daniel said. "I just get dizzy now and then."

"You always was," she said, closing her apartment door after him.

"Was what?" Daniel sat down heavily in a chair.

"Dizzy. Crazy."

"For you, Lil. Just for you."

"And how many hundred other women?" Lil stood before him wiping her hands on her apron. She laughed at the look he gave her. "Coffee? Whiskey?"

"Water."

"My God," Lil said. "Never thought I'd see you being friends with water." She brought a glass.

They said nothing until Daniel had drained it.

"Where's your brother?" Daniel said. He rubbed the cool, wet glass against his cheek. "Working?"

"He keeps saying he's old. Says he'll put his foot in a grave one of these days if he don't retire." Lil went downstairs, calling, "Charley."

Charley Xavier appeared with Lil in a moment or two, tucking his shirt in his pants as he came to shake Daniel's hand. "Long time no," he said. "Thanks for the help."

Daniel shrugged, looked at Lil and tipped his head toward the door. She left. They heard her footsteps going downstairs. "You think I'd charge you rent?"

"Old time's sake," Charley said.

"Right," Daniel said. "Suppose you could do another little job for me if I needed it?"

"Anything," Charlie said. "Somebody you don't like?"

"You can make good money. I'll let you know."

"Sure," Charley said. "Anytime."

It rained in Chicago, and then it snowed: a blizzard that piled inches of white on the Loop.

Anne and Tom bought high boots and walked in new snow gleaming with neon lights, block after block. "We're together, and it's all right," Anne said, her arm around Tom and Tom's arm around her. "Everything will be all right. You'll see."

"Let's take a taxi to the zoo," Tom said. "Who else will be at the zoo in this weather?"

Anne climbed in a taxi with him, as peaceful and contented as if they could spend the rest of their lives in each other's arms, watching a white city. "This is like a second honeymoon," Anne said. "Snowbound honeymoon."

Nobody seemed to be visiting the zoo but Anne and Tom. Perhaps the snakes in the reptile house sensed they were not on show: they slept together in enameled arabesques.

One king cobra was awake, and they stopped before his cage. "You'll see. Everything will be fine," Anne said. The snake raised its hood, its eyes as alert as two gun barrels, brass circles on black. "Doesn't Dad see the six of us happy together: our houses, the gardens, the boys?"

Tom's eyes were on the snake's flicking tongue. "He knows."

"But no one will ever mention it, will they?" Anne said. Behind glass, the cobra rode its coils high, watching them walk on.

"How about the lion house?" Tom said.

The lion house had no people in it. It was feeding time, and the big room seemed small, crammed as it was with the heavy pacing and scent of the lions. Every gleaming cat eye turned to Tom and Anne: a ring of malevolence behind bars, a caged hatred so intense that the two stopped just inside the door. Then the roaring began, and they fled, only to stop with sheepish faces in the snow outside. "Do we look that good?" Anne said.

"You do," Tom said. She kissed him. Winter air filled their lungs with tingling like a mouthful of champagne. They took deep breaths in a silent world as they broke through snow banks to circle the lion house and stop at a fence.

Behind heavy wire two panthers played in the snow like kittens. When their eyes were shut, the panthers were black silhouettes on white. When they opened their eyes, their gaze was as bright as a lighted candle: lemon-yellow staring from black. Sometimes, tumbling in snow, they licked each other with long, languorous tongues.

Snow fell on Iowa. Raina paced Emily's living room, moving from a window's view of snow to Emily seated on a couch. "I'm stuck in Anne's sweet little friendly life," she said. "I have to tell someone, and you're like a mother. The only one I have."

Emily said nothing.

"Anne's found out!" Raina cried. "I know she has. I feel it. I think she knows everything."

"And what's this 'everything'?" Emily said.

Raina didn't answer.

"That Jamie isn't Daniel's?" Emily said.

"You can see that?"

"*I* can, but that's because I have a reason to. Daniel doesn't, does he?"

Raina threw herself on the couch and hid her face in her hands. "Now, now," Emily said, putting an arm around her. "You told me once I'd never hear you complain."

"I'm not complaining," Raina moaned. "But I'm frightened—"

"Frightened of what?"

"I'm not afraid of Anne." Raina's voice had faint scorn in it. "And Tom won't talk. I beg him to tell me where we stand whenever I can get him alone, but all he'll say is, 'Nothing has changed.'"

"So it's Daniel."

Raina stared at Emily with tears in her eyes.

Emily said, "Even if Daniel finds out, look what he's got to lose if he says a word." She gave Raina a tissue and Raina dabbed her eyes. "He'll ruin Anne's perfect life. He'll make Jamie...what he is. He'll make Anne admit what her husband has done. He'll make you..."

"I'm alone! That's what I am!" Raina cried.

Emily said nothing

"We were so happy," Raina said.

"You and Daniel?"

Raina gave Emily a look. "You've never been on our side, and Tom's your nephew. I'm your best friend's daughter!"

Emily got up and went back to her chair. "Once upon a time I thought Anne was just a plain little rich girl."

"She hasn't got anything to be afraid of, like us."

"Yes, she has. She's afraid for Daniel, and Tom, and you, and the boys. She's afraid, I think, that she isn't strong enough to bring it off all by herself."

"What?"

"Saving all of you. I think she's going to try."

"By telling Daniel? We *never* thought—"

"You didn't know her. None of us did. She won't tell Daniel. Watch her: she's already starting to block him, just in case. She's reminding him every day that he's got too much to lose...smiling as if she's happy...showing him that she *wants everything just the way it is, and he should, too*. If she can, she'll save everybody. You'll have to help her."

"Help her?" Raina left the couch to stand over Emily. "Why should I help her? I've got what she wants."

"Tom?" Emily asked.

Raina gave her a hard look. "You wait and see."

When their lemon-yellow eyes were shut, the panthers were black silhouettes on snow.

20

When Tom and Anne came back from Chicago, they had dinner at Daniel's. Afterward he led the way to one of his garages. He had a surprise, he said, for Raina.

Anne and Raina took one look at the car inside and said, "Oh!"

Tom said, "A 'fifty-three Corvette! How'd you get one of those?"

"With difficulty," Daniel said. "With great difficulty. Only 300 of them were made, hand-built, and they were all white."

"It's mine?" Raina said.

They walked around the gleaming fiberglass body. The grill looked like bared teeth. "All yours," Daniel said. "Your early birthday present." He handed Raina the keys and got a kiss in return; Raina opened the door, sat in the driver's seat, and looked about her at the scarlet interior.

"Blue Flame Six?" Tom said.

"Hundred and fifty h.p.." Daniel wore a proud smile.

Tom walked around it. "You're taking an interest in cars?" he said to Daniel. The two men began to explore it.

The garage was cold; the women finally went back into the house. "Daniel enjoys giving you nice things," Anne said, putting her arm around Raina. Then she yawned and apologized and said she was tired from the trip—she'd better go home to bed. She walked to her own house through swirls of snow on the wind, remembering the look on Daniel's face, the tone of his voice.

Tom came from Daniel's house to say, "That's quite a car."

Anne said it was. She crawled into bed, and stretched her tired arms and legs.

"Daniel told me he thinks Raina's been a little depressed since Jamie's birth, and he wants to get her away, give her a vacation."

"He told you that?" Anne sat up in bed, her blue eyes shining. "He's trying! You see? To keep us happy. To keep us together."

Anne was cheerful in the morning, too. At breakfast Tom found her wearing heavy clothes and boots; he raised his eyebrows.

"I'll get fat if I don't get more exercise," she said. "C'mon and take a walk."

The night's heavy snowfall weighted every branch and twig. Tom and Anne shook garden firs and pines until boughs rose in the air again. When the trees straightened their backs, Tom and Anne were the ones covered in white.

They brushed each other off. Daniel sat alone at his breakfast table as they walked through his garden. He waved to them through the window.

Tom held Anne's hand when the wood path grew wide enough, until she cried, "I'm so happy," and ran before him through the snowy forest as if everything she saw delighted her. Tom smiled and shook his head, watching Anne racing ahead of him.

Her face was pink with the cold when they pulled off their coats and boots in Daniel's kitchen. "Saturday morning, and I don't have to drive to town through that snow," Tom said to Daniel. "Can't tell you how much I appreciate my assistant, especially in this weather."

Daniel didn't answer. A fire was laid in the living-room fireplace; Daniel set a match to it, and flames leaped between the window views of blue sky, black trees and white drifts.

Anne was in the playroom collecting Stevie and Jamie. Stevie spread one of his puzzles on the rug by the hearth; Anne cuddled Jamie in her lap.

Tom watched Raina bring coffee. As she handed cups around, her eyes were on Anne; she hardly glanced at the children, as if they were simply a part of the view, like her china elephants flanking the fireplace, or the intricately embroidered cushions scattered on the couches.

Anne looked up from the baby in her arms to see the expression in Raina's eyes. "You're simply perfect in that lavender robe,"

Anne said. "And you," she crooned to the baby, "you grew while Tom and I were gone." She smiled at Stevie. "So did you. You're almost five!" He pushed his puzzle along the rug to move closer to Anne.

Raina walked behind Tom's chair, a cup of coffee in her hand, and looked down at him. As she watched, he ran his ringed hand through his thick black hair. Tom knew she was there; she could feel it. He never looked up.

Raina left Tom to stand behind Daniel where he sat on the couch. The conversation was about schools for Stevie; everyone but Raina had suggestions. Tom talked of Montessori theories of education. The diamond on Daniel's left hand flashed as he gestured. Stevie had his cheek against Anne's leg now, and Jamie was almost asleep in her arms.

Anne saw Raina moving at the edge of the firelight; she left her chair and carried Jamie to her. "Would you like to hold Jamie? I think it's too hot for him by the fire," she said. "Sit where it's comfortable, now that you've given us our coffee."

Raina sat beside Daniel with Jamie in her arms. The little boy's hair was black against her lavender robe; Daniel reached out to stroke it, his diamond ring winking.

"We were smart to name you for my father," Daniel said to Jamie in the stillness around the fire. "You look like him."

Anne stared at Daniel. "You don't even have a picture of your father, do you?" she said.

"We were too poor for pictures," Daniel said.

Anne left her chair to go behind Daniel. She put her arms around his neck and her cheek against his and stayed there a moment, her eyes closed. *She thinks he's mending fences*, Tom thought, and looked at Anne with love in his eyes, a look Raina saw.

Stevie caught a bad cold. Since Raina was hard at work on a gallery show, Anne stayed the night on a cot in Stevie's room. Raina came home after midnight to find Anne lying beside Stevie in his bed, their sleeping faces close together.

Spring came with the first hepaticas in the bare woods: half-furled petals hanging their heads above leaves that were green all winter under the snow. Flowers of the Dutchman's breeches were scattered over the forest floor like long-johns hung to dry.

Raina slipped off her nightgown and stood at her bedroom window one sunny April morning. The big room was strewn with her clothes and shoes. The clutter gave her pleasure; she liked to see her possessions in heaps. They were all her own, her very own; she knew it was childish, but she'd sleep in a pile of them if she could, hugging them to her like stuffed toys.

Raina sighed again. From her windows she could see across the spring gardens and into the woodlands.

Someone was walking through the trees. She narrowed her eyes to watch Stevie with Anne and Tom: a family of three tramping through the sunshine.

They knew she slept late.

She kicked her slippers off, went into her bathroom and slammed the door, but the thought of Tom wasn't shut out. She stared at her bare self in a bathroom mirror, and remembered lying naked with Tom on a dark blue rug in a locked room. Stained glass had dropped rainbows on the muscles of his arms and thighs, and his thick black hair...

He was only a hundred feet away from her now. He was walking away with Anne and Stevie. She jerked the shower curtains shut, twisted the faucets on, and stood under water as hot as her anger. "Wait till you see what I'll do," she said under the water rush. "Wait and see."

Shadows of bare trees played over the forest floor. The April air was fresh and damp. "It's time for the Bluebell Wood," Tom told Stevie as the three of them walked single-file on the path.

"It is?" Stevie said.

Anne said, "You were too small last spring, but now you're almost five. This is a secret I discovered when I wasn't much older than you."

"When Jamie's old enough, you can show it to him, and surprise him," Tom said.

Anne lifted her face to the sun when she came to an open place on the path. "These fields and woodlands never change. They're the same as they were when I was your age, and my mother was still here," she said to Stevie.

Stevie's hand tightened on Anne's. "You always *be here*," he said.

"I will," Anne said in a surprised voice, glancing at Tom. "So will your mother and father, and Tom. We plan to be here almost forever. Now... are you ready?"

"Ready."

"Shut your eyes—shut them tight!." Anne told Stevie. "Now,

They lifted Stevie by his hands and swung him between them, uphill and down.

Tom, let's carry him to the secret Bluebell Wood."

They lifted Stevie by his hands and ran, swinging him between them, uphill and down. It was magic to Stevie: his eyes shut, his sneakers skimming the air, the pounding feet, the wet smells of the woods.

"We're here," Anne cried. "Open your eyes!"

Stevie's feet hit the ground. All he could see was woodland carpeted in such blue that he might have been upside down, looking at the sky. The sky-blue bells hung from thousands of green steeples, their buds tinged pink.

"Bluebells!" Stevie cried. "The Bluebell Wood."

Trees beyond the Wood framed a meadow full of sunlight and wild grass where a great oak tree threw far shadows.

Stevie talked about the Bluebell Wood at supper. He talked about it when Anne put him to bed. "It's magic," he said, pulling the sheet up to his chin.

"It's all magic." Anne put her arms around him, and laid her head on his pillow for a moment. "That we're all here together. A family." She gave a little "Mmm" of happiness in his ear. "Magic."

The next morning Anne met Raina at her gallery office. Raina hung Anne's coat in the closet and perched on the corner of the desk: a businesswoman in a scarlet jacket and narrow skirt, her hair coiled at the nape of her neck. "I've been meaning to talk a little with you, tell you how I feel," she said to Anne. "I know you'll understand. It's just that I'd rather you didn't come to the house quite so often."

The couch Anne sat on was as flat and large as a single bed and covered with tapestry; Anne stared at the appliquéd tigers parading across it, head to tail. She gripped her hands tightly in her lap. "I understand."

"Stevie's getting two sets of signals, and he's confused. That's my point," Raina said. "I wanted us to have lunch together so I could talk it over with you."

Anne picked at the whiskers of a tiger appliqué. "I'm too fond of Stevie and Jamie, I suppose," she said.

"It's natural," Raina said crisply. "They're your half-brothers, after all. I'm sure you want to do what's best. But Stevie's in nursery school now, and Betty can look after both boys in the afternoon." Her voice took on an almost accusing tone: "Stevie's having nightmares again."

"I've talked to Dr. Garrick several times," Anne said quickly. "I've tried what he—" she stopped.

"You see?" Raina said. "*You've* gone to the doctor. *You've* tried." A secretary came to the door. "Yes?"

"A long distance call, Mrs. Bonner."

"Take the number and I'll call back this afternoon," Raina said. She reached in the closet to give Anne her hat and fur cape, then put on her own coat and a small hat trimmed with roses and curling feathers. "I've reserved a table at Granny Meg's for us. We should be leaving."

They drove in Raina's Corvette, turning heads along city streets as they passed. A table was waiting for them at Granny Meg's. Several waiters called Raina by name. "I've never been here," Anne said, looking around her. "I'm a homebody, I'm afraid."

"That's another thing I wanted to mention to you," Raina said. "Of course you're like a sister to me, and I can't help but notice that you're cooped up. Shut in. I know you and Daniel enjoy the greenhouse and the gardens and playing with the children, but both of you are really meant for something...more challenging. How about Daniel's Center For Senior Citizens? The one you told us about, with the little old lady who was sleeping in her abandoned house."

"It has a full-time supervisor now," Anne said.

"I know you felt your visits to the nursery school took too much of your time, but there are so many charities. So much volunteer work to do," Raina said as a group of people came by and hailed her.

Raina left her chair to talk to them. She made no move to introduce Anne. Anne sat alone at the table, her head bowed over the menu.

She was thinking of Stevie. She thought of him during lunch. When she said goodbye to Raina at her office and drove home, she still thought of Stevie. She found him with Daniel between the two houses, muddy and hard at work setting primrose rosettes along a stone walk. The heavy fragrance of hyacinths came and went with the spring wind.

Stevie ran into the greenhouse, and Anne said to Daniel, "Raina wanted to talk to me this morning. She feels that Stevie's a little confused just now: he must feel that he has two mothers, not one, when I'm at your house so much of the time." She brushed her wind-blown hair out of her eyes. "I'm there too often. She'd rather I didn't come—"

"She told you to stay away?" Daniel asked in a sharp voice.

"Not like that," Anne said softly. "She's trying to be more of a mother, don't you see? Trying to balance us out so I don't... monopolize you and the children." Anne didn't meet Daniel's eyes. "I haven't any babies, but that doesn't mean I should shove in and try to take over yours. Or you, either."

Daniel sat back on his muddy heels. He didn't look at Anne; he looked at Stevie coming from the greenhouse. "The wind's picking up and Stevie's been out for a while," he said, getting up. "We'd better go in and have something hot to drink."

They kicked off their boots at the greenhouse door. Anne made cocoa, and the three wrapped their cold hands around the warm cups. Anne said to Stevie, "You and I won't be spending quite so much time together for a while. Your mother wants to be here with you instead."

Stevie stared at her, his blue eyes so much like hers, his hair the same warm brown. "No!" he said.

"Your mother wants to spend more time with you. She told me today that she'll be staying home every afternoon," Anne said.

Stevie licked off a chocolate mustache. "I don't want her."

"I'll always be at my house," Anne said. "You can telephone me and ask questions."

Stevie squirmed on the high kitchen stool, looking from Anne to Daniel. "I want you," he said to Anne.

"Tell your mother about what you're doing. She wants to know. About the bee box in the window, and our snake-hole map."

"She's scared of bugs."

"She just hasn't been close to bugs before, learning how they live," Anne said. "Let's put the bee box in right now. It won't have any bees in it for a while, so she'll get used to it, and you can explain it."

Stevie crawled under his bed and brought out the bumblebee box. Daniel and Tom had found a book that told how to build one. They had nailed four sides to a board to make it a box, and divided it in half with a board partition, so that the house had two rooms. They had bored a hole in the partition, and another hole in the front wall. "We'll stick a piece of garden hose in this front door, see?" Stevie stuck his finger in it to show Anne. "The bees'll have a tunnel to the outside. And here's the lid." Daniel helped him slide the sheet of glass in a groove to cover both bumblebee rooms, a moveable roof.

Suddenly a flash of jealousy shot through Anne: Daniel had never played with his daughter this way. Daniel's son, flushed with pleasure, knelt close to his father as they cut cardboard to fit around the hose and meet the open window's edges.

"Where is everybody?" Raina said, standing at the bedroom door. The sound of her voice made all of them start—Anne saw it—as if they were caught doing something wrong. Yet Raina was smiling at her son and her husband.

"My bumblebee house," Stevie said in a brave voice, flanked as he was by Anne and his father. "In my window. There aren't any bees yet."

"I should hope not," Raina said.

"We'll work on the bumblebee box later," Daniel said to Stevie. When they left Stevie's room, Jamie was awake; Anne could hear him crying. The day before she would have brought him to join the family; now she sat down like a visitor in the study where Daniel was going over grant proposals with Tom.

"Hundreds of requests for money, as usual," Tom said to Anne. "I've spent all day winnowing out the obvious fakes and crazies. Unfortunately most of them make at least a little sense."

"But, fortunately, we've set up a stiff list of criteria," Daniel said.

Raina came in with Jamie. She sat on a couch across from Anne to make a pretty picture of mother and son. Her fine, long legs were crossed; she lifted her heavy hair with both hands and seemed, so very slightly, to be putting herself on display...

Suddenly Anne was back in a ruined house on the Yorkshire moors. Raina had posed like that, teasing the man she was going to marry, making Daniel's eyes sparkle...

Making Tom's eyes sparkle.

Raina held Jamie during supper. While a spring storm drove rain against the windows, Raina cradled Jamie in her lap, crooning to him. She kissed his small curling fingers while she talked of a Chicago show she was hanging at the Rolinger. Sitting across from Daniel among his fine possessions, she was mother, wife and gallery director, and Anne could watch her if she chose.

It was Daniel who watched her; Anne saw that. His eyes rarely moved from his wife's face, and he said very little. But when Anne and Tom were opening their umbrellas at Daniel's door, he put an arm around Raina and said, "Since I bought that Corvette, I've been thinking that Raina needs a real vacation, a real change. She can get away from her work at the Gallery in August. If you two can keep the boys, Raina and I might drive to California for a month. She's always been in love with California. On the way we can stop at the Hideaway Inn that Patricia and I liked so well years ago. It's still there. Spectacular country."

"And we can have the kitchen remodeled while we're gone," Raina said. "We won't have to live in the mess."

"We'll drive the new car, of course," Daniel added, grinning.

"It's just what you should do," Anne said. "And we'll love to have the boys." She looked happy, but when she ran into the dark with Tom, she looked back at Jamie in Raina's arms.

Their path home along the woodland paths was muddy. Showers soaked the lawns and dimpled the river. Anne and Tom left their dripping umbrellas in the hall and sat in each other's arms by their warm fire. Anne told Tom what Raina had said at lunch. "I have to stay away from the children." Anne's voice trembled. "As much as I can," she said, and hid her face on Tom's shoulder.

Tom scowled into the fire.

Anne said, "I haven't touched Jamie all day. I miss him. And what will Stevie think? I didn't even tell him goodnight." Tom could tell she was close to tears. "It's as if the boys are mine, I love them so. They're the only—"

She didn't finish the sentence, but Tom heard it anyway: *They're the only children I'll ever have.*

They sat with their arms around each other, alone in their quiet house.

21

One morning at breakfast Daniel leaned back in his chair and said to Anne, "I want to build a play yard at your house so Stevie can use it this summer, and Jamie when he's big enough. If we start it now, it'll be finished by the time Raina and I go west."

"What a good idea," Anne said.

"And let's furnish a bedroom for Stevie and a nursery for Jamie at your house," Daniel said.

"Two children under our roof," Anne said. "You can't imagine how I look forward to it."

"Yes, I can," Daniel said, giving Anne a fleeting blue glance.

"Raina's going to miss them," Anne said. "She's a good mother."

They went to the Hancock house to look at rooms that had once been called "children's rooms." Daniel said, "Stevie's got to have twin beds, don't you think, so he can bring a friend home for the night?"

"And Jamie's nursery can be the room with the stained glass angels," Anne said.

The Hancock house and grounds filled with workmen.

After a few days, Raina said at supper: "What's going on? What's all the racket at the other house?"

Stevie said, "We're fixing up bedrooms for me and Jamie."

"We'll have swings in Anne's play yard," Daniel said. "And a sandbox for Jamie. I've designed easels along Anne's play yard fence, so a row of children can paint there in the shade. The boys might take after their mother and be artistic."

"And Dad's making me a surprise, 'cause I'm going to be five," Stevie said.

The birthday surprise took shape under Stevie's new bedroom window.

"What is it?" Stevie kept asking as he ran from Anne to Daniel to the carpenters and back again.

"What is it?" Stevie asked his mother for the twentieth time as he crawled into bed.

Raina said, "How do I know? I have no idea what's going on at the other house."

Stevie turned away from her and pulled the sheet over his head. When he fell asleep, he dreamed of the mysterious thing that was being built under his new bedroom's window: he smelled its fresh wood smell, and crawled inside it in his dreams.

"Stevie isn't having nightmares any more," Daniel said the next day. "He told me he dreams about his new room and the mystery under the window, and the bumblebee box."

"I don't want those bumblebees here," Raina said. "I've told Stevie that over and over, and you know it, too. He'll get stung. We'll get stung. Great black, fuzzy things."

"Well, you know best," Daniel said in a matter-of-fact tone as he left for the Hancock house. "Perhaps we can put the bee house in Stevie's new bedroom window."

When the six of them were having supper Stevie gave his mother a triumphant look and said, "Anne likes my bumblebee box. It's in the window at her house."

"I'm afraid Stevie will have to be at our house most of these days," Tom said to Raina. "Tracking bumblebees is an all-day job. You have to go at least three miles away and find a meadow and wait in the meadow until you see bees go down a hole."

"Can't you catch a bee right here?" Raina said.

"If you don't find a nest three miles away, your bees won't stay in your bumblebee box—they'll fly back to their old home," Tom said.

"And you don't want to catch just the queen," Stevie said. "You've got to get her workers and her nest, too. The queen bumblebee finds somebody else's house."

"And she makes herself at home," Daniel said.

"Sometimes it's a mouse's hole," Stevie said. "A mouse's nice, soft nest."

"But she gives herself away, if you watch her long enough," Daniel said.

Back and forth, back and forth went the bumblebee queens through the warming days. Tom, Anne, Daniel and Stevie hunted in a farmer's fields four miles away. The farmer told Stevie he was welcome to all the bees he could find there. Stevie came to recognize those fast fliers wearing gold jackets and rich velvet. Their thigh-high black jointed boots ended in long, delicate feet. Wings that looked as frail and useless as a cherub's shot them through the air.

At last Anne saw a bumblebee queen disappear down a hole.

"We've got her," Stevie cried at supper that night.

"Who?" Raina asked.

"The queen," Stevie said. "Anne found her nest in the meadow. We've got her."

"Not yet," Daniel said.

"But we know where she is," Stevie said.

"You'll have to catch her," Daniel said. Stevie followed his father as Daniel put his suitcase in his car. "I'm leaving before you wake up tomorrow," Daniel told him. "I'll be on a business trip to Chicago, but Anne and Tom can help get the queen bee. Give me a goodbye kiss and take care of everything while I'm away."

Raina woke late on Saturday morning. Daniel was in Chicago, and the house was empty and still.

The boys must be at Anne's with Tom.

Raina dressed and went into the woods to the Hancock house, scuffing her sandals in gravel. Where paths met, the fallen basswood's roots writhed above her.

"Tom," she whispered to the rough bark of a tree by the path. She put her cheek against it and sobbed.

When she rubbed the tears from her eyes, she could see the Hancock house through woodland trees, its walls as high and stony as if they had been built to keep her out. Lovers had hidden there... Raina's eyes filled with tears again.

She stopped at the edge of Anne's garden. Did Tom always see what she saw in his house—a second house only they remembered, where lovers kissed, then stopped, hot and out of breath, to listen for any sound? Did he remember lovers on a deep blue rug beneath stained glass angels—

"Mom!" A child's excited voice rang through the garden: Stevie had seen her. He came to pull her through Anne's living room door. (Did Tom remember that doorway, remember not being able to wait, carrying her?) Raina sat on a couch with Stevie, and listened to his chatter until Anne came in with Tom.

"Daniel called last night," Raina told them. She lounged on the couch in brief shorts and top, her eyes traveling from Tom to Anne. "He says he's arranged for us to stay at that mountain hideaway he stayed at once, before you get to Reno. Then we'll be in San Francisco for a while, and go on to L.A.." Raina stretched her long legs out, her eyes half shut as if her life completely satisfied her, then curled herself up with a smile and said, "I can't wait. It's been *six years* since I've seen California, and this time I'll really enjoy it."

Anne said, "You won't want to come back to Iowa."

"No," Raina said thoughtfully. "We might not. I've thought about that."

"About what?" Tom said.

"About not coming back. About living in California."

"For good?" Anne asked in a carefully flat tone.

"Why not?" Raina said. "Daniel's got no reason to live here in the Midwest where his gardens die every fall. Tom's taking care of the Bonner business and foundation—Daniel could garden all year round in California. The boys would love it."

The careful tone was still in Anne's voice. "Has Dad considered it?"

"I'll bring it up when he comes home," Raina said. "He knows where I'd like to live, of course—and the advantages for the children." She glanced around the living room. "We could keep our house here, and come for visits," she said.

"We'd have to take Anne and Tom," Stevie said. He had been listening with his mouth open, a shocked look on his face.

"They can live anywhere they want," Raina told him.

"You could come," Stevie said to Tom and Anne in a relieved voice. "You could live right next to us." He bounced on the couch beside Raina. "Come see my bumblebee box. Tonight we're going to dig up the queen and her brood."

Raina followed Stevie, leaving a silence behind her. Tom put his arms around Anne and said softly: "She's only daydreaming. Would your father ever leave this place for long? Leave his greenhouse and his orchids and his gardens?" The words he left out seemed to hang in the air: *And us?*

Anne pressed her face against him to muffle her cry: "Stevie! Jamie!"

That night Stevie could think of nothing but his bumblebee hunt.

"We're going to get the bumblebee queen," he told Betty Jacobs in the Bonner kitchen. She had kept clean, lidded bottles for him to use; he put tissues in each one.

"Why tissues?" Betty said. She was rinsing dinner dishes at the sink.

"Bumblebees get scared if you catch them, and make a mess. If it gets on them, they just die."

"Think of that," Betty said. "And what's that pincher thing?"

"Tom got it for me," Stevie said, brandishing long-handled forceps. "We pick the bees up by their hind legs. When they lie on their backs."

"Don't they fly?"

"Not at night. Not when you're at their nest. They can't see to fly in the dark. They crawl around looking for something warm to sting. If you poke 'em, they lie on their backs and buzz. With their stingers in the air."

"Ugh," Betty said.

"Amazing," Stevie said, and Betty laughed.

Darkness fell at last. Tom and Anne drove with Stevie to the farmer's meadow. When they left the car, their path was nothing but a faint trace around rocks and over roots. Anne carried a flashlight and a box of bottles, Tom carried another flashlight and a spade, and Stevie had the trowels and forceps and paper sacks.

They walked single-file, not saying a word, and Stevie was glad he was in the middle. Anne's flashlight shone a short way ahead; Tom's flashlight swung right and left behind them.

Insects sang. The scent of trampled vetch and bergamot rose from the damp meadow. Above them was a heaven of stars and the full moon.

At the far edge of the meadow Stevie whispered, "We're getting close."

"Stop here," Tom said. They halted to put their supplies down in meadow grass. They could see the white stick Anne had put by the hole.

They half-covered their flashlights and crept close to it. "The worker bees will be down with the queen," Tom whispered to

Stevie. "We'll pound around the entrance, to see if they're near the surface. Isn't that what the book said?"

"Let's pound," Stevie said, excited to have adults, for once, as interested as he was in his adventures.

They pounded, then stopped to listen. Below the sound of night wind in the grass, they heard a muffled buzzing.

"It's them," Stevie whispered, big-eyed with excitement. "Watch out. Workers will come up."

They waited in the faint light of their flashlights, but no bees climbed from the small hole.

"Push a stick down," Stevie said.

Tom found a stick in the grass, and poked it in the hole with care. Again they heard the buzzing; it was clearer and angrier now: a chorus of varied pitches. "They must be near the surface or we couldn't hear them so well," Tom said. "I'll pull away the grass if I can."

Tom cleared weeds and grass from the hole, and carefully scraped dirt away from it with a trowel. "I don't want to cave it in," he said. Anne and Stevie trained half-covered flashlights on Tom as he scraped deeper.

Suddenly a bee crawled out of the hole and turned on its back. "Give me the forceps and a bottle, and I'll get him for you," Anne told Stevie.

"Her," Stevie whispered. "All those bees are 'her.' There aren't any drones yet."

"Her," Anne whispered back. In a moment she had picked up the bee by a hind leg and dropped her on tissue in the bottle: a very small bumblebee, a first-generation bee, hardly bigger than a housefly, her wings glistening in the faint light.

No other bees crawled out. As Tom lifted away more dirt, a little at a time, they could see the dry grass of the mouse nest. Then another bee appeared, and Anne captured her, too.

"Let's make as many come out as we can," Anne said, and breathed into the hole. Bee after bee came out to be captured, until at last there was only a single loud buzz from below.

"Oh, look," Stevie breathed as Tom pulled the last grass away. There was the queen, beautiful in her black and gold, buzzing like a motor. She clung to a small, dull mass: egg shapes stuck together and coated with caramel-brown. The open cocoons of her workers, filled with nectar, glittered in the flashlight's glow.

"Catch her," Stevie whispered. "Touch her. She'll turn over."

Anne touched her with the forceps and she flipped on her back.

"Quick, quick," Stevie whispered, his whisper squeaking with excitement. "Catch her!"

Anne caught the queen's back leg with the forceps, Tom held out an open bottle, and Anne dropped the queen in.

Now Stevie jumped up and down in his joy. "The whole colony! We got the whole colony!" He could yell now; the bumblebees were under lids.

"But we have to take everything home for her nest, or she won't stay in your box," Anne said, and poked the caramel very gently. "It's so soft."

"The spoons," Stevie said. "We brought some."

Tom and Stevie, dark head by brown head, worked over the hole in the grass, bringing up the brood clump and mouse nest, closing them in a brown paper bag.

"Done," Tom said. "We can put them in your bumblebee box tonight." They gathered up their equipment in the moonlight.

But Anne stood for a moment by the gaping hole. The queen had found a safe home and begun to raise her brood. Now nothing was left in her empty nest.

Raina joined Daniel for a weekend in Chicago and shopped for clothes. She followed Stevie to Anne's house the next week with a suitcase. "How about helping me decide which of my Chicago things will do for California?" she told Anne. "I'll surprise Daniel when he comes home." She smiled at Tom and watched Stevie run off to the play yard. "I invite myself here because Stevie's always here."

"Come for supper while Daniel's away. We'll have style shows. It'll be like old times," Anne said.

"Remember wartime when you couldn't get a bathing suit with any rubber in it? And no nylons. Just those awful rayon stockings," Raina said.

"Remember Stalingrad? Lidice?" Tom said.

"Remember when Roosevelt died?" Anne said. "I can remember the very spot I stood on when I heard he was gone."

"Everybody can," Raina said. "Remember MacArthur? Which prompts me to say: *I shall return.*" In a little while she came from a bedroom to pose in a doorway for Tom and Anne. "How do you like this? I'm supposing Daniel will want to go dancing somewhere on our travels west."

They waited in flashlight glow, but no bees climbed from the nest hole. "Poke a stick down," Stevie whispered.

"You're a vision," Anne said, sitting cross-legged on the rug in her old jeans and shirt. Raina twirled in blue mousseline silk: a cocktail dress whose narrow shoulder straps hardly anchored the low neckline. The gown seemed to float from its sash to a delicate handkerchief hemline and the spike heels of Raina's blue sandals. "Beautiful."

"Tom?" Raina said.

"It'll do."

"Do what?" Raina said in a saucy voice, but Tom had turned his back and was gone.

Raina put on a green linen suit with a narrow skirt. The bolero jacket was trimmed in black to match her black turban. She turned round and round, posing for Anne.

Anne watched the parade of Raina's beautiful clothes: silk evening suits...a Lily Daché hat of flowers and green leaves to match a short cashmere cape...a royal blue lambs wool sweater-set above a pleated chiffon skirt. Raina had never cut her hair. No one else dared to be so fashionably unfashionable.

Just as Raina appeared in black shorts and strapless top, Emily rang the doorbell.

"Raina's been modeling her clothes for California," Anne told Emily. "Look at those shorts. They've got rhinestone suspenders."

Raina changed her clothes and chattered about the trip west during supper. Stevie told about putting the bumblebees in their glass house. He was delighted not to be left at home with Jamie, and was careful to remember his table manners.

"Are you coming here to your play yard every day?" Emily asked him, following the rest to the living room for coffee. Stevie nodded.

"I suppose we'll have to build another if we move west," Raina said.

"Move west?" Emily's eyes darted from Raina to Anne to Tom.

"We might," Raina said with a smile. "I've told you how I love California. Daniel knows that. Think of the gardening he could do there, and how the children would enjoy it."

"You'd go for good?" Emily said.

"We'd come back to visit, of course," Raina said. "Often. Keep the house here, perhaps. We haven't decided."

Emily looked at Anne and Tom.

"We'd have to come often," Raina went on in her careless,

contented tone. "Children forget so fast. Even if we manage to come back every year, Stevie will have new interests and new friends, of course. And Jamie—what will he remember? Nothing, I'm afraid."

Now Emily couldn't bear to look at Anne and Tom; she kept her eyes on her coffee cup.

"Jamie's got a cold," Raina said. She was the one reporting on the children now. "Betty's with him. He's so restless and unhappy, poor baby."

Anne took a deep breath. "Maybe we should go over to see him this evening," she said.

"Who?" Raina said.

"Jamie."

"Oh?" Raina said, as if such a thing had never occurred to her, as if it would be something new. Emily stared at her. "Well, we'll see," Raina said. "If he's not better."

22

Emily went home an hour later, sat on a kitchen chair and looked at Clara, who was mixing pound cake.

"You've been with the Bonners and Hancocks, so you're upset, as usual," Clara said. "You come home every time looking like that."

"I have to be so ferociously *peaceful*. Spread my sweetness and light. It's like pouring honey over a bomb."

"It's going to go off?"

"Not if Anne can help it. She'll throw herself on top of it if necessary."

"She's got courage, that girl." Clara began creaming sugar and butter in a bowl: creaming was the secret of her pound cakes.

Emily put her elbows on the table and her head in her hands. "Lie. Lie. Lie. We lie to Raina about our belief in her, lie to Tom about our belief in him, and, *especially*, we lie to Daniel—about our belief in all of them."

"And we have to pretend we *enjoy* the lying, every Sunday at dinner." Clara whacked her spoon on the edge of the bowl.

"We do it for Anne," Emily said.

"But how about Tom?"

Emily sighed. "He's as bad as Raina, of course. But his crime's the kind most people will excuse, isn't it? More than Raina's?"

"I love Anne the most. Always have," Clara said. "Since she was seven years old. She's sweet. Innocent. She ought to have what she wants, if anyone ought to."

"Anne's learning not to be so innocent. I told her about Daniel's affair with Rachel Harriman, and what he did to Bob Clingman,"

Emily said.

"Why?"

"She ought to know what Daniel's like. What he does about women."

Clara gave a snort. "About the women he loses."

"I told her, because she's got to lie to him, lie and lie. She can't let him have the least doubt."

"So she asked you to help her with Daniel."

"She didn't *ask*," Emily said sharply. "She gave me no choice at all. If the families break up, Anne will torment herself. She'll think she killed her mother and broke her father's heart. She couldn't have a family for Tom. Then she deserted Tom, and drove him into Raina's arms. Anne will think it's all been her fault, poor girl. And I'm afraid she's going to lose everything now."

"Lose? Lose what?" Clara stared at Emily.

"Just about everything...Stevie and Jamie..."

"How?"

"And Tom. Even Tom. I hope not, but I don't know..."

"What's happened?" Clara sat down on a kitchen chair. "Something terrible..."

"We were having coffee, and Raina told us all that she wants to move to California with Daniel and the boys."

Clara's face was blank with shock. "Has she talked to Daniel about it?"

"Who knows? But it's Raina's top card. We never saw it coming, did we?"

"Never."

"Anne and Tom simply sat there. Raina told us that she and Daniel and the boys might come back to visit 'at least once a year.' But, she said, 'Children forget so fast. What will Jamie remember? Nothing.'"

"Tom's going to lose his own Jamie?" Clara said. "And Stevie... anyone can see how Tom and Anne love those boys—"

"It depends, don't you think?"

"On what Daniel does? He'll go to California and leave Anne?"

"No. It depends on what Tom does. Anne knows that. Anne stands to lose everything. Even Tom. I saw it in her eyes."

The women were silent. Emily turned to look at her darkening garden. Moths were circling yard lanterns, hurling themselves like kamikazes at the hot light.

The next morning, Raina parked at a restaurant in Cedar Falls, an ancient building that had once been a factory on the bank of the Cedar River. When Raina pushed the huge door open, there was an early lunchtime crowd under rough-hewn beams. "Never mind," she said when the headwaiter greeted her and looked over the crowded room. "I see a friend. I'll sit with him."

Tom was by himself; his eyes were on the riverbank and railroad bridge. Now and then a train thundered across the trestle only a few dozen feet from the restaurant's linen-covered tables.

Raina sat down, opened a menu and whispered, "Why can't we talk at home? Why do we have to do it in a public place?" When the waiter had taken Raina's order and gone away, she said, "Because you don't want to talk," answering her own question.

Ducks waddled uphill from the river to eat stale rolls in the grass under the restaurant windows.

"Because Anne has it all," Raina said, watching ducks jostling each other. "She's got the money. She's got that sweet, friendly, unassuming little air that people like. She's got the house her father built for her. She's got the children, Oh yes. Daniel is arranging that, since she can't produce children for herself. It's obvious he'll do anything for her. So she's got him, too."

Tom's eyes were on the waddling ducks. Their necks and backs gleamed iridescent in June sunlight.

"Anne's so good, isn't she?" Raina said. "She's an angel, and everything she wants falls in her lap. So she's made of steel. She's a lethal weapon." When Raina leaned forward, her coronet of braided hair gleamed in sunlight falling through the window. "But the question is: Does Anne have you?"

Tom's gray eyes met hers for only an instant. When he looked down, Raina had a slight smile on her face. "*Daniel* certainly has you. You envy me. I've seen it. I'm so free to run the Gallery, make the decisions, do as I please. You work like a dog—even if you're his partner now. He hides at home and plays with Anne and the children because he's 'Bonfire Bonner,' and because he's *got* you."

Tom said nothing. Raina's eyes traveled over his face. "I'm a success, you know," she said. "The Rolinger's famous, and I've done it. I've had two children, one of them yours. And do you ever think about your experience, your prestige? You're a success, too. You could get a fine job anywhere. Why work for Daniel?"

The room was full; chatter surrounded the handsome couple at their table. No one but Tom could hear Raina's low-pitched voice. "So I can earn a good living," she said. "There are plenty of private and public galleries in California. I'd have the children, and child support."

Now Tom stared at her. "Daniel would never—"

"Daniel hates publicity," Raina said. "How awful to have a messy divorce case with who knows whose names dragged through the mud. Maybe Bonfire Bonner's? Anne's? Yours and mine?"

The waiter brought their plates, filled their coffee cups again. Would they like more hot rolls? No, Raina and Tom said politely. No.

"Now I'm going to California with Daniel," Raina said when the waiter had gone. "My aim is to buy a house there, a 'second home' for Daniel and the boys and me—except that Daniel won't ever live in it. The children will love the west coast, and go to such good schools. I want the boys. I want you—you as a free man with a fine new job. If Daniel won't buy me a house now, I'll get it in the divorce settlement."

Tom was silent. Raina broke a roll in half, then looked him in the eye. "I'm not going west with Daniel for a vacation. I'm going to California to set us up for the rest of our lives. So don't be surprised at anything I do."

Tom hadn't picked up his fork, but Raina was eating her salad. In a few minutes she cut a cherry tomato in two and looked at Tom. "The only question I have is the one I've already asked: does Anne have you? In addition to her money and her sweet nature and her gardens—I mustn't forget the gardens—and her father?"

Suddenly Tom stood up and dropped his napkin on the table.

"Or will you come to California with me and raise your son?" Raina said. "And Stevie, and more of your own children, too, if you want them. Think about it."

She watched him make his way through the restaurant tables. When he was out of sight, she ate both halves of the tomato. A train went by, so close that she could see words chalked on the sides of the cars: messages traveling from one train yard to another across the miles.

When Daniel came home from Chicago, Stevie ran to his father. "We're going to live in California," he cried. "We'll move there." He hugged Daniel in his excitement. "California," he yelled. "I can swim in the ocean."

"Welcome home," Raina said, kissing Daniel. "How was the trip?"

"What's this Stevie's talking about?" Daniel asked. He kissed Anne and shook Tom's hand. "Moving to California?"

"He's certainly jumping to conclusions," Raina said with an indulgent laugh. "You can see he wants to go."

"You've talked to him about it?"

"Now and then. Just to see how he feels, of course."

"It's the first I've heard about it," Daniel said.

Raina shrugged her bare, tanned shoulders. "We can talk about it sometime. I've thought that maybe you and I would like to have a house out there, a second house? We can all discuss it. We decide these things as a family, don't we? And do what's best for the children?"

Daniel said nothing more, and talked very little during supper. He was tired, he said, but he wanted to see the gardens before dark. He went with Tom and Anne along a stone path to see new plants in the perennial borders.

"How about more supports for the delphinium and perennial asters?" Tom asked. "Before they get any taller."

"And we'll have to reset them," Daniel said.

"The peonies are going to bloom this year—the pink ones, anyway," Anne said.

"The cold-frame seedlings are ready to plant," Tom said.

Anne left the path for the lawn. "And there are tons of phlox seedlings."

"All of them, of course, that ugly magenta," Daniel said.

"Somebody didn't dead-head in time," Tom said. "And we've got moles under the birch trees."

Tom and Daniel went off to examine mole tunnels. Anne waited under a sky full of pink and lavender angel-wing clouds. As the men returned, forest birds gave their last cries before dark, sharp and clear—as sharp and clear as Anne's feeling that the gray-haired man coming to her through the gardens wore his ordinary life for his disguise, as she did, as they all did.

Tom was close behind Daniel as Anne said, "It's chilly now," and picked up her jacket from the grass. Tom reached for it, but Daniel snatched it and helped Anne put it on. Anne turned quickly enough to see the coldness in two pairs of eyes meeting over her head.

"I'm tired and I'm turning in," Daniel said. He kissed Anne and went into his house.

"Story blanket," Stevie called, running to Anne, a blanket trailing behind him on the grass. "Lots of stars to watch while you're making up stories!"

"Oh, Stevie!" Anne said, hugging him. "Your mother wants to read you a story every night. She told me so. Find her and maybe she'll lie on the blanket with you."

Stevie turned around without a word and went in, dragging his blanket behind him. Tears came to Anne's eyes. He thought she didn't care for him any more. He couldn't understand. He'd blame himself, the way children do.

The late spring night was a perfect night: warm, deep green, starry. When Tom and Anne went to bed, they lay awake for hours, watching a streak of moonlight creep across their bed, repeating Raina's careless, contented words as if there must be some answer, some way out: *We'd come back to visit, of course. Keep the house here, perhaps.*

They held each other close, listening to the loneliness of the midnight forest. *Even if we come back every year, Stevie will have new interests and new friends. Children forget so fast. Jamie—what will he remember?*

At last Tom slept, but Anne roamed the house. When she stepped into Stevie's newly-furnished room, she glanced into the garden, and saw someone coming along the woodland path beyond.

It was only a shadow at first: a flicker of dark against dim trees. Anne froze, startled. Who was out there, slipping from one patch of moonlight to another?

It was a man. She thought of calling for Tom—running to tell him—but stopped: a garden light fell on the man's face. It was her father who walked across the lawn. Anne stepped backward in Stevie's dark room and watched Daniel come.

He circled the play yard, opened its gate, and touched the swings and the sandbox and the easels built into the fence. For a moment he stood still to look at her house, the patio, the terraces, the river below.

Her father came toward her. She stepped back farther. Daniel put his hand on a windowsill of Stevie's room, and stood for a moment with his head lowered on his hand. Insects in the gardens

Anne saw someone walking on the woodland path through patches of moonlight.

kept up their chirping, throbbing, ticking.

Then he turned and disappeared in the dark woods.

Stevie woke at dawn on his birthday, and ran down the hall. His mother didn't like being waked up; he went to his father's side of the bed and touched him very softly on the back of his neck until he woke, turned over, then slid out of the slippery sheets whispering, "Happy Birthday."

The living room was empty and half-dark; they sat together on a couch. "Five years old," Daniel said to Stevie. "Do you know you become a man of the house when you're five years old?"

"You do?" Stevie said, sitting up straight in surprise.

"You do," Daniel said. "And you change your name."

"You do?"

"You do. No more of this baby-Stevie stuff. It's all right for Jamie—he isn't old enough to be called James. But you're Steven. That's your name."

"That's my name," Steven repeated solemnly.

"And you have responsibilities now," Daniel said. "You have to promise to take care of your brother always, even when he makes you very mad and disgusted. That's what the man of the house does. I was never lucky enough to have a brother."

"What did you do?"

"Went out and found one, but he wasn't a good one," Daniel said. "I let him teach me to do bad things."

"Bad things?" Steven's eyes were wide open in surprise.

Daniel said, "Let's get dressed and look outside your new bedroom window."

They put on their clothes, stuck their feet in sneakers, and went through the patio door. Dew was falling, a constant patter, and the woods were misty. Crossing Anne's garden, they passed a bed of red begonias that would blaze like fire in the sun. Now they were glazed with dew.

"There are somebodies asleep under your window," Daniel whispered to Steven. "Go quietly and don't scare them."

Steven tiptoed with Daniel to the windows of his own new room. "Oh," was all he could say. There were two spotted rabbits behind the wire of the new pen. They slept close together, their spoon ears flattened, their paws out of sight under their long fur.

"Something else for you to be responsible for," Daniel whispered. "And you'll have to give them names."

Steven gave them names. "They're David and Jonathan," he told everyone at his birthday breakfast. "We learned about them at Sunday School. And I have a new name, too."

"A new name?" Tom asked.

"I'm Steven. I'm too old to be Stevie. I have to be a man of the house now, Dad says. And take care of the rabbits, and the bees, and Jamie."

23

The August morning was clear and cool when Daniel and Raina drove to the Hancock house to say goodbye. "I'm going to stay at Anne's!" Steven chanted, jumping up and down. Tom, Anne and Steven waved as the Corvette rolled down the drive. "Goodbye!" they chorused. "Goodbye!"

Raina looked back as she rode away with Daniel, and saw Jamie in Anne's arms, and Steven hopping and smiling beside her, and Tom's arm around Anne. Then a curve in the drive hid them. Raina closed her eyes. She imagined Tom in the seat beside her... Tom in a strange new bed with her that night...

"Forgotten anything?" Daniel asked. Iowa fields were green from horizon to horizon: the blue-green of soybeans, the yellow-green of corn.

"No." Raina shook her head and didn't say: *I haven't forgotten a single look in Tom's eyes. I remember how his skin feels under my hands. I haven't forgotten.*

"Anxious to see California?" Daniel asked.

"Can't wait to get there," Raina said; she leaned back and stretched her long legs before her. "Don't you love the first hour of a trip? When you've made the decisions and plans, can't change anything, and suddenly you're so free?" All the beautiful clothes in her luggage were new, and she rode in a car that even Californians would notice. The cash in her gleaming calfskin handbag would have paid a year's expenses in her poor-girl days.

Daniel, his eyes on the road, said, "You've missed California."

"Oh, yes," Raina cried.

Daniel said nothing. His expressionless face was what she would see, mile after mile. Raina looked down at her sparkling rings. Goodbye to Iowa farmyards, full of pigs and August mud. Goodbye to the children. She hadn't spent enough time with them, ever. The Gallery had to come first. Someday she'd tell the boys: *I had to get ready to support you.*

"It's surprising you want to go back," Daniel said. His voice was friendly and relaxed. "You've always said you were so unhappy there."

"Weren't you unhappy, growing up in Iowa?" Raina said.

"But I love the place," Daniel said. "I wouldn't want to live anywhere else."

"Even if you had to live over a bakery again?" Raina said, trying to treat what he'd said as part of a joke. "Or sleep on the floor, like I did in Berkeley, with my pillow against one wall and my feet against the other." Raina shut her eyes to see the candle stuck in a bottle, smell the soup bubbling in a pan, feel Tom...

Daniel was silent. Raina, her eyes closed, was living with Tom in California...they had found good jobs...

"A lot of times I never went to bed, when I was a teenager on the streets," Daniel said.

Raina opened her eyes to see that they were waiting at a stop sign on a narrow country road. She closed her eyes to imagine waking in Tom's arms in their beautiful California house...

"We robbed stores," Daniel said. A semi passed and he pulled on to the highway behind it, then glanced at Raina. "I never got caught."

"Robbed stores?"

"We had knives and guns. They were easy to get. Easy to use. I had a friend named Bill Drucker, and we ran a gang—a big gang. Tough. It was our neighborhood. If anybody wasn't for us, he was against us, and he'd better watch his step. A good philosophy."

Raina wasn't listening: she was roaming the new California house...

"Don't you think so?" Daniel asked.

"What?" Raina said.

"Sleepy?" Daniel looked at her, his cold blue eyes glinting. "I was talking about the philosophy my friend and I believed in: 'If they aren't for us, they're against us.'"

"Yes," Raina said. She yawned, then closed her eyes so Daniel would think she was asleep. He knew she couldn't stay awake in a moving car. But she was imagining that the divorces were over, hers and Tom's...the children were hers...she was on a beach watching ocean waves, and Tom...

"One guy in our gang was two-faced," Daniel said in a pleasant tone. "Sneaked behind our backs. He had two faces when we finished with him: an eye on either side and no nose."

Raina opened her eyes.

"But we were just kids with high-flying ideals." Daniel smiled at Raina. "We grew up soon enough and found out that life was full of bastards, and most of the world was against us, too, since we grew up on Wasserman Street. So we began to learn from the businessmen and the politicians. Hung around, analyzed their methods, you might say."

Raina said nothing.

"What's the first rule of life?" Daniel went on in a genial voice, "It's: *Get them before they get you.* We'd been young and stupid: we'd been getting them *after* they got us. Isn't that pathetic?"

"Pathetic?"

"Pathetic. The bastards do you dirt, and then you get them. Pathetic. Get them first. That was our new motto. Let them be happy. Let them feel safe. Take your time. They're not going anywhere. They think they're in your life like a worm in a nut."

Raina said nothing, but sat turning her rings around and around on her fingers.

"Oh well, I was young and green," Daniel said. "Hadn't gone into the navy yet. What do you think the first rule of the armed forces is?"

Raina looked at him.

"You guessed it." Daniel laughed. "So I felt right at home."

Raina gripped her hands together in her lap. "You had a hard life. So did I," she said. "We talked about it the summer before we married. Remember? After the night down by the river when you kissed me the first time, and kept calling me those wonderful love-names, Irish love-names."

"My mother said them to me," Daniel said, frowning.

"We talked about our grandparents the next morning, and neither of us could remember our fathers, but we had strong mothers. I felt so close to you, but after we made love and you asked me to marry you, I wandered around your beautiful house and felt so poor. You were asleep. I stood and looked around your living room in the dark and cried."

"What for?"

"Because I was thirty-one and I couldn't bring anything to you: my whole life added up to nothing. Then I said to myself, 'I do have something I can give him. I can give him a son.'"

"Yes," Daniel said. "And you did."

"Two," Raina said. "And we went to Haworth to tell Anne and Tom that we were engaged, and had rooms next to that awful graveyard. I came creeping into your bed, remember? Because I was so scared."

"Scared?" Daniel said. "Was that why you came?"

"I wasn't scared of you, silly, I was scared of the graves. I've always been afraid of corpses and skeletons."

"Dead people don't make trouble," Daniel said.

Raina sighed and said in a more cheerful voice, "Remember having strawberries and cream *and* ice cream for breakfast in Florence? Remember the dress you bought me to wear to the opera in Paris?"

At lunchtime they stopped in a small town. The big square cafe had blinking beer signs on the walls, and town regulars lined up along the bar to sneak looks at Raina with Daniel at a corner table. A plump lady brought home-cooked food: the potatoes were mashed with butter, and there was thick cream on the apple pie.

"Remember the reliquary we bought near the Ile de la Cité?" Raina scraped the cream off her pie and ate the apples. "The silver one with ashes and bits of bone in it? The shop owner kept talking to you, but I was the one who knew about silver," Raina said. "He wouldn't listen to me."

"And it turned out to be a fake," Daniel said.

Raina shrugged her shoulders. "We tried."

"Yes. We tried."

All day Raina had felt Daniel dragging her conversation down, dropping his heavy words into it like stones until she could barely kept her happy words afloat—words to remind him of how she loved him, how he loved her, how they had lived almost six years together…

When she climbed back in the car, she felt exhausted with the effort, closed her eyes and remembered Jamie in Anne's arms as they waved goodbye. He had a tight grip on Anne's long brown hair. Raina dozed, thinking of Anne perched on a kitchen stool talking to Mirabelle by the hour. Anne knew all Mirabelle's problems, and Betty's, and their gardener's too.

She remembered the day she'd first made love to Tom in the "angel room." Afterward, she could still feel his kisses when Anne came home from gardening and found them dressed, thank goodness, and sitting in her living room. Anne was wearing her old shirt and jeans and floppy gardening boots. She'd be plump in another ten years. She tipped her head to one side sometimes when she talked, and raised her eyebrows too much: the wrinkles were there already. For a minute that afternoon, Raina had felt Tom's warm body under her hands yet, and she'd pitied Anne, who had everything and nothing. No lover. No children. No career.

Raina's mouth kept falling open as she slept, mile after mile. She half-woke, shut it, and dreamed of herself, a skinny young girl leaning on the sill of a tenement window in the smell of asphalt and coal smoke. Below her the street gangs fought in hot New York nights, and she watched muscles ripple on their bare backs and sweat sparkle in the hair on their chests. Their deep-voiced shouts echoed from brick walls and store fronts and made her shiver.

Half-awake, she remembered New York summers when her mother had been young and pretty: pretty Olga Weigel. She had a good friend: Emily Hancock. Emily was younger than Olga, and pretty, too, and hadn't married rich Wendell Snyder yet; the women took Raina for chocolate sodas on hot afternoons. The three perched on stools at the drugstore soda fountain; Raina remembered ice cream bobbing in froth.

She dreamed again of her pretty mother washing herself before she went to bed, fighting the smell of restaurant grease she carried home to their room on her skin and in her hair. "Your father loves it when I smell like flowers," Olga told Raina almost every day, and scrubbed herself at the cracked sink where cold water from the one faucet left a long brown stain. "If he comes tonight and I smell like stale lard…"

Raina woke, her mother's face still before her, and felt as if she were drowning in sadness. Stop it, she told herself, keeping her eyes shut as if she were sleeping. Tom will come. She dreamed of his lean cheeks that were almost like an Indian's, and his teeth that were so white, but a little uneven. No man should have such long eyelashes, or such gray eyes…

She woke again, gulped, sat up, and licked her dry lips. Daniel was parking the car in a restaurant lot. "Looks like a good place to eat," he said, smiling as he opened the door for her.

Now he was a different man. He told her how beautiful she was, seated her at a table, and held her hand in the candlelight.

They ordered dinner. When the waiter left, Daniel said, "So you'd like a California home, would you?" He kissed her fingers with their diamond rings.

"Oh, yes," Raina said softly. "A house on the beach. That's always been my dream."

"The boys would love it," Daniel said. "We'll see. You and I can drive along the coast and look."

The Victorian hotel where they spent the night was charming. They made love in their big four-poster bed. Raina couldn't sleep; she lay open-eyed, pretending that Tom was lying beside her...

Tears filled her eyes. She wiped them on the sheet and imagined a California dawn. She dreamed she was lying with Tom in their soft bed, until Tom crawled out to bring Jamie to her, and Steven came to burrow under the sheets and cuddle. Suddenly she longed to hold her babies again: Jamie with his black hair and dark eyes, so much like Tom already, and Steven with his skinned knee he'd banged on the patio stairs as he chased bumblebees. She shouldn't have been so silly about that bumblebee nest. When she went back, she'd tell him he could have all the bumblebees he wanted.

Raina sighed, and pictured sunlight on a patio table. Beyond it was the rush and hiss of Pacific surf. When breakfast was over, Tom took Steven to play with a beach ball on the sand: one big brown body and one small one against the thundering incoming waves. She held sleeping Jamie and read the newspaper, sipping her coffee. And when Tom came back, cool and salty and amorous...

"He'll come," Raina said to herself over and over, until the phrase had the rhythm of breaking waves. "He'll come for me."

The next morning veils of mist lifted from the Hancock cottage garden. Anne woke to Steven's chatter: he stood beside the big frost-white bed tugging at Anne, then Tom.

Tom woke and turned over. "We've got a family," he said to Anne. "At least for now." He went out of the room in his pajamas,

Steven at his heels. In a minute he was back with Jamie. Tom slid under the sheet, put Jamie on his chest, and the man and boy looked at Anne with the same look: father and son.

Steven crawled in bed and curled close to Anne. "How's your knee?" Anne asked him.

Steven brought his knee up under his chin to show off the bandage. "Better," he said.

"Good," Tom said. "What we need is breakfast."

Anne dressed Jamie in the nursery. "Oh, my sweet one, my dearest dear, Tom's baby boy," Anne crooned softly as she carried him to his high chair on the patio.

Tom was reading the paper when Mirabelle brought breakfast. "It's fun eating outside," Steven said, inching himself up on a grown-up chair. "You can hear the river."

Steven and Tom ran into the garden when breakfast was over, and played catch. Both of them had turned brown in the summer sun. Anne held Jamie while she sipped her coffee, read the newspaper, and tried to close everything out of her mind but this perfect, rare morning.

Steven went around the house to feed the rabbits. Tom came to kiss Anne, and then Jamie. "I don't know anyone in the world like you," he murmured to Anne. "Love me?"

"Yes, yes, yes," Anne said in a light voice, kissing him and running a hand through his thick black hair.

"I love you. Do you trust me?" Tom asked.

"Yes," Anne said. "I do."

"Then I want to tell you what Raina said to me just before they left," Tom said. They could hear Steven talking to the rabbits. Anne put Jamie back in his high chair and stood in Tom's arms, held close.

"She's going to persuade Daniel to buy a seaside house in California first," Tom said. "Then she'll divorce him, and she wants me to divorce you. She says she'll be given the new house, and custody of the boys, and money. And she's sure I'll join her."

"And you will?" Anne asked. She felt Tom's body stiffen, but she pulled away and covered his mouth before he could speak. "Wait. Think. What if it's your only chance to have your own son?"

Tom took her hand away from his mouth, then kissed the palm. His gray eyes looked into her blue ones. "It's you I choose, always you."

For a few minutes they stood in each other's arms, so shaken that they saw nothing of the river or trees or gardens.

"Jamie," Anne whispered. "Steven."

24

Daniel said very little the next morning as he drove on Wyoming highways. Raina drowsed in the seat beside him, filled with hope: Daniel had liked the idea of a California house. If she were careful, if she were as warm and loving to him as she could be...

They stopped for lunch, and the lunch made her sleepy; the motion of the car lulled her. She pretended it was Tom beside her as they drove west to their new life.

It was late in the day when she roused herself, hearing Daniel's hard, precise voice."Bastards," he said, glancing at her to see that she was awake. His blue eyes glittered.

"What?"

"I've been thinking about the bastards I've known. About my friend, Bill Drucker, and how we got them first, before they got us. Remember?"

"Yes," Raina said. They passed a truck. For a moment Raina saw the wild, bulging eyes of live cattle through gaps in the wooden sides.

"There's a wall at home in Waterloo, down by the river off Webber street," Daniel said as he glanced at the truck in his rear-view mirror and drove back in the right-hand lane. "If you know where to look, about eight feet up, you can still see two marks in the wood. Two nail holes. Nobody's painted it after more than forty years, so the blood stains show a little yet." He smiled at Raina. "One of our smart friends had made some money with us. We heard he was going to keep it all. Selfish. Itchy fingers. Hands in our pockets. You know the kind."

Raina said nothing. Daniel's voice changed to a thoughtful tone. "My mother never asked where my money came from. I bought her food first when I got some cash. Then I made her buy a good coat and dresses and shoes, and quit her job. We moved to a nice place with a bedroom for each of us, and a kitchen and bath. We'd been sleeping on the floor like you did at Berkeley, but we weren't students. We were a kid and his mother, and she'd been on her feet all day every day since my dad died."

Daniel's voice had roughened with the last sentence. "Bill Drucker and I didn't let anybody rip us off. We got the money this rat owed us and then paid him back with a little climb to a box by that wall off Webber."

Daniel caught Raina's grim look.

"Good, solid wooden wall," Daniel said. "He wasn't going anywhere; he was tied up. When we had him standing on that box, a little teetery box, we untied one of his hands at a time and nailed them to that wall. He was screaming, but he was out of luck: Webber Street is warehouses. Who'd hear him? It was Friday night. Nobody would be around there until Monday."

Raina saw a small town's speed limit sign flash by; Daniel slowed to twenty-five obediently. "Never go over the limit in small towns," he said. "They always need money. They want to paint their water tower. The cemetery fence is falling down. The high school basketball team's got to have a steak dinner to win some trophy."

Daniel stopped for a red light. A family went into a drugstore and vanished behind posters and handbills plastered on the windows. Raina wished for a second that she could get out, get away, hide among the drugstore aisles with the corn plasters and toothpaste.

But her new Corvette was leaving the town now, passing a city park where ordinary people were picnicking in August shade.

"So we got this rat nailed nice and tight, standing on that little box," Daniel went on. "It was a hot summer night, as I remember. My friend Bill always had a sense of justice. He had a sense of style, too, a genius for just the right touch, so he'd brought a nice, ripe, dead rat tied to a string: a necklace for our human rat. We hung it under his chin."

Daniel eased the car back to highway speed. "It wasn't easy getting our human rat up there, but when we finally did, he was stuck like a fly on a pin. Two pins. No need to tie him up: he'd stay on that box. If he lost it, he'd be in the same fix as Christ on the cross."

Daniel reached over to help himself to a mint from the glove compartment. When he spoke again, Raina could hear the hard candy click against his teeth. "It's a bit tricky to get a nail in a hand. You have to go through the bones in the right place." The mint clicked again. "That dead rat smelled strong to begin with, and after a weekend up there in summer heat, I imagine our human rat noticed what was tied under his nose, all right, before Bill went back to pry our human rat off that wall and leave him nice and flat and dead."

Raina's eyes were open now, staring ahead.

"We took a lot of trouble with him. I guess we were perfectionists. I always have been: wanting my house neat and orderly, taking baths all the time." He glanced at Raina. "I know that seems silly to you. But Bill was just as finicky as I am, so we wanted this fellow with the rat necklace to send just the right message—if and when anybody found what was left of him."

Raina sat still, looking out the window. "Am I boring you, chattering away about the good old days?" Daniel asked. She shook her head.

Daniel finished his mint in silence, then said, "Bill Drucker was my best friend, along with Charley Xavier. They knew how to burn a business down and not leave a clue. Sure wipes out your competition: a good fire. He burned some people up along with my competition. Made a mistake there. Bill admitted it: he called me the next day and apologized. He said, 'At least you didn't have firemen and police all over the place,' and he was right. I didn't. He was police chief by then."

Raina's mouth was dry. She started to say, "Why are you telling me..." but Daniel didn't notice. "Before he burned down Clingman, Bill was a genius at the protection racket," he said. "That's where our money came from. We weren't even twenty. We had a great business—just the experience Bill needed to be chief of police later on."

Raina swallowed and moved her stiff legs. "It's a simple kind of business," Daniel went on. "What does it take to get a new client? Advertisements? Guarantees? You bet. First you go in and offer the businessman a guarantee. If you've been doing a lot of advertising on his street, he usually buys the guarantee, and everybody's happy."

Raina glanced at Daniel's profile. His bony nose looked as if it had been broken, and the dent in his chin was either a dimple or a scar. He was steering with the heel of one hand, and the diamond ring on his finger shot sparks of colored fire: blue, yellow, red.

"But sometimes he hasn't heard enough about your business, so you give him some of your advertisements," Daniel went on. "One of our best advertisements was a smashed shop window. Windows are expensive. Better yet, when people pass by that broken glass in the morning, they say, 'Who did that?' and of course you make sure the whole neighborhood knows it was you. That's good advertising."

Raina was watching homemade signs nailed on fence posts. Every half-mile or so they faced the highway, proclaiming "HONEY" in black paint that trailed black threads downward from the letters.

"I joined the navy, but the war was almost over," Daniel said. "I might have gone back to the protection business with Bill and ended up in a sack of rocks at the bottom of the river like he did. But Patricia changed my life. She saved it, I think."

Raina met his glance for a moment. "She was beautiful. She was smart," Daniel said. "She was faithful. She loved me. And I lost her, and my first son—smashed on a pile of rocks under a tree."

Daniel's voice was cold; the dry edge of it cut Raina away, shut her out. All she could do was put her head back and shut her eyes.

She tried to sleep as the day ended, but Daniel talked of cheating wives, double-crossers, bastards. He had grown up watching them "get theirs."

Just after dark, they stopped for supper, and Daniel smiled at Raina across a glass of wine. Candlelight ran along his bony nose. He was smiling as if he had said nothing to her all day but pleasant things. "I want you to enjoy yourself on your way home to California. You like to dance. You like to shop. We'll see some galleries." His hand closed over her ringed hand on the table.

Raina met his blue glance, surprised. "I brought a new dancing dress," she said.

"Then maybe you can wear it tonight," he said, and looked through a lodging guide.

Daniel found a hotel with a nightclub. "You can wear that new dress," he said when they were given a room. "They've got a band downstairs, and a good floor."

Raina put on the blue cocktail dress of mousseline silk that seemed to float from its low neckline to the handkerchief hem and her spike-heeled blue sandals. Tom had looked at her in that dress and said, *It'll do.* She lifted her heavy hair, and Daniel fastened a chain of diamonds around her neck.

After dinner it was a pleasure to walk to a table at the edge of the dance floor with so many eyes watching. "This is what I dreamed of when I was lonely and poor and watched the boys from my window," Raina said.

"This is what you miss in Iowa?" Daniel said.

"We could have it all, you know," Raina said, leaning forward, her breasts only half covered in blue. "Your beautiful gardens—you can really garden in California. Art galleries. Shows. Dancing. A dash to Hawaii every now and then."

"That would make you happy?" Daniel asked.

"Oh yes," Raina said. "But I'm thinking of the boys, too. The good schools...the choices they'd have..."

They left their drinks and danced on the black and shining floor. "What about Anne and Tom?" Daniel asked after a while.

He heard Raina's soft laugh close to his ear. "Tom's a convert to the Iowa way of life, and Anne loves it. If they miss us, they could commute. Stay with us every other weekend. Go to plays and concerts...lie on the beach..."

Daniel held Raina very tight and said nothing more.

"What fun!" Raina said, back at their table. "We almost never dance nowadays, do we?"

"I'm not much of a dancer," Daniel said. "You deserve better. There are plenty of men here with their eyes on you. Enjoy yourself. I'll be at the bar."

Raina opened her mouth to reply, but Daniel was already walking away.

Raina felt her cheeks burn. She couldn't run after him. She sat alone beside the shining dance floor. Before her drink was gone, she looked up to hear a man asking her to dance, and sudden anger made her say Yes.

Her partner was a handsome, belligerent young man with half-closed eyes and big hands. He was a good dancer, and kept his eyes on Daniel at the bar. "That your father?" he said.

"My husband," Raina said.

"Yeah?" the belligerent young man said, and grinned. He held her tight. "How'd he get you? He's got to be sixty."

"Sixty-two," Raina said.

"Then he's got money," the man said. "You got to have money in the bank, Frank." Raina didn't answer; the band was loud. Her silk dress clung to her breasts and hips; her long hair spread behind her like a fan when her partner swung her.

Daniel, leaning on the bar, watched Raina dance. He sipped his drink.

When the young man swung Raina close to Daniel, Raina said, "Thanks for the dance. Excuse me," and left her partner for Daniel. Her hand was sticky from the man's sticky palm; her dress was damp at her back where he'd held her. "Danced enough?" Daniel asked her, and she said Yes.

They went to their room, undressed, and lay side by side in their dark bed.

"We'll be at the Hideaway Inn by Saturday night," Daniel said.

"The place you stayed with Patricia," Raina said.

Daniel didn't answer; he turned over. Raina wondered what was in his mind as he lay so close to her, not touching her.

Tom, she told herself. For so many years she had thought of Tom for comfort.

Raina stared at the big, fancy hotel room she could see now; her eyes were used to the dark. *Tom will come. He will*," she said to herself, and remembered her mother washing the smell of grease out of her long brown hair, saying, *He'll come tonight. I know he will. He'll come back.*

Sudden fury shook her until she was sure Daniel must feel it, lying beside her. She could still hear his cold voice telling stories of smashing store windows, burning a business down, nailing a man's hands to a wall...

He had left her at their table alone like a used napkin, a dirty plate.

She lay awake, hour after hour. Before dawn she dreamed she

saw Daniel left behind her on the highway. She was driving away from him, making him walk all the way to California.

The days passed slowly: Raina dozed, and her night dream haunted her: Daniel was left behind, and she was at the wheel of her white Corvette, driving to San Francisco, her whole new life before her.

Daniel hardly talked at all. The road map lay open on Raina's lap, and she found herself memorizing the roads to the coast, as if she were living her dream.

She pretended to sleep during the long afternoons, but late in the day Daniel began to talk. The brown and gray desert beyond the car windows was as dreary as the shame in Daniel's voice. "Anne's never been wanted," he said. "Her mother called her 'a milk toast child.' I let her do it. I was too busy to care."

Was that Daniel's voice, so slow and full of regret?

"And I left her alone, and blamed her—seven years old!—because she was scared at the top of a tree. She planted a garden, and I ruined it."

Now Daniel's tone was suddenly low and vicious. "But nobody hurts my kid." He gave a dry laugh. "Nobody? Nobody but me."

Raina kept her eyes shut. At least he wasn't talking about rats and crucifixions. She began to imagine, one by one, every room in a California house. White walls. Vivid rugs. She'd shop with Tom for some wonderful antique furniture... a wall of clever storage pieces with green plants...

Daniel pulled into a gas station in Nevada and went to the rest room. Raina was alone. Her car key was in her purse. Suddenly her dream was screaming at her: *Leave him!*

Every muscle in her body tensed. "Don't be stupid," she told herself. She'd studied the map. He hadn't filled the tank yet, the road ahead had no towns for miles, and it was growing dark. If she drove off, she wouldn't get far, not without any gas stations still open at night. *Wait*, she told herself. *Just wait.*

They followed a narrow, lonely road. Finally they ate dinner late in a small town restaurant, and she drank too much wine. What did it matter? It would put her to sleep in the car.

While they drank coffee, Daniel said, "I've thought about buying a house in California all day. I think I see why you want to live there."

"Yes," Raina said. "Good."

"Very good," Daniel said. "I hadn't quite thought it through."

"Yes," Raina said again. The wine made her mind fuzzy.

"It's Anne," he said.

Raina nodded, running her finger around the edge of her cup.

"We can't take the boys away from her," Daniel said. "So a house in California is out of the question."

Raina's face was pink with the wine; now it flushed with anger. She wanted to scream, pound the table. It was Anne. It was always Anne.

But she kept still. She didn't look at him. She picked off pieces of her red fingernail polish and laid the bits in a line on the tablecloth like the trail of some tiny bleeding animal.

"It's always cold at night in the mountains," Daniel said, tossing bills on the table for the tip. "We'd better get heavier clothes out of the luggage and change in the rest rooms here before we leave."

Raina changed her clothes. Her heavy jacket and jeans warmed her when she climbed into the car without a word.

Daniel wore his heavy clothes, too. "Sleep for a while," he said as they left the town's last lights behind. "We'll be at the Hideaway by bedtime."

Raina closed her eyes. He'd never meant to buy a California house, the liar.

But she would please Daniel, get around him somehow. Of course she could. She imagined walking through beautiful California houses, choosing the perfect one. She was the director of a world-famous gallery. At night Tom waited for her.

Comforted and full of food and wine, she half-slept, then sat up and licked her dry lips.

"Is it much farther?" she said.

"Not very far," Daniel said.

Raina peered out the window. The car's headlights shone to the edge of the road, then spread a white fan into nothing but the blackness of a mountainside falling away. She said, "It's late."

"Not too late," Daniel said.

Raina, her eyes half open, saw nothing but their headlights on a curving road ahead. "Can't you find the place?" she asked.

"Yes," Daniel said without looking at her. "I can."

"Isn't this road dangerous?"

Her moon-white car was moving and on its way.

"For a mountain road, it's good," Daniel said. "It's the best one."

Raina sighed and shut her eyes.

"It's the only one," Daniel said.

Raina watched Daniel through her eyelashes. He was gripping the wheel so tightly that he seemed to be powering the car with his own knotted muscles; his face was sweaty in the dashboard light. A man would never ask directions. He'd drive forever in the mountains. Look at him, gritting his teeth like grim death.

Let him wander around. Who cared? She wasn't hungry. She could sleep. She was coming home to California.

Mile after mile, the lonely car followed the mountain road in the hours after midnight, its lights traveling on the edge of nothing but sheer rock face. The driver of the car stared straight ahead; the beautiful woman beside him slept, her face half-hidden in her long hair, her head rolling slightly with the curves. Once, when a town came out of the dark with a scatter of lights, Daniel murmured to himself, "I could turn here. I could."

He drove on. The highway began to run along an edge that was hollow beneath: a shelf jutting over black space.

Raina had fallen into the dream she'd had at dawn. A tremendous, triumphant joy filled her: she saw Daniel left behind. She was in the driver's seat of the white Corvette with the highway and her new life before her.

Still in the grip of her dream, she woke as the car motor died. She heard Daniel open his door. Gravel grated under his shoes as he walked away, and the door swung shut. Gone! He was gone! The key was in the ignition. She lunged for it with the rhythm of long hours on the road still in her bones, and her moon-white car was moving and on its way.

25

"That was Dad calling!" Anne said, wide-eyed with shock. She put the telephone back in its cradle as Tom came from the shower, a towel around him. "Raina left him on the road yesterday morning! He got out to go, and she drove off!"

"Just left him?"

"Left him on the road after midnight! In the mountains!"

"Where?"

"Before they got to Reno."

"Is he all right?"

"He says he is, but he walked miles, and finally a driver stopped when he saw Dad lying beside the road, and took him to a hospital in Reno!"

"Should we go out there?"

"The doctors say there's nothing wrong, except that Dad's exhausted. He's coming home by train late Thursday."

"Did he say why he thought Raina did it?"

"They'd argued a lot about buying a house in California, he said."

"He isn't going on to California to find her?"

"He's not sure she's going there. She might drive back to Iowa."

Tom crawled back in bed. Anne lay in his arms and sighed. "When he called, I'd been lying here thinking everything was almost perfect."

"A house full of children?" Tom asked.

Anne's blue eyes gleamed. "Yes."

"Never mind if I'm there or not?"

Anne swatted him lightly on his cheek. "Silly. You're the most important thing."

"But you've never liked our house much."

"I haven't?" Anne looked startled.

"You spent so much time at Daniel's."

Anne's eyes grew wide. "I..." She stopped, then started again slowly, as if she were examining her thoughts as she spoke them. "I guess...I spent so much time there..." She stopped, then began in a low, ashamed tone. "Dad's never liked me much. You know that. So I must have felt I could make him love me, or at least make a habit of me, if I gardened with him, had breakfast and lunch with him, helped him run his house. And then, Steven was at Dad's house. I couldn't leave him alone when Raina..."

"She didn't care about him. Didn't care about Jamie, either. And who cared about you? Daniel? Me?" Tom said. "I was gone all day, and all you had here was the 'children's rooms.'"

"Empty," Anne said, watching her fingers pleat and unpleat the front of Tom's pajama top. "But so often you woke up alone. And when you came home from work, I wasn't here."

"You were here the night Raina and I came back from Drayton Point," Tom said.

"Yes." They both smiled, but suddenly Tom grabbed her to hide his face on her shoulder. "You forgave us," Tom said in a muffled voice. "Both of us. I couldn't believe it. Raina couldn't. She thought you were her enemy."

When Daniel met them on the station platform, he was wearing a jacket and jeans and running shoes. Anne threw her arms around him. "You look so tired and pale."

Tom said, "Where's the luggage?"

"There isn't any," Daniel said.

"You had two suitcases..."

"They were in the car," Daniel said. "We were heading for the Hideaway Inn."

"And Raina was upset?" Anne asked.

"She...we'd had quite a fight, and she drank a lot of wine at dinner. We changed our clothes at dinnertime because it was cold—I was lucky there. But I couldn't hike all the way to Reno—kind of passed out on the side of the road. A car saw me and stopped, and the fellow in it took me to the hospital. I had my wallet, so I could catch a train home."

"Oh, Dad!" Anne cried. "Lying by a mountain road in the dark and cold? Are you all right?"

"I thought of going on to 'Frisco and renting a car, but I figured she was hours ahead of me, and where would I start looking? She'll probably be hiding. She doesn't want to see me again. She said so." Daniel rubbed his eyes. "And I thought she might come back here."

They had an early supper on the patio. Steven asked questions about riding on a train, and when his mother would come home, and whether they'd seen any mountain lions. As they ate, Anne felt Raina's absence, and the emptiness of Daniel's house beyond the forest trees.

The sun went down. Tom lit candles on the patio table, and took Jamie from the highchair to sit on his lap. Steven ran off to look at his bumblebee nest.

"The boys are settled-in here." Daniel stood up. "Can they stay for a few nights more?"

"Of course," Tom and Anne said in chorus.

"Not much sleep the last few nights. I'll be off to bed," Daniel said. He called a goodbye to Steven, clapped Tom on the shoulder, kissed Anne and went away through the gardens.

"Steven?" Anne called through the gathering dusk. Moths were coming to the patio candles.

"I'm feeding the rabbits," Steven called back.

"Bedtime," Anne said when she found him beside the rabbit hutch.

"Do I have to go home?" he asked.

"Not tonight. Dad's tired after riding a train for so long, and he'll want to sleep very late in the morning."

Steven blew out the patio candles, and they carried supper dishes into the kitchen. By the time Anne had changed Jamie and sung him a bedtime song, Tom had read Steven a story about riding a train, and tucked him in.

Tom and Anne went into the living room. "What do you think?" Tom asked.

"Dad's furious," Anne said. "Who wouldn't be? Left on a mountain road in the middle of the night? And he must have fainted. Maybe I can get him to check with his doctor." She sat close to Tom on a couch, and he hugged her. "How are we ever going to find Raina?"

"She's reckless," Tom said. "And she doesn't think much about other people; she's the center of her world."

"But she'll come back to get the children, won't she?"

"Did she ever care much about them?"

Anne pulled out of Tom's embrace to look at him.

"A lot of this is my fault," he said.

"That Raina went off by herself?"

"I've told you that she talked about her divorce and mine one day at lunch," Tom said. "I didn't tell her I wouldn't get a divorce. I didn't say anything. I just left her at the table, walked out."

"You certainly didn't say Yes."

"But she's counting on it. She hasn't given up."

"It's my fault, and Daniel's," Anne said. "We—" Tom's kiss stopped her in mid-word, and for a while there was no sound in the big living room. Finally Anne gave a little flustered laugh, escaping him for a minute to get her breath.

Tom said, "I love you so. I do," and she whispered, "I love you, too."

Anne put her head on Tom's shoulder. "I tried to make them both see we were a family. And I was afraid. I walked around our house in the dark for hours sometimes, thinking about losing the boys, thinking about Dad."

"Why didn't you wake me?"

"Why would I? You had to go to work in the morning, and I didn't really have any reason to be prowling. But I almost woke you once. It was after midnight, and I saw a man come from the woods."

Tom leaned away to look at her with concerned eyes.

"It was Dad."

Tom smiled. "Out on a late-night check of his territory?"

"That's what I thought. He does that sometimes. But he wasn't just looking: it seemed almost as if he acted out his feelings when he felt he was alone. He went to the play yard first, and then the rabbit hutch. He looked up at our house. And then..." Anne looked into Tom's eyes. "He came to the window of Steven's room, and put his hand on the sill, and put his head down on his hand. He stayed that way for a long time. And then he left."

"That's all?"

Anne nodded. "As if he were lonely, it seemed to me, or shut out. Mourning something?"

They sat in each other's arms listening to the night noises of the woods through open windows.

Daniel slept late the next day, then came through the woodland to find Anne and the boys in her garden. "How are you?" Anne asked him. "I stayed awake last night, thinking of you lying along a road. Hadn't you better check with your doctor?"

"I'm fine," Daniel said.

"Well," Anne said, "It's a cool day. We can do some weeding to lift our spirits—all but Tom. He left for the office."

"Can I weed? Can I?" Steven asked.

"You can look for one special weed," Daniel said. "It's a nasty thing. You can rip it right out. Can't have nasty things here."

When lunch was over, Anne and Daniel knelt in the flowerbeds, tossing dandelions and crab grass and chickweed into bins. Yellow sunshine striped the garden grass where Jamie sat in his swing. Now and then Steven ran to give him a push, then was back to find the ground ivy that was his weed to pull. The plants came away from the earth in long chains of small, ruffled leaves, and left a strong smell on his hands.

"It's a nasty thing," Steven said every now and then, copying Daniel's tone. "Can't have nasty things here."

"No," Daniel said in a sharp voice. "We can't."

Anne stopped weeding to look at him. When Steven ran off to see his rabbits, she said, "You're so angry."

Daniel never looked at her or answered, but kept at his weeding in the sunshine.

"You and Raina fought about going to California."

The force of Daniel's voice startled her. "I don't need her. Let her go."

Anne said nothing, but lifted Jamie from his swing and sat with him on a bench under young paper birches. Raina had helped plant those trees just after she married Daniel; now the birches moved in the afternoon breeze, scattering their shade.

Jamie threw his toy on the grass. Anne picked it up for him. "She could never leave you," she whispered to the little boy. Sunlight glinted on his black hair.

Daniel was grubbing under the peonies, knifing beneath the

surface so that every weed—leaf, stem and root—was cut away clean. His knife struck over and over.

The next week Daniel climbed the stairway at the Xavier apartment. His face was red, and he was panting. "Dan!" Lil Xavier cried. "How you doing?"

"Not bad," Daniel said. "Got some coffee?"

"Sure," Lil said. "Coming right up."

Charley Xavier came in as Daniel sat down heavily on a swaybacked couch.

Lil brought them coffee. They heard her high heels go downstairs.

"Got a little job for you," Daniel said. "If you'd care for, say, ten thousand?"

"For that," Charley said, sitting down, "it's got to be a hit."

"You get half the cash before. The rest, after."

"Somebody you don't like?"

"Right."

"In town?"

"Right."

"Business trouble?"

"Personal. Very personal. Family, you might say." Daniel sipped his coffee. "A family rat, eating me out of house and home. That kind."

"That kind," Charley said in a thoughtful tone.

"You'll have to do it someplace quiet. He works late here at my office, gets his car in the parking ramp next door. Good place. Could look like a robbery."

"When's it going to be?"

"I'm taking him to 'Frisco next week for a few days. When I get back, I'll give you a call, so be all set." Daniel got up with an effort, said goodbye, and passed Lil on the stairs.

"What was he here for?" Lil asked Charley in the kitchen.

"He's giving me plenty for doing a little job for him in a week or two. Very nice money, sis. How about you and me go to Vegas?"

"Vegas!" Lil yelled, and grabbed him to whirl him around. "O, you sweetheart—won't we do that town?" Then she stopped. "You'd better get a move on. He looks like death warmed over, and how old is he? Sixty-something?"

Days went by. Every ring of the telephone made Anne pause, hold her breath and think, *Raina?* But Raina's voice never came across the miles.

"Doesn't she wonder how her children are?" Anne said to Daniel one morning. He had come for breakfast; he drank his coffee and watched Anne work with her violets on the light carts. Anne lifted a plant sidewise to look for suckers, and broke them off from the main stem. "Maybe she's hurt, or killed."

Daniel's only answer was the chink of his cup on the saucer.

What did you say to Raina to keep her from calling home? Anne couldn't ask Daniel such questions. She tapped the plant out of its pot, checked for mealy bugs on its roots, then fitted it in the pot again and said, "It seems to me that Raina was the one who was uprooted, had to change, fit into our routine, live where we lived, try to find space enough to live herself, and take what she had to have."

Daniel's eyes had been on the garden beyond the windows, but now he gave her a startled glance.

"Look at that," Anne said, stooping behind one of the tables. "Violets grow so fast they knock each other off the shelves." She picked up the fallen violet and said to it: "Not much left of you."

Tom came in, and Daniel said to him, "I've been thinking that we'd better go out west and hunt for Raina. We can drive to where she left me, then go on to 'Frisco. Raina knows the city; she's probably there. We've called the police, and friends, and every California gallery and museum. The best thing is to go look. Maybe Tuesday early."

Tom hesitated. "I don't know that I can leave the office. The Jepsen sale—"

"I want you along," Daniel said.

There was nothing Tom could say. Anne broke the uncomfortable silence: "If you don't find her, you might hire a detective."

"A good idea," Daniel said.

Anne hugged Tom and told him she was so glad he was going with Daniel. "You'll be sure to call me whenever you can," she said.

Tom drove west with Daniel: long miles with little conversation to shorten them. He called Anne every night. She said the boys were fine, and he asked, "Any word from Raina?" It was an old question now. Anne's answer was the old answer.

Tom called her when they found a motel in Salt Lake City. "Tomorrow we'll find the place on the road where Raina drove off and left Daniel," Tom told her. "Then we'll go on to 'Frisco."

Daniel and Tom drove out of Salt Lake City in the hot, late summer sun. They listened to the radio as the hours passed, and watched the mountains slowly slide their peaks across the view, catching sunlight on their rocky slopes.

Night fell before they finished supper at a restaurant. "Should we wait until morning to find the place where Raina left you?" Tom asked as Daniel pulled on to the highway. "You want me to see it, you said. We might miss it in the dark."

"It's not far," Daniel said. "Have you seen that photograph of Patricia and me on our honeymoon?"

"The two of you standing in front of a rock wall?"

"There's a white streak on that rock that's easy to see in the dark," Daniel said. "The night Raina left me I was watching for it. It's a sentimental place for me. Raina had asked about the picture, and I wanted to show her where that rock face was. So I parked there. And she drove off and left me."

Miles passed as their headlights showed the highway edge, then spread their fan into empty space where the mountainside fell in sheer rock hundreds of feet below. Tom was riding a few feet from that brink, and tried not to look at the black emptiness outside his window.

At last Daniel pulled over and stopped. "Here we are," he said.

Tom opened his door, and it hung over empty, dark air—the sheer drop of the cliff was less than two feet away. He climbed out, edging along that blackness, pressing his hip against the car.

Daniel waited on the highway. Tom joined him, and they looked up. A cliff jutted against the dark sky, wearing a face with a long white gash for a nose, and two deep rock holes for eyes. The empty eyes stared down.

"Not hard to find, even in the dark, that face," Daniel said. "I thought I was lost that night with Raina, but when I saw that streak I knew where I was."

"And you stopped here," Tom said.

"Stopped right here," Daniel said. "Here's where Raina left me. Couldn't forget it, could I? Not with that face up there."

237

Tom followed Daniel back to the cliff edge of the narrow road. They looked down into black space together. Daniel kicked a stone off. They heard it strike far below, skitter for a moment, then strike again and then, far off, strike again and again until the tiny sounds ticked away into silence.

26

"Any news about Raina?" Tom asked when he called Anne from a motel that night.

"No news," Anne said, and told him the boys were fine and asleep in bed.

Tom said goodbye to Anne. Daniel sat back in a motel chair and put his feet on the bed. "What about the Hideaway Inn?" he said. "Raina could have gone there by herself, then driven west in the morning. I thought of that today."

"Could she find the Inn after midnight?" Tom said.

"She had all the maps with her. She might have mentioned where she was going to someone at the Inn that night."

"Wouldn't she have worried that you'd think of the Inn? She probably went right on to the coast."

"I'm off to bed," Daniel told Tom, and went to the door, then turned, his bushy eyebrows raised over his cold blue eyes. "You'd better call the Inn," he said.

Tom watched him leave. The urgent undertone of Daniel's words still hung in the air. He called the Hideaway Inn.

No, the Inn clerk said, no woman named Raina Weigel or Raina Bonner had spent the night there on August tenth.

"But Daniel Bonner made reservations for that night," Tom said.

The clerk said no one of that name had made such a reservation. She checked again. "No. No one," she said.

"Nobody with a white Corvette checked in?"

"Oh, no," she said. "I'd remember that."

No reservation. So Daniel had forgotten to call the Inn. Tom thanked her, hung up, and left his motel room for some fresh air. The cold struck through his shirt. He looked up at mountains that were dark against darkness; only the lack of stars showed where their slopes blocked half the sky.

Tom shivered. The road they had traveled that day was in those mountains somewhere—and a rock face to mark where Raina had left Daniel. She was in the sunshine of California, waiting for him.

"You lived here for quite a while," Daniel said to Tom the next day as they drove into San Francisco. "When Emily had a house here. And you knew Raina."

"Yes," Tom said. "I met her at Emily's."

"You met her at Emily's," Daniel repeated in a dry and meditative tone.

They drove to the detective's office. He was middle-aged, fat and thorough: he took notes and sometimes examined Tom over his dirty glasses as if he, too, might be a bit of interesting data. He missed nothing about Daniel, either: Tom saw that. A detective would investigate a man whose wife had disappeared.

Daniel supplied information: "My wife's maiden name was 'Weigel,' and she was born in New York City in 1920. I've written most of the facts down for you. She graduated from U.C., Berkeley with a B.A. in 1946; then she came back to U.C. the summer of 1948 and received her master's degree in 1949, before we married in 1951. I don't know much about her Berkeley years, except that she worked in a gallery, I believe, and lived in a one-room apartment. She left for Iowa in 1948." Daniel spread pictures of Raina on the detective's desk. He glanced at Tom as he put down the last snapshot: it was of Tom and Raina, young students in the 'forties with their arms around each other. Where had he found it? He didn't look at Tom.

Question after question, fact after fact. At last the detective shut his files away and showed them out.

Dread followed Tom from the detective's office like an agent assigned to tail him.

He rode the long way home with Daniel, and dread went with him.

"You've done all you can. We'll just have to wait," Anne said to Tom and Daniel as they sat at supper on their first night home. "Such a long trip. You both need a rest."

"The detective's one of the best in the business," Daniel said. "He's got all the information we could think of, and he'll follow every lead. For now, we've done all we can do."

Tom heard the finality in Daniel's voice, as if something had been settled, a problem had been solved. Had it? He felt cold, though they sat in the shade of a hot summer garden.

Daniel finished his coffee. "I think I'll say goodnight," he said. "I promised to call an old friend when I came back from the west. I'll do it and then turn in."

When Daniel was out of sight, Anne said, "Dad looks awful—so gray-faced and exhausted." She poured another cup of coffee for Tom. "Not a single clue? Did you ever call that inn where they planned to stay?"

"She never went there. I checked. She must have driven straight on to 'Frisco." Tom's voice deepened; he was staring at Anne. "Daniel's going to find out."

"Find out what?" Anne asked. She left her patio chair to put her arms around him. There was a shamed, intense look in his eyes.

"How long I lived with Raina. That detective has an old '46 snapshot of Raina and me with our arms around each other. He's going to find people who knew us both."

For a minute Anne was still. Then she said, "You lived with her a long time?" She hid her face against his shoulder as if she didn't want to be there, didn't want to hear.

"Neither of us had any money, so I moved into her closet of a room and we cooked on a hot plate and were stupid and young—and when she was going to marry your father, I wanted to tell you, but she said, 'You know what kind of a life I've had so far. You'd never ruin my chances.'"

"And you couldn't." Anne held him tight. "You couldn't do that. You wouldn't."

"But now Daniel's going to have his face rubbed in the fact that Emily and Raina and I hid the truth from him—from you—Oh, God, I was so stupid, so blind—"

"So was I," Anne cried. "So was I." They held each other tight, there on the darkening patio.

After a while Tom asked, "What will he do?"

Anne shook her head and walked back to her chair. "Emily says that if Raina's gone for good, I ought to be happy." Anne covered her face with her hands.

"I'm happy," Tom said. "So are the boys. Would Daniel ever miss her much?"

"She'd give up her boys?" Anne cried, dropping her hands to stare at Tom. She hesitated. "Give up *you*?"

Tom's face was turned to the garden; he didn't answer.

"Dad must have said terrible things to her," Anne said. "How could he drive her away from you and the children?" Her voice was full of despair. "How *could* he?"

The next afternoon Charley Xavier sat at his kitchen table and watched his sister pour coffee. "Bonfire called after you went to bed last night," he said. "The deal's on. We'll get that other five thousand."

"Charley!" Lil cried. "Listen to me! I've never said nothing, but I been thinking—it's not worth it! Give Bonfire that cash back he gave you! Tell him you're too old or something!"

"You crazy? So we lose his money for the rent? Car payments? You want to be out on the street at our age? Or maybe they find us in the river?"

"I'm so scared!"

"Bonfire's no joke. He and I got a deal—"

"I know! I know! You burned Clingman's —"

"What Bonfire wants, he gets. If Bonfire wants his son-in-law out of the way, I got no choice. And you always land on your feet, don't you? If I mess this deal up, you'll have Bonner's first five thousand. Clear out. Disappear. Bonfire won't come after you for that measly five."

"Clear out? Clear out to where?"

"Or you can just have some guts and stay put. Tell Bonfire you're keeping the cash because you know too much. Tell him if you get your rent paid every month and that two hundred we always get besides, he won't never be in trouble. What you think I'm spilling this deal to you for? Did I have to tell you a thing? Did I?" He got up and went into the bedroom. "Time to go."

She followed him. She watched him put on a black coat over his dark jeans. He loaded his gun. "Where's it going to be?" she said.

"It's got to be tonight. Hancock's going away for the weekend. The parking ramp by Hancock's office. I've tailed Hancock for a week now. Sometime between five and six he leaves work, and he always parks on top of the ramp. Old Floyd Dougherty's down in the booth taking money that time of day, when the last people drive out. I know that ramp from way back. We kids always checked the place out for unlocked car doors."

"Oh, Charley," Lil said, putting her arms around him at the door. "Charley."

"Remember: you're my alibi. I been here all day and night," he said. He looked out a window. "It's getting dark. Dark at four-thirty—we're going to get a storm, and that's good. Nobody'll be around to see me."

The streetlights came on under a black sky. Charley went down alleys to Fordwell Street.

The parking ramp stairs echoed with the storm's thunder as he climbed to the top tier and saw Tom Hancock's fancy car. There it was: the only car among empty spaces.

He backed into one of the niches in the ramp wall. It was deep enough to hide him from the door. Hancock's car waited hardly twenty feet away.

The rain began, and struck hard. Gaps in the ramp wall gleamed with a downpour that glittered when the lightning flashed.

Charley shifted from foot to foot, leaning against the wall. Lightning flared, vivid as searchlights; it probed the ramp, bringing Tom Hancock's lonely car out of blackness, then burying it in dark again.

Five o'clock.

Five-thirty.

Five minutes more, and the rain died to a soft shower. Steps on the stairs were easy to hear. They grew louder, coming up the ramp, level by level. Charley waited, his hand sweaty on the gun. It had to be Tom Hancock: he was coming to the top. When he came out and went for the car...

But he heard a second set of footsteps now, like an echo of the first steps, coming along behind...

Tom Hancock was there, not ten feet from Charley. Lightning flooded him for a moment. Floyd Dougherty shuffled behind him.

Charley flattened himself in the niche and hid his face against the cold wall.

"Damn kids," Floyd said, following Tom to his car. "Always sneaking in behind my back. They was up here about four, but I couldn't tell was there anything missing from your car. You ought not to leave it open."

"I was in a hurry," Tom said, opening the car doors, looking front and back. "Not much in here they'd want. But thanks for watching out. How's your wife doing?"

"Can't tell you how much it means to us. You gave us enough to bring one of our daughters from Ohio. I'm not much of a nurse, but the daughter is, and the wife's better, and we've got enough to eat for the three of us."

The men stood with their backs to Charley. Tom reached for his billfold. "If you can use more…"

"No…no, I put some in the bank to tide us over."

"Well," Tom said, getting into his car. "Just let me know."

Floyd watched Tom drive away down the ramp, then went downstairs, step by slow step.

Night rain darkened Iowa fields and roads. The Cedar River was only a black flow between dripping trees. When Tom, exhausted from long hours of work, drove past Daniel's house, every window in the Bonner house was lit.

At midnight Daniel's house showed lights on every floor.

At dawn, every window in the Bonner house still glowed.

Before sun lit the treetops, a doorbell at the Hancock house rang. "Doorbell?" Tom said in a dazed voice, crawling out of bed and grabbing a bathrobe.

"This early?" Anne said, sliding from the sheets to put on a robe and follow him.

Tom opened the front door. John Bateman, a doctor and their neighbor along the river, stood on their doorstep.

"I'm sorry," he said. "I had to wake you. I was called to your father's house by the men working there. About fifteen minutes ago."

"Dad?" Anne said. "It's Dad?"

"Yes," Bateman said. "You'll both need to come." He turned and hurried away through a forest shrouded in drifting mist.

The boys were still asleep. Tom and Anne rushed to dress, and ran through the soaked gardens to Daniel's house.

Dr. Bateman waited on Daniel's doorstep to take Tom's hand and put his arm around Anne's shoulder. "I'm so sorry," he said. "The workmen arrived here a half hour ago and called me. They found Mr. Bonner in his big storeroom next to the garages. They hadn't seen much furniture in that room yesterday, but it's full this morning, so it looks like he moved a lot of heavy pieces sometime in the night. He had a heart condition, and perhaps the exertion killed him. I'm so sorry. He didn't suffer, I don't think. A massive coronary."

They followed the doctor to the storeroom. The big room was heaped almost to the ceiling with furniture. "This way," Bateman said, and took a narrow path through tables topped with upturned chairs on top of chairs under mounds of framed pictures, rolled rugs, tumbled books, and dresser drawers stacked and spilled.

Daniel lay face down in a dark corner. "Dad," was all Anne could sob. "Dad." Tom put his arms around her. A woolen shawl had fallen from a pile of dresses to half cover the body.

Anne left Tom's arms and knelt in the narrow space beside Daniel. She kissed the side of his face. "Raina's shawl," she sobbed, running her hands over the shawl's red wool. "Do you remember?" she asked Tom.

For a little while they were quiet while Anne stroked her father's face, crying, and pulled the fallen shawl over his shoulders as if she could warm him. At last she stood up, clinging to Tom, and he led her back to the living room.

Anne stared around her. "So many things are gone," she whispered to Tom. "You see? *Raina's* things are gone. It looks as if Dad cleared out everything she bought."

Tom went back to speak with the doctor. Anne wandered through the half-empty rooms. Half-emptied bookshelves gaped like mouths with missing teeth.

She went into the master bedroom as furtively as a robber, or an eavesdropper listening to intimate conversations. The wide dressing table had always been heaped with Raina's clutter of tubes, brushes, bottles, perfumes, used tissues and wadded cotton. It was swept clear and clean. Her closet was a long, high emptiness; Anne remembered dresses on hangers thrown in heaps on the storeroom floor, and a red shawl.

Tom stood in the doorway. "It looks as if he wanted nothing of hers in his house," Tom said.

Anne was crying again. "Dad told me when you two came back from San Francisco: 'I don't need Raina. Let her go.'"

They went through a garage and into the early light. Anne took a deep breath of September air. "I'd better go back to the boys. Mirabelle will be here before long, and I'll come back." She looked at the big house behind them. "So terrible," she said. "A terrible, empty house."

A woolen shawl had fallen from a pile of dresses to half cover the body.

27

"Hey, Charley!" Lil Xavier ran upstairs with a newspaper. She found her brother in bed, half asleep. "Dan Bonner's dead! Look here!"

"Dead?" Charley groaned, turning over and squinting at the paper.

"Where'd you go last night?" Lil said. "I waited and waited, stayed up till maybe four. How'd it go? I was scared to death—you didn't come! Did you get Tom Hancock all right? Nothing's in the paper about Hancock that I can find. Where'd you go after? Some bar?"

"Did I get him? Hell, no!" Charley glared at the paper, then at Lil.

"You didn't?"

"Hell, no! I was all set, up on the H level where Hancock always parks."

"And he didn't come?"

"He came! Right on schedule. But hell—old Floyd Dougherty's with him!"

"Why?"

"Some kids got by Dougherty at the ramp, and he comes up with Hancock. Thinks the kids could of got in Hancock's car."

"And they saw you?"

"Nope, but they jabbered right there, ten feet from me, about Dougherty's wife who's sick and Hancock's given him money, and on and on, and then Hancock drives off!" Charley fell back on his pillow.

"Drives off? You couldn't get him when he was in his car?"

"Dougherty's right there, watching him go."

"Well," Liz said.

"Well? That all you got to say?" Charley sat up. "What's well about anything? Bonner's a dead rat, and there goes our trip to Vegas. *And* our free rent. *And* payments on the car."

"Oh, Charley!" Lil cried, crumpling the newspaper in her hands. "He was only sixty-two! Why'd he have to go and die before you got the other five thousand?"

"Why'd he die? Because he was mean enough. Haven't I told you a dozen times? Plenty of people in this town'll dance a jig when they see the paper. They'd have been glad to kill him theirselves."

"But how'll we ever pay the rent? And we were gonna have such a good time!"

Leaves were beginning to fall along Waterloo streets. Emily Snyder's September garden was a mass of blooms; they moved together in the wind like a ripple of chorus girls in perfect step.

Emily watched them from her upstairs hall window, patiently waiting for Clara to fasten the back of her dress. "If I dared, I'd stay home from every funeral," she said.

"People will certainly wonder where Raina is," Clara said. "His own wife. And she's left her children?" She hooked the last hook of Emily's dress and gave it a pat.

"She's probably sold that fancy car," Emily said. "She'd have to get a new kind of job, maybe, birth certificate, name…"

"It's not that hard if you have money." Clara's tone said that it was an old conversation they were having, dog-eared at every corner by long wear and no answers.

Emily sighed. She sighed often as she drove to Daniel's funeral service, then joined the procession of cars driving slowly to the cemetery. Townsfolk were at work in their gardens in a soft, almost misty late afternoon.

Daniel, shut in his brown casket, lay over the brown hole of his grave.

Steven stood beside Anne, his face solemn. Jamie stared from Anne's arms at the faces around him; he was as black-haired as Tom, and his eyes were as dark as Raina's. Emily remembered that Raina had said: *Children forget so fast. Jamie—what will he remember? Nothing.*

"Mr. Bonner's will was updated early this year," Daniel's lawyer said, spreading papers on his desk before Anne and Tom. "The fact that we can't locate Mrs. Bonner will keep us from finishing our work and closing the estate, but the will is very simple and straightforward, as you'll see. Mr. Bonner left your house and half the river bluff land to you, Mrs. Hancock," he said to Anne, "although Mr. Bonner told me that he has been reimbursed for much of the cost of that property. Any remainder of that debt will not be due. And he left you the Bonner Rubber and Supply Company. The rest of his estate goes to his wife."

Anne and Tom had identical looks of unbelief and shock on their faces.

The lawyer hurried on: "However, all of Mr. Bonner's holdings will go to you, Mrs. Hancock, if your stepmother dies, as you will see when I read paragraph two. I questioned Mr. Bonner about such a decision. He seemed to feel that his daughter would have the Bonner Company and her husband to rely on, but his widow would be left with his two children and no resources but her position at the Rolinger Gallery."

Anne and Tom looked at each other in silence.

"I will now read the will in its entirety," the lawyer said. When he had finished, he said, "I am merely informing you of the will's contents. No settlements can be made or signed, of course, until Mrs. Bonner has been located. We must wait until she is available."

The lawyer gave Anne a copy of the will, showed them out of his office, and the two drove home in silence, until Tom said, "We have our house and land, and the Bonner Company."

"But Dad left a fortune!" Anne cried. "You've worked for him for ten years to double that fortune, and improved everything you touched! He called you his partner!"

"That was just a word he used," Tom said. "You know he always kept me on salary—a very good salary, but no partnership about it, and after Raina and I…" Tom stopped, then went on in a bitter voice. "I couldn't bring it up."

"What can we do?"

Tom gave her a hopeless look. "Raina wooed him and won him behind our backs. Now she has nearly everything, even the boys. He hated me. Of course he hated me. But he loved you, didn't he? Weren't you the only one he could trust?"

Anne said nothing. "You even forgave Raina and me!" Tom cried. "Tried to keep him from ever suspecting."

"I suppose he thought I was stupid, and didn't know," Anne said in a dull voice. "Or if I did know, that was even worse: I was spineless then. Weak. He always wanted a son, not an ordinary kind of daughter."

Tom pulled off the road to stop the car and reach for Anne. He held her close, smoothed her hair, and rocked her a little in his arms as if she were a hurt child.

Where was Raina? Tom went to his office as usual. He brought a young man from Chicago to serve as interim director of the Rolinger Gallery. The detective put notices of Daniel's death in newspapers. Surely Raina would learn soon enough that she was a rich, free woman.

"Steven asked me yesterday if you and I were going away, too," Anne said to Tom after a week.

"The boys miss Daniel and Raina," Tom said. "We should try to give them extra attention. I'll spend more time at home when I can." He took the boys into the woods often, and they came home happy with some secret they didn't want Anne to know.

Anne watched them come across the gardens one afternoon. Tom was carrying his own Jamie. Anne hurried to meet them. "I'm living a dream," she said, kissing Tom. "A family living in our house, and you..." She stopped and laughed. If Tom had wooed her before Jamie was born, now he was showering her with every joy he could think of—roses on her pillow at night, gifts beside her breakfast coffee, lovemaking whenever he caught her alone for ten minutes, five minutes, two. She found his notes rolled around her lipstick, or rustling in a negligee pocket, or hidden in her gardening boots.

The four of them stopped in the patio's shade. "Don't you ever-ever-ever go into the woods!" Steven told Anne. "It's a secret, what we're doing. Don't you ask us." He flopped on a hammock and set it swinging. "I want to live in this house whenever I'm in Iowa. Can I? I can't live in the other house. Dad's gone. It's locked up," Steven said.

Anne looked at Tom, then said softly, "We'll see."

"And you're our mother," Steven said to Anne. "Until our real mother comes back. You know all the games, and we've got to study the insects, and there's my bee house, and the riverbank..."

"Mama," Jamie said, holding his arms out to Anne. "Mama."

Anne picked Jamie up and said to Tom, "Emily just drove in.

I'll put Jamie to bed for his nap."

Emily had begun to lunch with the Hancocks on weekends. She came through the house to sit with Steven and Tom on the patio, surrounded by the brilliant colors of the autumn woods.

Steven said to Tom, "When are we going to California? Mother said she wanted to. She said we'd live by the ocean and have good schools, don't you remember? And you and Anne'll go there, too, and live right next to us. When Mother comes to get us." There was a wavering, uncertain tone in Steven's voice. "It's taking her so long because she has to find the right house."

Emily and Tom looked at each other. Pity kept Emily silent. When Steven ran off to the play yard, she was alone with Tom. "It's so sad," Emily said. "For all of you."

"Anne's lost two parents, like I did," Tom said. "But mine loved me. Did hers ever love her? And now her own father has left her so little, and she's going to lose Steven and Jamie when Raina comes. How can she stand it?"

"You'll lose them, too, and one of them is yours," Emily said. "Unless…"

"I can't live with Raina!" Tom said. "She's hard. She's as calculating as an adding machine. She'll turn the boys into grabbing, selfish men!"

"Could you work for her?"

"Never!" Tom cried. "And I won't even get a chance—Raina's not going to stay in Iowa! When she comes and finds out how rich she is? No! She'll sell Daniel's house and all his Iowa property but the Bonner Company, and build a gallery finer than Daniel's in California. Won't she?"

Emily couldn't answer; she watched Tom bent over the patio table, his head in his hands. His voice was muffled when he said, "And the worst thing of all is that Anne knows I left her for Raina. Nothing I can do will ever make her forget that." He sat up suddenly and cried, "And *her own father* planned all this!"

"Did he want revenge?" Emily said. "He's left you with nothing but your house and land and the Bonner Business—you'll never live his kind of wealthy life."

"Raina will have the boys," Tom said. "They'll be a rich woman's sons."

They sat together in silence, looking at the autumn forest.

Emily's voice dropped into angry despair. "I don't understand Daniel Bonner. I never have." She pressed her lips together, as if wondering whether she should go on. "And what about Anne? How can Anne be sure that you'll choose her and the Bonner Supply Company?"

Tom stared at her.

"Anne may be trying to face her life without you," Emily said. "She might suppose you'll leave her—that she can't hope to compete against Raina *and* the money *and* the boys."

They heard Anne coming to the patio. Steven ran back from the play yard. "Can we?" he asked Tom, grabbing Tom's hand. "Now? Can we?"

Tom made an effort to smile at Steven.

Steven grabbed Anne's hands to turn her in a circle. "A surprise! Just for you!" he cried. "All three of us did it for you, and Emily helped, too! Now we're all here, and you've got to go on a walk with us! Anne! Come on!"

Steven led the way, skipping along the forest path.

"How beautiful your woods are," Emily said. Leaves caught the sunlight, falling in showers.

They came to the edge of the field where Patricia had died. Steven ran into the meadow yelling, "Surprise! Surprise!"

"Oh!" Anne cried. "Oh! Look!"

It couldn't be there. But there it was—a new garden hidden in weeds and long meadow grass: a small spaded plot: black earth, green rows, blooming flowers.

"It's your garden you made when you were little!" Steven shouted, jumping beside the glowing colors of marigolds and zinnias. "All of us made it for you!"

Anne was so quiet that Steven ran to her and cried: "Tom helped me! We planted it all." He looked into Anne's face. "Don't cry. It's a present. Aunt Emily gave us the plants out of her garden, already grown—she said they'd bloom for a while yet."

"It's wonderful," Anne said in a faint voice. "Such a present. Such a secret present."

"You can keep it this time," Tom said.

"Until the frost comes," Steven said.

Anne acted her parts: the surprised mother, the pleased wife, the grateful friend. Tom was comforting her because he remembered. Anne hugged all of them with tears in her eyes.

"Don't feel bad," Steven said to Anne, a worried look in his blue eyes. "The frost won't come for a little while."

28

This *is yours for a little while.* Anne told herself this, over and over. For a little while she had a family: Stephen and Jamie were in her house day and night; their father's house was locked and empty. They climbed on her lap, played with her hair, whispered in her ears, wanted a book read or a sore bandaged or a toy mended. And Tom made love to her like a man on his honeymoon.

But Raina was somewhere out there. Every morning Anne and Tom woke to think: *Raina might come today.*

People watched the Hancocks. Raina Bonner was missing. Who would inherit the Bonner business, the properties, the money, the two sons—if Daniel Bonner's wife came home? If she were never found?

Summer ended, Stephen was in kindergarten, and the four of them at the Hancock house celebrated Halloween, Thanksgiving and Christmas in every delightful way Anne and Tom could imagine.

Then it was January. How could a new year come, and not Raina? Week after week the detective called with nothing to report.

February arrived, and the Hancocks celebrated Valentine's Day with a festival of lace doilies and red construction paper. When Easter came, they wove Easter baskets of paper strips and filled them, of course, with candy and chocolate rabbits and chicks.

Jamie was two in April.

In May they planted Anne's garden in the woods, her birthday present.

June brought Steven's sixth birthday.

July set them to making noise for the Glorious Fourth: pots and pans beaten, pails clanged together, in rhythm with "The Stars and Stripes Forever" sung at the tops of their voices. "Fun!" Steven yelled. "Fun!" echoed Jamie.

Summer days passed with the smell of hot earth and the acrid sweetness of gardens in rain. At night while the boys slept Tom and Anne made love on the dock by the river, or in moonlight under garden trees. In those nights Anne almost forgot Raina... there were hours that summer when she almost forgot.

Raina never called, never came. The detective wrote and telephoned. Agencies they were using kept in touch: they would try this, try that.

Finally Anne told Tom: "We've tried everything. Should you go west and look for Raina again?"

"We'll go together," Tom said.

"Together," Anne said, keeping her voice level. "All right. In a week or two?"

But in a week or two Jamie had caught a bad cold. One night Anne looked up when Tom came into the kitchen, home from work. She had been listening for any sound from Jamie, asleep in bed.

They heard the telephone ring. Tom answered it.

Jamie called from the nursery. He had been fretful all day. Anne was rocking him when Tom came to the nursery door.

"Who called?" she said. Seeing Tom's face, she put Jamie to bed and sat beside Tom in the living room. He didn't look at her; he looked down at his hands gripped together. "The detective. It's the Corvette. They traced it by the license plate."

He heard her gasp. "Raina's?"

"The police found it at the bottom of a steep mountain drop fifteen miles from Reno."

"Oh," was all Anne could say. "Oh." Her eyes were full of horror.

"He said there's a body. I'll have to go there."

"It's a woman?"

"I asked. He said they couldn't tell yet; the bones are scattered. They brought up the car. It had Raina's suitcases still in it, and Daniel's, all with their names in them. They say the body could have been down there for a year."

Anne put her arms around him, and his arms came around her.

Anne was so happy. Sometimes she almost forgot Raina.

She said, "Maybe it's not Raina. Maybe somehow..." she pulled back to look in his eyes. "Somehow... maybe someone stole her car?" She stopped, hearing how hopeless her words were. Tom hugged her close, his cheek against her hair. She murmured, "I wish I could go with you."

"Stay here," Tom said. "Jamie isn't well. Stay here."

"But if it's Raina..."

Tom gripped Anne so fiercely in his arms that she could hardly breathe, and murmured, "Oh God."

"Maybe she was coming home," Anne said. "Maybe she was bringing Daniel's things and coming home."

Tom drove west, saying to himself, mile after mile: *It must be Raina.* Who else could it be?

He gripped the wheel as if he held the rest of his life in his hands. Mile after mile he was triumphant, ashamed, horrified, saved. *It must be Raina.* A dead woman could claim nothing, own nothing. Stopping at a motel on his way, he picked up a magazine left in the motel room. A beautiful model smiled from a double page, a bottle of whiskey in her hand, and he saw Raina modeling a dancing dress in his living room, or lying on a deep blue rug in nothing but the gleam of her hair. She ran to meet him across Berkeley's Sproul Plaza with every man in sight turning his face to her the way sunflowers follow the sun. "Who is that beautiful girl? Is she human?" he had asked Emily the first time he saw Raina. He'd been in his early twenties; his mouth had probably been hanging open.

It must be Raina. He remembered a voice in his one-room apartment where Raina's clothes were scattered near a toy soldier: *You'll know I'm here, waiting.*

The sheriff's deputy spoke to Tom Hancock with the subdued voice of official concern. Tom would need to identify the body, if possible, he said. The coroner had decided it was a woman's body: it had been thrown from the falling car, and was mostly bones. What was left of the car was in the impoundment yard.

"How long ago does he think it happened?" Tom asked.

The deputy licked a thumb and turned typed pages. "About a year ago, the report says."

Tom moved through the monotony of police procedures as if

he were an actor in a detective film. Mention of "the body" was scattered through the conversation in the same way that the bones, they said, had been scattered among rocks.

Mostly bones. About a year. Summer sun and autumn rain had fallen on her, and a winter of mountain snow, and spring rain and summer rain.

He followed the deputy "to view the body."

Raina.

Walking behind the deputy, Tom remembered Raina lifting her heavy hair in both hands; he heard her laughter...

Raina. The body. Bones jumbled together in some official box, dumped out for his inspection?

But when he followed the deputy through a last door, a sheet was lifted from a steel table, and he saw that someone had paid the body a last kindness: they had returned what was left of Raina to the familiar human pattern. Although some of it was missing, her gray and dusty skeleton leaned backward, fleshless, breastless, arranged neatly with its shreds of cloth. One set of her toes was still together. Here and there the bones were linked by brown webs; they lay under her skull's constant jolly grin.

A few strands of long brown hair lay along her spine. There was a single note of color: one of her red-enameled nails had stuck somehow to a finger bone.

The top of the skull was smashed. Pieces of it had been fitted together. Tom lifted a strand of hair from her spine, and it moved with static electricity and clung to his sleeve.

"She had long, long brown hair—below her waist," Tom said. He plucked the long hair from his sleeve, but when he tried to lay it along her spine again, it came back to him, until the deputy held it away with his pencil.

"We found these rings among the rocks," a man at a desk said, handing Tom a small envelope.

Tom shook rings into his palm. They were dusty, but they sparkled yet. "My mother-in-law's engagement and wedding ring," Tom said, and stood—for a moment—before an altar, handing the wedding ring to Daniel.

Tom signed papers for "valuables found," and put the rings in his shirt pocket. A woman at a typewriter in the corner looked at him with sympathetic eyes.

"You think it happened in August 1957?" the deputy said, consulting his typed papers. "She was traveling out here?"

"Daniel and Raina left home for California on August seventh last year. My father-in-law said before he died that they were on their way to Reno early August tenth when his wife left him on the road and drove away. I guess she never got to Reno," Tom said. He stood near Raina's splayed feet and the long bones of her shins and thighs and explained that his father-in-law, Daniel Bonner, had died without ever knowing where his wife was. Daniel had said that Raina was tired and depressed after midnight in the morning of August tenth when she drove away and left him.

The deputy scribbled busily.

"Daniel told us that he walked miles until he fainted. A couple in a car saw him lying beside the road and took him to the hospital in Reno," Tom said. "He called us from there on August eleventh to say that his wife had driven off without him, and he was coming back to Iowa."

Tom hardly heard what the deputy was saying. He had made love to the flesh that was only a few brown shreds holding bones together on a steel table. Raina's teeth grinned there—he knew them: that one small gap between the bottom ones that had kept her smile from being perfect.

"After a few weeks, I drove here with him and we checked with your office," Tom said, forcing himself to go on. "You've got a record of that. We hired a detective: the one you called in San Francisco."

"That's about it," the deputy said. He closed his notebook and led the way past Raina to the hall. "We've tried to get the state highway administration to put more guard rails on that road." When they reached his office, he handed Raina's purse to Tom. "Thousands in cash in there," he said.

Tom signed papers and made arrangements for the body and the car. The deputy said, "We'll send the rest of your mother-in-law's effects to your motel."

Tom said, "Thanks. I'd like to see the place where she went off the road. I'd be glad to pay if one of your people could take me there when they're off duty."

"Murphy can do it," the deputy said, and a plump deputy named Eldon Murphy was assigned to drive Tom. As they pulled out on the mountain road, Murphy said, "One of my friends sighted your mother-in-law's Corvette. He's got a small plane." He glanced at Tom. "That sure was a fancy car to total like that."

Tom didn't answer. Murphy said, "You should've seen the big truck-hauling-size wrecker they had here, pulling that Corvette up. And the EMTs had a hell of a time getting down there."

The two rode in silence until Murphy said, "Here's the place," and stopped. "This was some mess of cars that day. Sergeant Gorwin was yelling about 'scene management' when the TV crew got there. They all fought over whether the body belonged to the medics or the coroner or the sheriff." Murphy opened his door. "She went over about here."

Tom's legs were stiff; he got out and stretched, then looked up. He whispered, "My God."

The rock face above him had been knifed in half by a slash that gave it a long white nose. Holes on each side of the slash gaped like sightless eyes.

"Funny looking cliff up there," Murphy said. "It looks kind of like a real face, don't it? Real landmark. Headlights always pick up that streak when you come round either curve."

Murphy walked to the highway edge. "Guess the car must have went down fast, you know, hitting all the way, smashing so damn far off you'd hardly hear an echo. Wonder anybody ever saw it down there. Didn't catch the frame of that Corvette on the edge, hardly—the road runs along a kind of shelf right here. Hundreds of feet straight down." He kicked a stone over, and they heard it strike far below, skitter for a moment, then strike again and then, far off, again and again until it ticked away into silence.

Tom called Anne. He heard the tremor in her voice when she asked, "Raina? You're sure?"

"She went off the road last summer. The coroner says she's been dead that long. The car's her Corvette. They found the suitcases, and her diamond rings."

There was silence on the line. Then he heard Anne sigh; that was all.

"How's Jamie?" Tom asked.

"His cold's gone. He ate breakfast and lunch, and now he's napping. Steven's visiting Gwen at the nursery school. I miss you. I love you."

"Wish you were here," Tom said. "I'll start home tomorrow, love. Goodbye."

When Anne said goodbye, the click of the phone going dead was like the flick of a switch in her head—in her whole body.

Raina was dead. She ran to Jamie under the stained-glass angels. He was awake. His face, so like Tom's now, wavered through her tears. She dressed him, and roamed her house with the two-year-old in her arms.

Memories of Raina sat at a dining room table, posed on a sofa, modeled clothes in a living room doorway.

Anne took a deep breath of July's fragrant air as she carried Jamie into the gardens and looked back at her home. Two boys slept under her roof now, and toys scattered on the patio were silent witnesses to the "children's rooms" in her house.

Daniel's house was locked and silent under its trees.

"You wanted me dead, but I'm not dead," she whispered to Daniel outside his front door.

Jamie toddled beside her on the woodland path to the meadow, her garden, and the oak tree. "I didn't kill my mother," she told the oak, flattening her hands on its rough bark. "It wasn't my fault. If he'd loved me, he'd never have thought it was."

Zinnias and marigolds blazed in her small meadow garden. "Never again!" she whispered to their red and yellow. "My garden stays. Tom and Steven and Jamie made it for me. You never loved me." Jamie sat down by the rows of flowers, and Anne crouched beside him, hugging herself. "But now I love Tom and the boys, and they love me," she said. She stood up and yelled, "They love me!"

"Love me, love me, love me!" echoed Jamie, and echoes beyond a faint trail at the meadow's edge called, *Love me...Love me....me...*

When Tom said goodbye to Anne, he put down the phone and looked at Daniel's and Raina's suitcases waiting along the wall of his motel room.

Daniel's bags had broken open, and were roped shut. What was left of them was stuffed with dusty clothes and a camera with a cracked lens. Raina's matched luggage had survived; her initials still shone gold under the handles, as if Raina had imagined that the two cases might lie on a bed before Tom and speak for her: *You've come to find me.*

Tom opened one and lifted out a creased green linen suit, jackets, sweaters, dress after dress, frilly underwear, slacks, a turban. Rhinestones glittered. Polished cotton still shone like leather.

At the bottom of the case was a blue dancing dress he remembered. He had looked at Raina modeling it, and said, "It'll do."

"Do what?" Raina had asked before he turned his back and walked away.

There was something lumpy beneath the blue silk.

Tom pushed the blue silk out of the way. His hands shook as he lifted out a small stuffed toy: a Buckingham Palace guard in red and black.

29

"Somebody took a dive down the mountain?" Deputy Sloan said.

"Drove off," Deputy Murphy said. "Wendell Perkins was flying over—saw the car way down there. This rich dame was driving west with her husband, and she went over the edge. Where that face on the rock is." The two deputies stared at mountains beyond the office window.

"The husband did it?" Sloan asked.

"You might think so, but he's dead now, and nobody'd believe he did it, anyway, 'cause you know what she was driving?"

"A Caddy?" Sloan said.

"Hell, no!" Murphy said. "A 'fifty-three Corvette! Hand built! They only made three hundred of those babies. Pitch your wife off a cliff? Yeah. But not in a car like that. Her Iowa son-in-law came, named Hancock. Young. Lots of dark hair, light eyes. After he finished signing everything, he said could somebody show him where she went off."

"And you lucky s.o.b.—you got paid."

"Twenty bucks." Murphy said. "I showed him where she took the dive—at that big white split in the rock there that makes that face, and he looked over the edge."

"Ought to be a guard rail."

"Sure. And you know what? Hancock must've not gone back to Iowa right away."

"Yeah?"

"I was coming to work the next day, you know, and when I went by that face in the rock, I saw this pink thing right on the edge of the cliff— I was just curious, you know, so I stopped. And it was a big bunch of roses. He must have gone on to Reno and bought 'em, and brought 'em back—he'd found some rocks and made them roses kind of stand up on the edge."

Sloan grinned. "And you didn't leave 'em there?"

"Hell, no," Murphy said. "My wife's alive. She knows what to do when I bring home roses."

A week later, Clara answered a knock at Emily Snyder's door and found Tom on the doorstep. "Come in!" she said. "Welcome home!"

Emily was in her living room. The summer garden glowed beyond her pale reflection in a wall of plate glass.

Tom sat by Emily, and Clara brought cups of coffee. "You look exhausted," Emily said. "What a horrible trip you had."

"Yes," he said.

They sipped for a while in silence, looking at the garden. "But it must be such a relief," Emily said. "Anne inherits everything... you two have the boys...you don't have to work for Raina, or move away." She regarded her coffee cup with satisfaction. "I'm sorry Daniel and Raina are gone, but won't the future be so much better for the four of you?"

"You're the only relative I have," Tom said. "And you know how lucky I've been in Iowa, thanks to you." He looked at her with a sober face. "I still count on you."

"You're not a foreigner any more. You used to say you were."

"I've learned the ways of the country." Tom's caustic tone made Emily look at him sharply. "I remember I asked you to keep me from making a fool of myself, because Anne and her father didn't act the way I expected them to act."

"We joked about it, I remember," Emily said. "I told you it was our good old farm values."

"And I asked you to warn me if you saw me on thin ice."

"I did," Emily said.

"Yes," Tom said. "You did."

"And, goodness knows," Emily said, a slightly righteous ring in her voice, "I warned Raina."

"Yes." Tom jumped up and walked back and forth in tree shadows falling through glass. "But now the ice is very, very thin."

Emily put down her cup and saucer in surprise. "Why?"

Tom looked into his own cup and didn't answer. Emily said,

"Raina's gone, and Daniel, and that's a shame, but you and Anne–"

"I have to tell you how it is. How it's been since they found Raina..." Tom put his coffee down and came back to half sit, half crouch on a chair close to Emily. Suddenly he smacked his fist into his other hand, then threw himself back in his chair. "Since I've known how I helped to kill her."

"*Kill her*? No such thing." Emily waved her hand, waving the very thought away. "If anyone killed her, she killed herself, made all the wrong turns...had that accident—"

"I see her," Tom said. "I see her in a thousand places in both houses, in the woods, down by the river. Sometimes she's beautiful and sometimes she's bones."

"Now stop that," Emily said sharply.

"Jamie's got her eyes. I helped to kill her."

"You can't talk that way. Raina's gone, but she's gone, that's all. She didn't ruin your life."

"Yes," Tom said. "She did. And I did."

"I can't imagine it," Emily said in a resolute tone.

Tom jumped up again to walk back and forth from a window's view of Emily's garden to a mirror's view of the room. "If you can't imagine that," he said, "try imagining this: you find that a man you thought you knew very well—a man who had given you so much you couldn't repay him—had killed his wife."

"Now, *really*, " Emily said.

"He was clever," Tom said. "He knew a mountain road that had unprotected curves, and an obvious landmark on one of them: a big face in the rock above the road that you couldn't miss even if you were driving in the dark. You've seen it. In Daniel and Patricia's honeymoon picture in our living room."

Emily stared at him.

"Then he put up a smokescreen at home. He pretended he didn't know what Raina and I had done—pretended he'd forgiven insults nobody like him could ever forgive. Could he? Forgive his cheating wife? Forgive a man who'd been unfaithful to his daughter, and stolen his wife, and given him a son who wasn't his?" Tom's face was bleak. "But worse than all that—the minute Raina began to talk about a house in California, he must have suspected that Raina meant to divorce him and get custody of the children. Then she'd use the boys to entice me to join her in California and leave Anne. And he loved Stephen, and Anne, too, didn't he? In some twisted way. Because they were his?"

"Yes," Emily said. "I think he did. But—"

"So he drove his wife out west, saying he'd take her to the perfect mountain hideaway; she'd love it. It *was* the perfect hideaway. While she was asleep—didn't she always fall asleep in a car?—that Corvette plunged hundreds of feet down, and she hid there until she was nothing but bones."

Emily raised her hands before her, and her earrings sparkled as she shook her head. "But you don't know that," she cried. "Nobody can prove that."

"You'd think so," Tom said in a cold voice. "You'd think that this man would make absolutely sure no one ever suspected. Wouldn't you? And who would believe that a man in his right mind would send a millionaire's car smashing hundreds of feet down a mountain? He'd get rid of his wife, maybe, but not in that car."

"Well, he was proud of it, and it cost—"

"But this man isn't just any man revenging himself. This is Bonfire Bonner." Tom's eyes met Emily's in a somber stare. "So after Raina disappeared last year, he and I went west to look for her," Tom went on. "I thought it was peculiar that he wanted me to see the place on the road where Raina 'left him.' Why should it matter *where* she drove off and left him? Oh, but it did, though I couldn't imagine it then. So we drove to that place. You remember how we stopped at that strange face on the side of the mountain—I told you—the one in Daniel and Patricia's honeymoon photo?"

Suddenly Tom stopped in his pacing to cry, "Oh, God!" He had tears in his eyes. "I can't stand it. Do you know what Daniel did when we stopped there?"

"Tom!" Emily went to put her arms around him, but Tom shook her off and cried: "Daniel Bonner stood on the edge of that steep mountain drop, and he kicked a stone into it. We stood there. We listened to it hitting the cliffs on the way down, down, down—Oh, God! How could I have guessed that stone was falling on Raina?"

"On Raina? She was already down there?" Emily stared at him. "And you and Daniel went to the detective in California then? Looking for her?"

"Yes! Looking for her. And all the time *he knew where she was*. A deputy out there showed me *exactly* where the Corvette went over, and it was exactly *there*. Daniel knew where Raina was when he came home and told us she'd 'left him.' He'd watched her fall

—right there—and he wanted me to know it...if they ever found her. Can you imagine how it amused him to see me hunting for her?"

"So he always knew where she was?" Emily said in a dull, stunned voice.

They stood together for a while, looking at the garden.

"But why would he ever want you to know?" Emily said.

"He made absolutely sure that I would. He made absolutely sure that I'd discover that Daniel Bonner never made reservations at the Hideaway Inn on that road, because he'd never need a bed for Raina Bonner that night or any night, would he?"

"You found that out?"

"He *told me to find it out*—insisted I should call the Hideaway Inn 'to see if Raina had stayed there.' He knew she hadn't, and never would. I called, and was told the Inn had no record of the Bonners. But I thought he'd just forgotten to make a reservation."

"Oh, my." Emily could say nothing more.

"And a final touch, to make sure that I understood, in case I'd never figured out who killed Raina. Daniel intended me to ask myself (after he died and we saw his will) *Why would Daniel Bonner leave almost his whole fortune to his unfaithful wife?*"

"Oh, when he did that, it hurt Anne!" Emily cried. "She tried not to show it."

"He had to cover his tracks. When he drew up a will like that, nobody but me would ever suspect he'd sent her over that cliff. And he was after revenge, wasn't he? Did he care whether he hurt Anne, as long as he got even with me?" Tom said in a low, intense tone. "*And didn't he make sure that Anne would inherit everything someday?*"

"But he left it to Raina—" Emily stopped mid-sentence, her eyes wide.

"Yes," Tom said. "Daniel explained to the lawyer that Anne would have a husband to support her, but Raina would be left a widow with two children to raise."

"But he knew she'd never be a widow. She'd never inherit a cent of his."

"And that final question," Tom said. "Why did Daniel Bonner feel so safe that he could show me where he killed Raina, and when, and how?"

"He didn't have to tell you a thing."

"No." Tom grabbed the back of a chair with white-knuckled

hands, and leaned toward Emily, his eyes wide and furious. "But this is Bonfire Bonner. He kicks that stone over the edge and he says to himself: 'I sent Raina Weigel to her death. Now I've taken her lover to the very spot where she died—Tom Hancock, who cheated my daughter and stole my wife and fathered one of my sons. And if they ever find what's left of Raina Weigel, *only one man* will know what I've done—know it the rest of his life, and never say a word. I'm Bonfire Bonner, standing here above my dead wife to show Tom Hancock—some day—how far...'" Tom put his face in his hands... '*How far a cheating wife can fall.*'"

They were silent for a long time. Finally Tom said in a flat tone: "We can't guess, can we, what anyone's like inside? You told me that once. We're all just little kids forever, maybe? Wanting, wanting, wanting...dressed up as grown-ups—even looking like mothers and fathers, for God's sake." He sighed. "I've told you. I thought somebody beside me should know. And I suppose I'm doing it for my own relief. I'm hurting you. I'm sorry."

"You had no one else to tell," Emily said.

Tom turned his back on Emily to look at the blooming garden. "I'll never tell Anne. Bonner was sure of that."

"Anybody could see how Anne loves you. Even Daniel could see it," Emily said. "And he did leave her everything. He meant to."

"But Anne will never know that he did. It would make her so happy, but she'll never know."

"You can't tell her of course. Never."

"And there's a final thing, a thing I can't understand," Tom said. "Why would Bonfire Bonner leave all he had to his daughter, knowing that I'd share it? After what I'd done to him, *why wasn't I first on his list to die*, not Raina? At least Raina had given him a son. He hated me enough, God knows. He could have killed Raina and me, and expected to live the rest of his life with Anne and the boys: the king of the castle."

"Then..." Emily stared at him. "Was it Anne who saved you? Daniel didn't want to break her heart?"

Tom crouched in a chair and said in a low voice: "Then I have Anne to thank for one more gift."

Emily's face was grave. "You're alive, thanks to Anne?"

Tom stared at her with a grim smile. "So we have to lie again, don't we? Keep still and lie. Everyone lies to Anne. What else have we ever done? But it's the one thing I can do for her—the one thing. Isn't it?"

Emily stared back at him. "I hardly know you," she said. "I was wrong about Anne. I've been wrong about you." She shrugged her shoulders. "But who's to say what you're really like, or Anne? After all—can you tell me why we think Anne never hated us?"

"She forgave us. Even me. She said so."

"But did Raina ever believe her? Don't you think Raina knew that Anne was simply...very powerfully...pretending to be blind...pretending to be sweet...boxing you and Raina in? Raina tried so hard to get away from the world Anne was making... she told me how hard she was trying...trying to escape with you and the boys..." Emily gave a small sound that was almost like a laugh. "Well, Anne must have done the smart thing: she forgave everybody."

"She did. She always said she did. I hate myself," Tom said. "Can't you imagine how much?"

"But now..." Emily rose from her chair and picked up their empty coffee cups. "Anne's rid of Daniel, who never loved her. And she's rid of Raina, who robbed her. She's her father's heir. And she even has a family of her own. And you."

The doorbell rang, echoing through the house.

They heard Clara go to answer it, and then a woman's voice. Emily whispered, "Nobody in town knows about Raina yet?" Tom shook his head.

"There you are, Emily. And Tom." Sally McDonald stood in the front hall. "I'm just delivering the City Club program, and I'm in a rush."

She turned to leave. "Goodbye! I won't interrupt your happy talk."

T he funeral director's wife sat up in bed when the doorbell rang after ten on Friday night. "Who on earth would come this late?" she said. The director got out of bed to put on pants, and grabbed a shirt.

After a while he came back.

"Somebody dead?" his wife asked.

The director was taking his clothes off. "No. It was the Bonner son-in-law. Tom Hancock, you know?" He kicked off a shoe. "Wanted to put something in Mrs. Bonner's coffin. He could tell I didn't think he should, so he said, 'Don't worry. I saw the body when they brought it up the mountain.'"

"So he put something in?"

"One of her son's toys. A little British soldier."

"Ohhh," the director's wife said softly, moving over as he climbed back in bed. "How sad."

It was such a shame, people said, taking their seats in church the next day. Two little boys. Orphans now. She was so young…lying dead for a year on a mountain.

Autumn sun poured through stained glass. Raina Bonner's casket lay before the altar where she had married Daniel seven years before.

The boys sat between Tom and Anne, being very good. Their last name was going to be "Hancock" now. It was their mother in the box, but she had died and gone to heaven.

"Jamie's too little," Steven had said on the way to church. "He doesn't even know he's going to have a new last name."

The organ Daniel had given to the church sent its powerful bass through wood, flesh, metal and stone. Small things trembled: the baby's breath in the funeral bouquets…ferns among the roses that covered Raina's coffin.

The minister spoke of wifehood and motherhood and a life devoted to others. Tom looked at Anne: an eloquent glance that brought a little color to her pale face.

Roses covered the coffin lid. Beneath it a skeleton grinned, wrapped in satin. A small toy guardsman nestled beside the bones of a foot, his helmet strap like a gag across his mouth.

THE END

A small toy guardsman with his helmet strap like a gag across his mouth.

Critics praise Nancy Price's novels:

A NATURAL DEATH

Who is Nancy Price? Not since Mary Boykin Chestnut has there been such a biting voice, such an accurate eye. —*Charlotte Observer, N.C.*
A rich first novel...quite remarkable.—*Kirkus* Vividly-recalled times past.
Persuasive and saddening.—*N.Y. Times Book Review* —Chicago Tribune
BEAUTIFUL, TERRIBLE, HEART-BREAKING—A POWERFUL EVOCATION OF WHAT IT MEANT TO BE BLACK AND A SLAVE.
—PUBLISHERS WEEKLY
My God, what a film it would make. It's not just fiction: it's Literature. —*Mary Carter*

AN ACCOMPLISHED WOMAN

Seductive...I found myself racing...excited by all its elements. —*Chicago Tribune*
Moving, even terrifying... a rare richness, subtlety and depth.—*Publishers Weekly*
Elegant detail.—*The New Yorker*   Heady and powerful. —*Booklist*
INNOCENTLY PASSIONATE AND ACHINGLY EROTIC. —DETROIT NEWS
Strangely haunting story. Finely written. Read this book. It will change
—*Cleveland Plain Dealer* —*Kirkus* your heart. —*Sacramento Bee*
Compelling and poignant...More than just an accomplished novel; it is a work of art.—*Houston Chronicle*

SLEEPING WITH THE ENEMY (filmed by 20th Century Fox starring Julia Roberts)

Rich characterizations, an ability to move the reader emotionally, and a lovely sense of atmosphere...right on the money. —*San Francisco Chronicle.*
A tense, tightly woven novel...so vivid that one is troubled, longs to know what becomes of these people. —*Louise Erdrich, Minneapolis Star and Tribune.*
Every woman's nightmare...you won't be Powerful, moving.
able to put it down. —Houston Chronicle —*Publishers Weekly*
ABSORBING...SENSUAL...THE READER ROOTS FOR SARA/LAURA ALL THE WAY. —WEST COAST REVIEW OF BOOKS
Terror grips like the coils of an anaconda. —*London Observer*

NIGHT WOMAN

Brilliantly disturbing...Price is masterful in her characterizations. — Houston Chronicle
Well-written and engaging...gritty, wry characterization, chilling images...will keep readers flipping pages. —*Publishers Weekly*
THE TENSION RISES ALMOST UNBEARABLY. Highly recommended.
—EXPRESS NEWS (SAN ANTONIO) —Library Journal
NIGHT WOMAN is so well-written that it raises the psychological thriller to another level. —Orlando Sentinel
Fine...moving...highly *Gripping...a nail-biter of a climax*
recommended.—Chicago Tribune *...engrossing.—Kansas City Star*
A terrific suspenser...Don't even wait for the movie. —*Kirkus*